Down the Hatch

Many of the incidents in **Down the Hatch**, even though they are humorously accounted, will be horrifyingly familiar to many long-distance yachtsmen. The story line in **Down the Hatch** is more an extension of the confessional than a tall yarn told in a quayside watering hole. Here we have a long-distance, modern sailing adventure by a crew so ill-equipped to deal with the many variances of sea and weather that a disaster is inevitable. What should be the adventure of a lifetime quickly becomes a nightmare. Some crew members regain their senses and jump ship, while others continue to the bitter end. Their hilarious experiences on land are second only to their trials at sea. If ignorance were bliss this would surely be the happiest crew ever to set foot aboard a yacht. Having never sailed before they conquer Biscay and cross the Mediterranean.

To our very good friends Roger & Kate

Jim Tyrrel?

Happy sailing.

Down the Hatch

Jim Tyrrell

Illustrated by M. Peyton

A rollicking tale of long distance yachting,
of imbibing and gybing, boozing and carousing.
Could this be how it really is?

SailAway Books

SailAway Books, Publishers,
St Georges Road, Sevenoaks, Kent England TN13 3ND
Tel: Kent (0732) 450311

Distributed by:
Barnacle Marine, Hazelbury Manor, Corsham,
Wiltshire, England SN13 9ZZ
Tel: (0225) 812024   Fax: (0225) 812025

Simpson-Lawrence 218/228 Edmiston Drive, Glasgow G51 2YG
Tel: (041) 427 5331/8   Fax: (041) 4275419
List No 47 20747

Categories: Sailing, Humour, Fictional long distance yachting adventure.

ISBN 0-9520747-1-0

Printed and bound by
HarperCollins Manufacturing Ltd, Glasgow

For Margaret

Acknowledgments

Many of the incidents in Down The Hatch, even though they are humorously accounted, occur with frightening regularity and will be horrifyingly familiar to many long distance yachtsmen. No representation of any person living or dead is implied or intended.

A word of thanks to Katherine Peyton, Brian, Siobhan, Jenny, and a very special thanks to Bob, Tommy, James, Chris, Jim, and Bruce, and others too numerous to mention, for so many mad and memorable sailing experiences. Without their help and support this book could not have been written.

Charts by Carolyn Gilsenan.

Preface

It is often said that the best way to learn to sail is by simply going out and doing it. Hardly a hundred years has passed since Joshua Slocum sailed around the world single-handed in a thirty-seven foot wooden boat, which at the time was regarded as no mean feat. Today this is regarded as an everyday occurrence. Regardless, the romance and challenge still remain. Many still believe that long distance sailing is one of the few real adventures left to man. Eric Hiscock, Robin Knox Johnston and many others have written highly informative books on extended voyages and have contributed immensely to the enjoyment of the sport. But, what about Mr. Average, un-able seaman 'Joe Bloggs' who has drifted into yachting almost by default and has acquired all the characteristics of a disaster looking for a place to happen? He is the one, whose every free moment is spent reading and talking about boats. He aimlessly wanders around marinas and chandlers simply dreaming about the time when he will sail off into the blue yonder never to return.

Sailing becomes an obsession far more insidious than narcotics and probably just as expensive. Outwardly his physical appearance changes: The novice yachtsman no longer walks upright but stoops slightly, adopting a strangly rolling gait. He grows a beard for the first time in his life. His clothes look as if he permanently sleeps in them. He wears navy blue and nothing else; navy blue trousers, navy blue jacket, even navy blue shoes with strange laces.

He also babbles in bizarre tongues and can no longer communicate with his family or friends. Words such as: fender, gimbals, windlass, baggywrinkles are uttered in a seemingly endless torrent as are looard and forrad which do not appear in any known dictionary. Phrases like: lying a hull, sailing close-hauled, or round turn and two half hitches, roll off the tongue with frightening ease.

This unsung hero of our time, would never normally buy three screws in a plastic packet for a pound at a D.I.Y. super-store when he could buy a box for ninety pence wholesale, is now paying seven pounds-fifty for a square of rolled up paper, called a chart, that will be out of date in six months. He recklessly throws away ninety pounds on a box of fireworks that will never be used, but will have to be replaced in a few years.

The madness continues with the purchase of a thirty-seven foot piece of floating plastic that depreciates faster than a Lada in Alaska. It will cost him six hundred pounds a month in interest and a further four hundred for the privilege of parking it in someone else's swamp, surrounded by mud and sewage. This vessel, which he can neither handle nor afford, will be used once a month if he's lucky, creating havoc and despair at every turn. We all know him. He's the one caught in mid-channel about to be run down by the Isle of Wight Ferry. He's like Lot's wife, frozen to the spot, unable to react and leaves someone else to remedy the situation.

Undaunted he will brave on through unsurmountable odds to earn the cherished title 'Captain', or better still 'Skipper' A term used only for those who have earned the respect of their . . . can we say it? 'Mates'!

He will eventually become Captain 'Joe Bloggs', conversant with 'yacht-speke', craft management, boat parking..oops sorry..berthing, and ready to utter maledictions on those less competent than himself.

The following is a light hearted story, telling how one man strives to earn the respect of his sailing companions and become a fitting recipient of the title 'Skipper'. Unfortunately, he has to sail almost three thousand miles to do so and is never quite sure if the term might not be derisively used. However, he does learn by his mistakes and those of others. Like the true fanatic, he soaks up pertinant information like a sponge, which he disburdens on the unwary in a deluge of rambling words.

The tale is based on factual experiences. The more bizarre they seem the more likely they were to have actually happened. Does the boat Deceptive actually exist? I am pleased to add that indeed she does. However, I have sworn on a stack of R.Y.A. sailing memoranda never to disclose who the real owners are. Those who imagine they took part in this voyage may read on safe in the knowledge that their names will never be divulged. Their secret I will keep with me, even to the grave, but only as long as each continues to send those little monthly considerations.

1

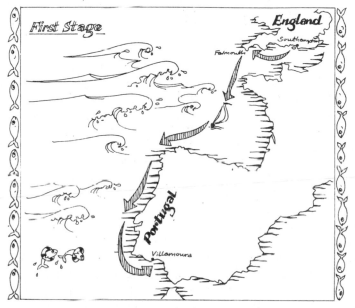

Deceptive by Name

The sailing yacht Deceptive lay secure at her moorings, next to Berthon's boatyard in Lymington, peacefully awaiting the return of her new owners. The Autumn sun glinted faintly off her slightly dusty topside, causing the row of portholes along her side to vanish, momentarily lost in the wide, dark blue feature-strip that wrapped itself gracefully around her sleek, white fibreglass hull. Her teak deck had taken on that silvery grey sheen which quickly confirms to an experienced onlooker that a boat had not been used for some time.

Fred had bought Deceptive on impulse. It was love at first sight. The very moment he had set eyes on her all rational thought was gone. He had not wanted anything so much in all his life, with the exception of his first bicycle, his first car, his first camcorder, his first set of skis, and the first time he saw Madonna on T.V. adding a totally new concept to the term, 'Like a Virgin'!

She was hardly two years old when Fred first saw her and had

1

been lovingly cared for by the previous owner. 'A real dream machine,' was how he first described her to Nigel and he wasn't far wrong. Sixty-four thousand pounds had been the asking price. Deceptive was offered to Fred at a *remarkable* discount, by a keen young salesman with a habit of repeating himself. He assured Fred that it was in *remarkable* condition and also was *remarkable* in that it came complete with an engine and sails and a host of complex gadgetry, totally confusing, but nevertheless, *remarkable*. This would, in all probability, not have been *remarkable* to anyone else, just to Fred, who knew absolutely nothing about boats. If he had been asked to 'man the winches' would have muttered an embarrassed apology. Stammered that he was a happily married man and satisfying wenches was of very little interest to him. But could he have a look at one anyway. Just in case!

Fred made an offer of just over fifty thousand pounds, secure in the knowledge that it would never be accepted. After all, who would drop the price by twenty percent? He had never been so wrong in his life. He still had a chance to get out of the deal without losing face as the boat had yet to be surveyed. Hopefully, there might be something wrong with it. Alas, the surveyor's report was good. The boat was undervalued and a good buy. There was no sign of osmosis. Nigel had been particularly happy about this as, coming from non-farming stock in Ireland, he thought that the disease could only exist in cattle or sheep.

Fred had become the confused owner of a rather expensive and complex piece of sailing machinery. To make matters even worse he was short ten thousand pounds, his mother's recent demise and the subsequent legacy not being quite enough to cover the full cost. He thought of asking his wife Marge for a sub, but thought better of it.

'Your mother's savings have been frittered away before her poor body is cold in the grave,' Marge complained. Marge ran the family business as Fred couldn't get excited about fish and chips, hamburgers or pizzas any longer. The truth of the matter was simply that Fred's fast food enterprise had been spectacularly slow while Fred was in charge, but was blossoming since Marge took over. Fred's mother had no illusions at all about her son's inability to look after money and had often threatened to leave the lot to a dog's home or to a donkey refuge. Shortly before her death she had relented, deciding that if an ass was going to benefit she may as well keep it in the family.

Nigel, until then, had been only a nodding acquaintance of Fred's. He had come into Fred's restaurant for take-aways as he no longer had a dutiful wife to cook for him at home. He no longer had a home either, because the aforesaid dutiful wife made sure that that had remained her property when she'd thrown him out, for what he'd considered was a slight *misdemeanour*. A certain *miss* in his *demeanour* caused the problem. Fred and Nigel finally came together at a 'Rotary Club' dinner. Nigel was the unpaid guest speaker and was trying to give a humorous talk on 'Broadcasting' while a couple of overfed, designer draped, marshmallows kept up an infuriating high-pitched conversation between two tables. He had a sudden urgent compulsion to scandalise his prattling tormentors, and also surprise their husbands, whom he wrongly assumed to be a stiff-shirted bunch of boring old farts. To gain their attention he gave an unexpected rendition of 'Roll me over in the clover, roll me over, lay me down and do it again'. Much to his surprise everyone had joined in.

Nigel later had blamed his impromptu performance on a few pints of Guinness which he was partial to. It had been a bad day for him. Earlier he had been injected with a cocktail of highly potent antibiotics, and told to avoid alcohol, by a turbaned, half-blind needlework expert from Bangalore who seemed to be perfecting his petit-point. It was for a viral infection which he was prone to and, as he joked, he was usually prone when he got it. The combination of both distillations and then another few pints of Guinness had somewhat lowered Nigel's resistance. Fred had made his sales pitch. Before the night was out they had shaken hands on the deal and Nigel became a part owner of the sailing yacht Deceptive.

Fred chose Nigel as a sailing partner for two reasons. First, he could be endlessly entertaining, just press the play mode button in the morning and he would prattle on all day. This suited Fred who was a little on the dour side and couldn't tell a yarn if his life depended on it. Secondly, he was the only person Fred knew who had a few thousand pounds lying around doing nothing. The only concession that Fred really had to make was to sail the boat under the Irish flag once every three days, but only when they were on the move. Nigel, a Dubliner, felt it was little to ask as his investment was sizable and before long, he knew that further contributions would be necessary. It didn't cross their minds that international marine law would have to be changed to accept this particular arrangement.

Fred and Nigel were about the same age, but there the similarity ended. Fred looked much older than his forty-three years. His thick, greying hair, and lined, newly bearded face, suggested a maturity sadly lacking in reality. However, his long sinewy frame had reserves of strength and stamina not found in many men in their early forties. Deep within his soul Fred was still a twenty year old and was seeking new frontiers, new discoveries. He was already a good skier and a keen sub-aqua diver and now he was going to add yachtsman to his list of accomplishments. Yet, despite Fred's physical achievements, he inwardly lacked self-confidence. This was the catalyst that drove him on, making him strive harder to prove to himself and to others that he had what it takes to succeed. Once he got his teeth into something he wouldn't let go until it broke him or he had it completely mastered.

Nigel, on the other hand, looked ten years younger than his years. He was of stocky build, slightly pigeon chested, with a full head of brown wiry hair which he wore a bit long. His beguiling smile could charm the birds off the bushes and it often did, straight into his bed!

Fred and Nigel couldn't have been more different, yet they got along well together. They had complete faith in their ability, rarely disagreed or quarrelled and respected each other's privacy.

Their new boat, Deceptive, was a sleek, thirty-seven foot Dehler sloop, twelve feet at the beam and drawing just five-foot-six inches. Her displacement including ballast was eight and a half tons. Her maximum sail area was six hundred and eighty square feet. She had a thirty horsepower Yanmar diesel engine which would give her a maximum speed of seven and a half knots, given the right conditions. Her fuel tank held 180 litres and her fresh water tanks 300 litres. High coamings with handrails had hidden conduits which led her halyards and reefing lines back to the cockpit, keeping her decks clear. A self-tacking jib arrangement was provided for handy tacking to windward in restricted waters. Her sail wardrobe, besides the mainsail and self-tacking jib, was made up of a storm jib, number 1, 2 and 3 genoas, and a radial spinnaker. She was masthead rigged with a mast height above decks of 44 feet

(13.4 m.). Her teak centre deck and blue stripes gave her a sporty appearance. This was definitely not the boat for a traditional string and tar sailor. Neither was it an ideal boat for Fred and his cronies to learn the basics of sailing.

Her three double cabins had wash basins and full-standing headroom. In the main saloon there was a large navigation desk, a settee that wrapped itself around a large folding dining table, a U-shaped galley with hot and cold taps, fridge and gas cooker. The toilet (heads) and shower room were to the starboard of the chart table where a V.H.F. radio, Decca navigator, a sailing monitor and depth gauge were conveniently mounted on the dividing wall.

The importers first referred to this model as the 'Mercedes Of The Sea', which may have sounded fine in German, but not too clever in English. However, they had changed their slogan to 'The Porche Of The Ocean.', no reason given. This also didn't sound too good in English.

'The nearest she ever got to earning either title was when she was towed along the M25 at over ninety miles per hour by a lunatic trying to get to Southampton before the pubs shut,' Nigel had been heard to remark over a few pints of Guinness in his local.

Fred and Nigel thought of bringing the boat back to Liverpool but on investigating mooring charges and transport costs decided otherwise. They suddenly realised that they had a boat which they just couldn't afford to keep in England and they'd only had it a few days.

'Twelve hundred pounds to get her to Liverpool on a flaming transporter, or eight hundred to pay someone to take us to Portugal,' Nigel had whined, sinking deeper into another pint of his beloved Guinness, 'and then there's the mooring costs! Cheaper to park the flaming thing in a N.C.P. car park in Central London.' He convinced Fred of the possible financial implications. Fred didn't need convincing. He was skint.

'Four and a half flaming thousand pounds in marina costs.' Fred moaned, head in hands. 'If only I'd known, if only I'd listened to Marge.'

'There's nothing for it, it has to be somewhere abroad, anywhere but England. Anyway,' Nigel crooned in his mellow brogue, 'wouldn't the sailing season be that much longer in the Mediterranean than here? And furthermore, there would be no need to buy sailing gear at all. We could live in shorts and T-shirts and damn all else.'

The decision made, they were off. Fred, sometimes known as Sputnik, and his friend Nigel had to sail Deceptive from Lymington to Falmouth, and then non-stop to the Algarve. As neither had sailed before, they were grudgingly assisted by a mildewy, complaining, garrulous old yacht delivery captain named Bert.

A mildewy, complaining, garrulous old yacht delivery captain named Bert.

Bert, or Pugwash as he was called, when out of earshot, had plenty to complain about. Prior to taking on this job he had brought an old, leaky, sixty-foot fishing boat from Holland to Grimsby single-handed. Due to appalling weather, frequent engine failures, and an almost worthless bilge pump it had taken him almost a week to complete a journey that should have been over in a few days. On his arrival the new owner had complained about Bert's delay and refused to pay him for the extra days worked. But Bert had already removed two fuel injectors from the old engine, as a precaution against just such an eventuality. He had dumped them in the sea, satisfied that honour had been served.

Without a break, Bert jumped on the next train to Southampton for what he hoped to be a fairly routine delivery. The forecast was good and he would earn eight hundred pounds for eight or nine days work. He didn't like yacht owners as a rule but since the incident at Grimsby they had ascended just a little in the pecking order. 'At least they have plenty money and pay their bills,' he told himself. However, when he finally understood that Fred and Nigel wished to be taught how to sail en route to Portugal, and this their very first voyage, his mood changed somewhat. An unshakable, brooding depression settled firmly on his not so broad shoulders and refused to budge until he arrived in Portugal.

Actually, it would be Fred and Nigel's second outing. They thought it prudent to hide from Bert that just two days previously they had run aground within hailing distance of Berthon's boatyard in Lymington, hardly two hours after being launched, and while negotiating the wrong side of a channel marking buoy.

'You want to learn on the way to Portugal, do you?' Bert said. 'My, my. And you've never ever sailed before, neither of you? You wouldn't like a few quick turns round the Isle Of Wight just to get your hand in, would you?' he asked sarcastically. He needn't have bothered. The irony of the situation was lost on Fred and Nigel. If ignorance were bliss they would surely be the happiest crew ever to contemplate a long distance voyage.

The weather could be highly unpredictable and was certainly not the time of year Bert would normally venture through Biscay. But, he badly needed the cash, as he was a little more strapped than usual due to a particularly slow summer.

Later that evening Bert was impressed with Deceptive's handling as they motored to Falmouth for their one and only stop before heading South. He instinctively knew that she would sail well, but he had serious misgivings about Nigel and Fred. Unquestionably, they would not sail well. What if there was an emergency . . . ? He shivered at the thought.

'Do they really expect to learn to sail on the way?' he repeated to himself again and again. This was the last in a very long line of broken camels' backs for Bert. Another last, un-grasped, straw had been added to an already overburdened hump. After this trip he would hang up his canvas plimsolls, sell his sextant and reply to an advertisement he had recently seen in a barber's shop in Stoke which read:

Lonely?

Refined young Philippino girls from good families seek lasting relationships with British males. Marriage considered. Age no object. Three months probation. If unsatisfied there is a no-quibble, money back guarantee.

Send $100 U.S. with S.A.E. for full colour catalogue. [Pre-marital agreements not considered] to: Hilda, ex-American Naval Base, Manila.

At Falmouth, Fred purchased extra charts as Bert was not too impressed with the two Fred had already bought. This was hardly surprising as both were for planning purposes only, one covering the entire Atlantic from Boston to Bordeaux, and the other, the whole of the Mediterranean. Nigel raided a chemist's shop for every cure known for sea-sickness. He returned to Deceptive with arm bands, patches that stuck behind the ear, and tablets of all shapes and sizes. It was an over-kill situation, hopefully one would work. His trip from Lymington had been horrific. He had been sick the whole time and he wondered if it might not be better to jack the whole thing in and simply head for home. Fred took great pains to point out that there would be no turning back once they headed out past The Lizard.

They topped up with diesel and water and added some sensible provisions to their list. This was on Bert's specific recommendation and included two large bottles of brandy and a few cases of Newcastle Brown ale!

'In case of unforeseen emergencies,' Bert said.

The next day their minds made up to get going, Bert hoisted the self-tacking jib, raised the mainsail, pointed Deceptive in the right direction, retired to his bunk and wasn't seen on deck again for eight days, or so it seemed to an over-anxious Fred. Bert was untroubled, he felt that he had earned the rest. As long as Fred and Nigel kept a look-out, maintained the headings, and cooked the meals, why should he worry? He had the brandy, even though it was of a particular poor quality and not the five star he'd asked for, and the two cases of beer. This would see him through. 'Cheap skates,' he decided. 'If they want to learn to sail this will really teach them.' Hands-on-training, was how he would describe it in his demand for extra money. He smiled wickedly, once more burying himself in the latest Jackie Collin's best seller, taking a good swig from the cheap brandy bottle. The acrid taste caused him to shiver involuntarily. 'They would pay dearly for this!'

Fred was on duty most of the time as Nigel wandered around in a somnolent state, doped up to the eyeballs with anti-sea sickness drugs.

When they arrived in Villamoura, Fred showed serious signs of mental deterioration. His speech was slurred and his eyes deep-sunk in his drawn, unshaven face. His clothes cast off odours of sweat and other body fluids due to errors of balance in both feet and mind. Urinating over the side in blustery conditions was an art he didn't quite have the hang of yet – hang being the operative word. 'Now, if I had three hands maybe, just maybe,' he reasoned.

Fred was happy. He knew within himself that he had won. He had beaten the sea like countless millions before him and now he could really call himself a sailor.

Bert, much relaxed, having slept the greater part of the voyage, confessed that he liked Fred and Nigel, admired their spunk, and could he have his eight hundred pounds, and his air fare home, please? Oh! and by the way, an extra hundred smackeroos for the special training, in cash, and could he borrow the boat for a month or two next summer? He had really enjoyed it so much he would like to bring a dozen or so of his friends out to see her? No! said Fred to all the new demands and especially the proffered offer of friendship.

Next time there would be no need for a delivery captain, Fred decided. He couldn't bear another Pugwash on board, especially not one that slept twenty-four hours a day and needed to drop his trousers at regular intervals in order to express a build up of unnatural gas so vile that the odour never seemed to dissipate fully. Fred believed that Bert got more pleasure from this unusual pursuit than he assumed an Arab gets from a really good belch. But why on earth did he loosen his trousers? Did he feel he should share it unselfishly with others? Fred couldn't work it out at all.

Nigel revealed himself as an unexpected expert on the subject and gave a long and informed commentary. 'He's probably made a flaming documentary about it,' Fred thought unkindly. As an erstwhile T.V. presenter this would very much be his wont. 'Obviously, he has done some serious research on the subject!!'

'It is well known that the surreptitious passing of gas can be an art,' Nigel began, giving Fred a knowing glance. 'A quiet look with a raised eyebrow can throw the suspicion to an innocent bystander. I can vouch for this method as I have often practiced it myself. But . . . ,' he paused for effect, 'Pugwash is to farting what Punch is to serious theatre -no subtlety, just plenty knockabout action and frequent encores. It was never a case of, 'Oh! no! he didn't.' You always knew that he damn well had.' Nigel searched Fred's features for a glimmer of amusement. There was none. Fred thought it better to ignore Nigel. Utterances from assholes left him un-amused, he decided. He was absolutely and categorically positive of this, even if one of the assholes was his sailing partner, Nigel.

All that remained now was for Fred and Nigel to fly back to their home town of Liverpool, get a crew together, learn a little more about seamanship and then sail Deceptive to her final destination, Greece. Greece was selected because it was about the only country they could now afford.

The next crew would be made up of their friends. Well, actually Nigel's friends, as Fred's were a little unstable and liable to drown themselves at the first opportunity. But, first they must take sailing lessons. After all, Fred decided, he would have to navigate, he would need to know which sails to use, when to reef and how to maintain the engine. But, not to worry, it was only mid-September and the trip would not take place until April.

2

The Press Gang

Immediately on his return from Portugal Fred had signed on for one week's training with a French yachting school. As a result, he now had sufficient proof, if proof was ever needed, that he was competent to sail. Well, it didn't actually state that. But who would be so presumptuous as to question the formal looking document in his possession? This took the form of an elaborate scroll given to him by the instructor who, obviously, didn't like Englishmen. Only after Fred had complained vigorously and demanded his money back did he receive his copy of the parchment.

'After all,' Fred explained to Marge, who had given him the course as a present, 'all the others got theirs and I wasn't leaving until I had mine. I had paid my money just like the rest!'

'Yes dear,' Marge uttered, trying to hide a willful grin that was just about to spread across her care worn face. She wasn't at all sure that sailing was as easy, or as safe as her husband kept telling her. 'Are you sure you understood everything they taught you? You know your French was never that good?'

Fred first produced the scroll on a cold, grey, dank, miserable, November night in a quayside bar in Liverpool which had retained none of its former dock-side charm. Its reputation for whores and press gangs had long since been forgotten. It was now frequented by their modern day equivalents, double glazing salesmen and bank clerks. Gathered round a laden drinks table was a diverse bunch of characters, all potential crew members, made up mostly of Nigel's rugby pals. Fred had the dubious task of convincing some of them that they should take time off from their work and businesses and sail with himself and Nigel to Greece. Two of the assembled bunch looked like fearsome characters. They reminded Fred of punch drunk, heavyweight boxers. He had an instinctive feeling that they could be trouble-makers. These thickset men with twisted noses and bent ears were probably great on a rugby pitch, but never on a boat, he decided. 'Like bulls in a bloody china shop!' If this was the answer to their crewing requirements Fred began to wonder whether or not the right question had been asked?

Fred, himself, had been transformed into a daunting figure. His much improved beard added stature to his streaky presence. He wore dark blue deck shoes, and had removed the plastic shoulder protectors from a donkey jacket which he wore over a navy blue, roll neck sweater, or 'tricot' as he now referred to it after his trip to France.

'I will 'ave to put on mon tricot as it is tres chilly outside,' he'd said to Marge, in a voice suitably inflected. This was to illustrate a working knowledge of French and a highly developed sense of humour. Marge knew only too well that he had neither. Nevertheless, Fred now looked the part. From head to toe he looked every bit a sailor, an old tar. Unfortunately, this illusion - for illusion it was- was reminiscent of putting a conch shell to your ear to hear the sea.

They had already studied the charts and the proposed route. Well, not really charts, but a Phillips World Atlas whose centre pages covered their intended route across the Mediterranean.

'No, no, this is Greece and that one over there is Portugal,' he thought he heard Nigel say as he joined them around the fire. They were busy working out the distance. Assuming, from the shown scale that two fingers equalled one inch and by walking the fingers across the page, carefully flicking stray crisps out of the way, they estimated that the journey could be anything from 900 to 2000 miles.

It was better than he'd hoped. Good enough for tonight's purposes.

'The less they know the more chance I'll have of mustering a compliant if not a too competent crew,' he thought. Wouldn't do to have the crew better qualified than himself.

'A little at a time and we'll get there,' whispered Nigel, anticipating Fred's thoughts and making room for him by the fire. 'We won't stretch their thought mechanisms too much at this stage, might break the elastic.' Fred glanced again at the two Orang Utangs and involuntarily shivered.

Fred had a half of lager and then thought it time to begin the hard sell. He cleared his throat noisily and stood up.

'This will be the voyage of a lifetime.' 'God!' he thought, 'I sound like a Time-Share salesman.'

'Ah'm no goan, if it's going tae take tha' long,' piped up Steve, in a broad Glasgow accent.

'Just think of the adventure. How often does one get the chance to sail straight across the Mediterranean?' continued Fred, slightly shaken. This wasn't going to be as easy as he'd hoped.

'Once a fortnight if you work for Cunard,' added George from Belfast, trying to better his fellow Celt's, Steve's, opening remark.

'Bloody comedians', thought Fred, 'I'm going to have a crew of bloody smart arses.'

'I work forcun ard all my life,' piped up Pat from Leeds, not wishing to be outdone, an' I've never sailed across the Med.' He laughed at his own joke. The slightly balding, tall one called Kevin didn't get it.

Fred glared at them and struggled on. 'Sun kissed, deserted, tropical beaches, white sands . . . palm trees . . . cheap wine . . .' He paused for effect. 'Topless women. Yes, even topless women!' Hit them where they think, and going by their comments so far he decided that was nowhere near their brains.

'Got it,' interjected Kevin laughing, 'for Cunard. It's a play on words, right?'

'Is anyone interested?' Fred asked in desperation.

At last they paid attention, and his words soon had the desired effect. Grey Liverpool ceased to exist. They were now far away on a sailing boat in a technicolour dream, and all they could hear was the faint whish as the yacht, Deceptive, cut her way through the azure waters of the Mediterranean.

'Bloody funny name forra boat,' Steve whispered to Nigel.

'Gibraltar, Ibiza, Sardinia, Italy, and then a leisurely cruise up the Ionian to Corfu.'

Fred could see that he was winning, he knew that he almost had them eating out of his hand. He needed just one more sentence to clinch it, a closer . . . then inspiration.

'I regret gentlemen, but we'll have to be sailing for three weeks . . . no work, no girl friends, no wives, no telephones, just . . .' He shrugged his shoulders as if further comment was unnecessary. He refrained from mentioning, no drinking. Fred was no fool.

In an instant there were cries of; 'I'm coming . . . me too . . . don't forget me . . . can we leave tomorrow?'

Fred had a fleeting feeling of guilt. He realised that Nigel had the ball rolling well before the meeting. But, it was he who convinced them to go, and as a result he would be their skipper. He had never skippered before. Deep down he knew he was far from ready for this voyage. He recalled his sail through Biscay, the confusion of darkness and the endless heaving and yawing as Deceptive beat into the wind in heavy seas, making it impossible to get comfortable. He remembered the inability to cook and the nauseating effect of trying to eat. He didn't mention what confined spaces could do to people deprived of comfortable beds, sleep, hot food, and their loved ones as he'd experienced on the way to Portugal. They change. All pretence of being civilised disappears. Deprivation of normal comforts triggers something in their long forgotten primordial past. They become monsters; they don't shave, they burp loudly during meals, they pass gas in un-ventilated spaces, they never wash themselves or the dishes, but use countless gallons of precious fresh water washing stinking socks. Worst of all, on night watch they relieve themselves into the wind, ensuring that those in the cockpit will have to use even more fresh water. It was pure hell!

Steve, George, Kevin and Pat were hooked, the others would be unable to get time off. Fred raised his eyes to heaven. Bent nose, and the one with the twisted ears were not coming. 'Probably couldn't get time of from their jobs as bouncers,' he decided, unkindly.

'Like clergymen in a brothel,' Nigel thought ruefully, looking at their raised hands. 'All coming and no real experience between the lot of them.

Fred elected himself captain.

Kevin, a lad from the Welsh valleys, would be first mate as he was a dinghy sailor and the only one with any real sailing experience. He produced his sailing club's rule book as proof of his ability to sail and Fred thought he threw a questioning look his way. Instead of being comforted, Fred had a sudden feeling of impending doom. He would have to do something fast. Nigel saw the problem and casually mentioned that there was quite a difference between handling a dinghy and a thirty-seven foot sailing yacht as he had found out on his first sailing lessons.

'Yachts don't fall over and dump you in the water. Well not too often anyway,' he joked.

This was the moment Fred had been dreading. He had no option but to produce his sole credential. He would have to bluff it. With a exaggerated flourish he produced his French sailing certificate. He hoped no one spoke French. This was important as he hadn't been able to get it translated yet.

Could he trust that French sailing instructor when he had tried so hard to deprive him of his just award? 'The bloody cheek of him.' The thought of it still made Fred's blood boil.

The scroll was passed around from hand to hand.

'I can't unnerstond a wurd of it, it's aw' in French,' said Steve.

'Obviously the wee man from north of the border has the same problem with English,' Fred thought harshly.

'Let me see thon,' said George, who considered himself a bit of an expert in things French after a brief liaison with a French-maid kissogram.

She'd arrived for a stag party and he suggested she should stay, and whilst she was there perhaps he could dust up his French, as it were. After a few months, George still hadn't learnt a single word of the language, hardly surprising as she really came from Lurgan, a few miles down the road from his native Belfast. However, she had dropped her French accent almost as fast as she had dropped everything else, which suited George fine.

'Looks fine to me,' he affirmed, handing it back to Fred, 'but, what does DEFAUT mean ?'

3

Bring On Them Dancin' Girls

Five months had already slipped by since that bleak night in the Liverpool bar. It was now the month of April and almost time to commence the trip from Portugal to Greece. Fred, still unsure of his ability to navigate, purchased a 2000 system satellite navigator for five hundred pounds to make sure he got their position spot on. For another four hundred he was offered a state of the art G.P.S. instant update system, but thought it not worth the difference as they would only average five knots, and who in their right mind could get lost travelling at only five miles per hour? Besides it wasn't his money, Nigel had paid for it, as he had for a collection of other essential yachting items purchased from a second hand chandlery with the wonderful name 'Yot-Grot'. Included in his list were a five man inflatable rubber boat, a hand bearing compass, a book on navigation, an old nautical almanac, and an out-of-date pilot book for French Mediterranean ports, which they had no intention of going anywhere near. Nigel couldn't resist it as it only cost fifty pence. They also purchased the necessary charts and an up-to-date Reed's Mediterranean pilot, also life jackets, a deck harness, and, in Portugal, a small second hand outboard motor for the dinghy and some extra rope.

Fred had run out of ready money and it was probably just as well he was leaving the country, because Marge was sick and tired of the whole business and, as she said often, she was quickly getting to the stage where she might not be responsible for her actions. A threat that Fred didn't take at all lightly as he had been down that well-travelled road before.

'The bailiffs are practically banging on the door,' Marge moaned, 'and you want more money?' Marge was quite determined that none of her hard earned cash would end up in this project, which she considered to be a total waste. 'We could have bought that new conservatory and some fitted carpets and still have plenty left to cruise round the world, being waited on hand and foot,' she'd whined. 'Let that announcer fellow pay,' she added vindictively, as she blamed Nigel for Fred's sudden entry into yachting. 'These television people get money for old rope. They have so much they don't know what to do with it. Leading honest people astray. More money than sense. What do ye need all that stuff for anyway?'

Nigel's charm failed completely to impress Marge. She was impervious to men's flattery as a result of her long-suffering marriage to Fred, which she regarded as some kind of penance and knew that one day she must get her ultimate reward in heaven. She had been taken in by flattery once and look where it had got her, she thought, looking daggers at her unsuspecting husband.

As Nigel picked up the bills his share in Deceptive increased. He paid the mooring charges in Villamoura and, as a result, he could now fly his flag every second day. Fred fretted secretly on how long it was going to be before Nigel owned more of the bloody boat than he did himself.

Nigel and Fred arrived one week early in Portugal to ensure that everything was ship-shape and ready for the crew's arrival.

'Ship shape and Bristol fashion,' Fred quoted, resorting to what he now considered to be mandatory language. He used nautical terms whenever possible and was surprised that Nigel could still refer to fenders as bumpers. Nigel retorted characteristically, suggesting that Fred was becoming a real pain. Whether he used the word bumper or fender was his business. 'What difference did it make anyway?' he said. He knew what he meant. Everyone else knew what he meant, so stuff you Fred.

Everything would be ready for the crew's arrival, they would make certain of that.

They found Deceptive much as they had left her. She was now a lot dustier but otherwise looked superb.

'With a little elbow grease she will look like new,' Nigel said admiringly, 'Isn't she a real beauty?' He stood back to admire her sleek lines as she rested, securely moored to the jetty she shared with a rather neglected yacht. Nigel couldn't help but remark on the sorry state of the other boat.

'What a mess! That boat looks as if it's been through the wars.'

'Hi, you guys, this yer boat?' said a beaming tanned face, with a pronounced American accent that had suddenly popped out of a hatch on the very same mess that Nigel had just alluded to.

'Name's Jimmy I've been looking after her fer yuh.'

Atop the beaming face was a mop of tousled sun-bleached hair. 'Name's Jimmy. I've been looking after her fer yuh. Thought you guys were never coming back.'

Jimmy professed to be an expert on all things to do with yachting, having sailed from California, through Panama and finally on to Portugal. Considering that his boat had been de-masted, and looked to say the least, un-cared for, did little to confirm his statement. His washing lay everywhere; it was on the guard-rails, on the bowsprit and hanging from a makeshift line, hitched to the end of the redundant boom. There were two rusty, racing bicycles on deck, as well as, parts of an outboard engine that had been dismantled and forgotten about. His de-masting was the reason he gave for having spent six months already in Villamoura awaiting a replacement, but there was another attraction. The clothes drying in the sun gave the game away. It was obvious that there was a young woman staying on board if one was to judge by the anorexic underclothes scattered about. Jimmy was having a romantic interlude with Laura, a dancer from the local casino. The whole pontoon was talking about their sexual gymnastics, which usually commenced after they returned from the casino at two o'clock in the morning. On Deceptive, alongside, Nigel could mimic Laura's cries and Jimmy's heavy breathing almost exactly, and had taken

18

to doing the odd impression when sure they were both out.

'Oh my God! Oh no! Oh no!' would suddenly shatter the silence from what was apparently Jimmy's boat, followed by a long exhausted asthmatic wheeze. Next morning Jimmy would be met with, 'You were home early last night!'

Fred had too much on his mind to be amused by all this. He had noticed a strange growth on Deceptive's hull and feared that this might be the dreaded osmosis. Jimmy assured him that they were just barnacles.

'Leave em there an' you'll lose a knot,' advised Jimmy. He offered to go out with them for what he called a breeze up. They would then anchor somewhere off a beach and while Laura, her dancing pals and himself had a picnic, Fred and Nigel could scrape the hull.

Next day, under Jimmy's instruction, they slipped the lines and headed out of the marina. Twice the engine failed, each time it only started after they had drifted onto other moored yachts.

'It just needs a good day's run and everything will be fine,' shouted Fred, his sailor's cap perched nonchalantly on his head, blissfully unaware of the real havoc he was causing on the jetties, as boat owners prepared to fend off the next assault.

Jimmy stood, perplexed, one leg over the guard-rail, ready to push off yet again and wondered if they would even make it to the harbour exit.

It was a perfect day, the sun was warm and Laura and her friends were already disrobing.

'Well!, it's a nice day and why shouldn't they?' Fred thought. He was no slouch when it came to admiring pretty women, especially now that Marge was not about, but wait! They were taking their bikini tops off as well and they hadn't even left the marina. This was really going too far. Fred was almost speechless. A deck full of bikini clad girls is one thing, but a boatload of brazen hussies was something totally unexpected. What could he do?. There was no law against it.

'It's a free world,' he considered, 'but we're not anywhere near a beach, they're on the deck of my boat exposing themselves to all and sundry!'

Fred was now in one of his regular blue funks. He hadn't bargained for this. It was like a bosom factory . . . boobs end to end. They were pear shaped, bell shaped, they twisted and turned and heaved up and down, but Fred couldn't get into the swing of things. Everywhere he looked they seemed to be pointing at him, silently accusing him of previously unsuspected voyeurism. If one could commit mental adultery Fred was in deep trouble, up to his neck in lustfull thoughts. He would have to avert his eyes, think of other things. He tried reciting the alphabet backwards. It was no use. He was mortal after all. He would have to peek, pretend what he was seeing was an everyday occurrence. Maybe staring might rid him of this moral insensibility. That must be the answer! He would give it a chance, see if it would dull his senses.

It really wasn't all that bad as there were only seven bare chested women on board, which was fourteen mammary protuberances, and fourteen into a thirty-seven foot boat would work out at thirty-one inches from boob to boob if equally dispersed. When you look at it from a mathematical point of view it didn't seem excessive. But, Fred wasn't interested in mathematics at that moment, he had already done his sums and the answer was plain. If Marge should hear of this, his number would be well and truly up! He would have to tell her of course. Make a clean breast of . . . aagh! It was no use they would have to cover up . . . at least until they cleared the harbour exit.

If one could commit mental adultery Fred was in serious trouble.

The stalled engine, and general commotion had given the neighbouring yachtsmen time to arouse themselves. They crowded on their decks, with broad grins on their now expectant faces, their whistling and caterwauling drawing even more attention to Fred's plight. Their many offers to come aboard were rejected by Fred who was unable to come to terms with the situation. He had yet to pass the customs building and the harbour police. 'Could I be arrested for this?' he asked himself, giving Deceptive full throttle, polluting the marina with thick blue smoke, which he most certainly could be arrested for. But Fred need not have worried as the girls waved to the customs officers who were now lined on the quayside intrigued by all the commotion. Some of them even waved back, they were well known to the dancers, frequented the casino, and even knew the girls by name.

Once outside the harbour they headed west. A steady fifteen knot wind was blowing and it was now time to get the sails up. As

Some of them even waved back.

this was a training exercise, Jimmy decided to use the mainsail
and working jib. Nigel had hanked on the jib in harbour and
now it lay ready to be hoisted, loosely tied to the guard-rail.
Fred wasn't sure how to fit the mainsail's reefing lines, having
removed them six months ago and feared that he may have
attached them in the wrong reefing cringles.

'Take her into the wind, Fred,' instructed Jimmy. 'Nigel, haul
the main up.'

Nigel hauled on what he thought was the main halyard but
nothing happened.

'Not that rope,' shouted Jimmy, pointing, 'That one there.'

Nigel pulled on the halyard and the main went up so far and
stuck. Nigel put the halyard round a self-tailing winch and
started to grind furiously. Jimmy went spare.

'If it's not going up there's a reason for it. Look first. Release
the reefing line jammers, ya son of a bitch,' he shouted, pointing
to the batch of clutches behind the winch.

21

With this done the sail moved a little, but as they had now lost headway Fred couldn't keep Deceptive into the wind as he had stopped the engine prematurely. The battened sail was pushed sidewards under the spreaders. Jimmy also noticed that the reefing lines were in juxtaposition and ordered the sail to be dropped. Half an hour later everything was once again ready. Unfortunately, the wallowing had caused two of the girls to become seasick and the rest to feel decidedly queasy.

'Don't mess around when you take her out, man, otherwise, you're gonna have everyone pukin' all over yer nice teak decks.'

With the engine on once again both sails were set without any further problems. With Jimmy now at the helm, Deceptive seemed to give a sigh of relief, and responded like the true thoroughbred she was. Within a short time they were tearing along at five and a half knots, once again the engine off, and only the sound of the bow slicing the waves giving any indication of speed. The girls were stretched out like sardines on the flat teak centre deck, all sensations of sickness gone.

'The only thing missing is the can,' thought Fred, sarcastically. They had slapped buckets of oil over their bodies and drips were creating dark patches on the beautifully greying wood. It would take months before the sun had once again bleached them out. Fred had already added this to his mental list of what not to do on boats.

Jimmy took great care in explaining to Fred the size of sails to use in different wind conditions.

'If you find her overpowered, either reef down or change your headsail. You can tell by the feel of the helm whether there is too much sail up or not. Got that?' He emphasised the need to come through the wind and to avoid gybing until they were more experienced. He covered the three main points of sail: running, reaching and sailing close hauled. Jimmy had decided that the only possible way this lot could survive the long voyage was to put them through this routine every day until they left for Greece. With the girls on board, this could very well be a not too unhappy prospect, as each girl was more talented than the next. Not only were they hoofers, but most were trained singers or actresses trying to gain their Equity cards. They good naturedly vied with each other, giving Fred and Nigel a demonstration of their less obvious talents.

Jimmy changed tack repeatedly, showing them how to come about safely and effortlessly.

However, other things had to be done today. The bottom had to be cleaned, the picnic had to be organised, and Jimmy had to wear, for the first time, a very special present that Laura had made for him.

The girls had now removed their bikini bottoms and were clad only in the briefest of G strings, which they continually adjusted to make sure that their well oiled bodies were sun tanned all over. Fred was getting used to seeing their well cared for, curvaceous forms stretched out on his deck and perhaps, just once or twice, he may have stared that little bit too long.

Jimmy had gone below to put on Laura's present and so attired came up on deck.

'What on earth is he wearing?' wondered Nigel 'Don't look girls!' he shouted, in mock horror, but it was far too late.

Fred too saw the apparition and searched for his camera. 'Where's the bloody camera?' he asked a gob-smacked Nigel. He had to hide that camera. He'd never be able to explain this to Marge. Bad enough having naked women on board, but now he had to contend with a pervert, as well. The only thing Jimmy was wearing was a canary yellow codpiece, with pink, red, and blue flowers. This was Laura's gift, fashioned from one half of his mother's discarded Hawaiian bikini top. It was hideous, it was obnoxious, it was obscene, it was revolting, and Jimmy was no Adonis, being a little on the plump side. In fact there were not enough adjectives in the English language to describe this abomination, but the girls loved it. They screamed and giggled and chased him around the deck. He admonished them,

'You may look, but doo . . . doo . . . don't touch! Unhand me, you varlet.' Or maybe he said 'starlet,' whichever was more appropriate.

'Jaysus, that white arse is something else.' Nigel whispered in mock earnest to a totally bemused Fred.

Jimmy refused to take the codpiece off, pretending that he actually liked it. He was delighted at the reaction and milked it for all it was worth.

Laura had meant it as a joke, thinking that he would never wear it, and now she thought he was taking it seriously. The girls were laughing at him. It had backfired badly. She made up her mind to do something about it.

As it was getting a little cold the girls dressed. A few bikini tops had gone missing and it was assumed they had blown overboard.

The girls went on stage that night, Jimmy went back to his boat and Fred and Nigel sat down to some serious reading. Their books were about cruiser sailing. Above them, blowing in the soft night breeze, just below the spreaders, were two bikini tops and a canary yellow codpiece with pink . . . !

4

The Final Preparations

As the days passed neighbours began to ask, sometimes cynically, when Deceptive planned to leave. They gave the most recent weather predictions and told stories of losses at sea, of de-mastings and collisions. They heard of a yacht lost off Cadiz last month, and of friends who had left on similar trips never to be heard of again. Nigel put this down to sour grapes as he reckoned that most of the yachtsmen remaining here were disillusioned, spent old men, who had probably lost their bottle coming through Biscay. Otherwise, why would they stay here, a mere stepping stone from the Mediterranean, the Canary islands or even the Caribbean? They had turned their backs on their families, chucked their jobs and spent all their savings setting out on the adventure of a lifetime, to get no further than Portugal. Even Jimmy fitted this category. He had sailed from San Francisco through Panama and across the Atlantic to cruise in the Mediterranean, but had now decided that, as soon as his mast was replaced, he would head straight back to America without even visiting Gibraltar.

Nigel thought he understood these men but he was well off the mark.

'They wallow in a sea of self delusion,' he decided, using a familiar broadcasting style to amuse himself, 'while I am an island of sanity. I am in their midst, but not one of them. I am going forward and they shall remain.' He was pleased. 'Might use it sometime,' he decided.

What Fred and Nigel didn't realise was that those sailors who remained found their own paradise. They could live aboard their boats at a fraction of the cost of living at home. The weather was possibly the best in Europe as the summer was never too warm or the winters too cold. The cost of eating out was reasonable and provisions were cheap if you avoided the imported foods. The social advantages of living in a marina surrounded by like minded individuals meant loneliness was never a predominant factor. Everyone knew their neighbours and looked out for the less able. Those who really wanted to move on did so. But why move on when everything you wanted from life was right here? Flights from home were reasonable. Families could come and visit. Those who found staying on boats claustrophobic could stay in nearby hotels or flats. If they didn't like sailing they could sunbathe on the vast expanses of beach or play golf in the endless courses that surrounded the harbour. The countryside was unspoiled and the people, the friendliest in Europe. It was Nigel who was wallowing in his own sea of self delusion, not those who had found their particular paradise.

Nigel mistook their innocent remarks and questions as interference in his affairs. When asked technical questions about the boat, he thought they were testing him. Some were, but in the main they were trying to be friendly. He treated every remark with unwarranted suspicion.

'Is your rigging masthead or fractional?' he mimicked. 'There's a high in the Azores; there's a low in the Ionian; the Mistral season is upon us; we're in for a katabolic storm, or you'll have it on the nose the whole way.' He wouldn't mind letting them have it on the nose, frigging, rigging and all!,' he decided. But, what did it all mean? Had Fred and himself learned enough about sailing to continue with this voyage? He wasn't sure any more.

'I must find out all about this weather forecasting business, lives might depend on it! It really wouldn't do to get caught in a ..carbolic storm,' he considered, 'Suds everywhere.' A broad smile split his lips.

Nigel read and re-read sections on atmospheric pressure, synoptic charts, barometric rises and falls, frontal systems and cloud formations, until his head was dizzy. Nothing was clear. He decided in desperation that yet another visit to Jimmy's boat was called for. Good old American Jimmy! What would they have done without him?

Jimmy's greeting was predictable. 'Hi ya bassard. Yuh got another problem?'

Nigel described his predicament.

'Sheet, man, there's nuttin' to it,' Jimmy informed Nigel knowingly, taking a swipe at a small creature that had just crawled onto the table. 'Bassaran cockroaches are everywhere, must have come on board in a cardboard box or somethin'. Can't get rid of the little bassards, tried everythin'. Just tune to yer local radio station when they're dishing out the weather

26

forecast for shipping or ask at the marina office. If you unnerstand plain English you can unnerstand dem forecasts, man.' Jimmy explained at length how to make use of the information, which sea areas to note and how to identify a general pattern. 'Look at it this way, the weather is left behind as the world spins. Right? It goes west to east an' the prevailin' wind is off the Atlantic, goddit?'

Nigel was impressed. Was that all there was to it? Was it that simple? He was so delighted that he invited Jimmy to Wellies, their favourite local bar, to celebrate. He would now have to wait up for the weather forecast which would be broadcast at six the next morning. Where better to wait than in a pub and then a disco? It was going to be a long night. One had to make some sacrifices if one was to ensure the safety of all aboard, hadn't one? Fred would pick up the crew from the airport. It was the least he could do given the circumstances.

'And by the way, all those cardboard boxes should be put out – cockroaches,' Nigel added, as he and Jimmy left the jetty for yet another marathon drinking session. All in the line of duty of course.

Fred feared cockroaches as much as Marge hated health inspectors. No matter what you did both species just kept coming back! He panicked, horrified at the thought of cockroaches on board. If they got into their boat they would never get rid of them. He got to work immediately, dumping boxes onto the quay, wondering why Nigel wasn't giving him a hand.

Later, Fred installed the new satellite navigation set. The instructions seemed simple. 'Power to the set, co-axial cable to the aerial, fix aerial to pushpit rail, turn it on and Bob's your auntie... Pieceacake,' Fred muttered to himself through his greatly improved beard. He always muttered when engrossed in something he knew little about.

Fred had already helped to install Hector's set. Hector was a seventy-five year-old who had just bought an old motor sailer along the jetty. As far as Fred was concerned, he shouldn't have bought more than an extra pair of socks, as it looked as if he would never get the chance to wear them out. He had tested his own unit on Hector's antenna and didn't have any problems.

Now its L.E.D lit up and to Fred that was a plus. The minus was trying to get the aerial wire to the receiver as the channel designed for the purpose was already full. An opened wire clothes hanger, much sweat, contortions more befitting a double-jointed circus performer filling in his tax return, a few loud oaths, and eventually Fred had the cable in place.

The single sheet instruction inferred that a one-armed, blind monkey could work the set. Fred switched it on, punched in some information that told it approximately where it was. This amused Fred as he had expected to be told by the bloody thing where he was supposed to be. After all, that was what he had bought it for! He then put on the satellite alarm which would bleep for ninety seconds whenever a good fix was obtained. Now he only had to wait for a satellite to pass overhead.

The set was user friendly. A self test series of questions and answers appeared on the L.E.D. screen:

Battery? . . . O.K.

Aerial? . . . O.K.

Installation? . . . O.K.

It was in love with itself. The questions it should have asked and didn't, were; 'Can I be guarantied to give a true position when required,' or 'Does this dipstick installing me know what the hell he's at?'

Three hours later a plaintive 'bleep' announced that a fix had been obtained.

'This is not good enough,' Fred thought, who sat staring at it most of that time praying for some sign of life. It wasn't like his, now redundant, Decca, but nevertheless it worked. 'Possibly the number of satellite passes is limited,' he reasoned. He already made excuses for it. 'Like waiting for the last bus on a wet night,' he thought. 'There must be something far wrong.' This did not reassure him at all. If they were caught close to shore in fog it would be useless. He decided to leave it on overnight to see how many passes registered by morning. He retired to his bunk with his Walkman and favourite Beethoven tape, as he didn't wish to be disturbed by one of Nigel's noisy returns.

Nigel's and Jimmy's visit to Wellies went as one would imagine. Laura left them early and returned to Jimmy's boat. They drank too much, sang out of tune, tried to chat up two very uninterested females and then assisted each other along the jetty stopping for a final natter. There was time enough for Nigel to get the six o'clock weather forecast as it was now just past four. They talked and laughed a little too loudly for a Canadian insomniac, who told them rudely to, 'Get the hell outta here. There's people trying to sleep.' Jimmy crashed out in the cockpit of his boat after noisily tripping over the two rusty bicycles and the dismantled Yamaha. Negotiating gangway steps would have been suicidal in his condition. The Canadian was up again and could be heard remarking to someone below decks that he hoped the daft bastard had broken his stupid neck.

Nigel turned the dial on the F.M. radio slowly and deliberately to the selected station as only someone blitzed out of their brain could. It was only four fifteen, so he jammed himself between the navigator's seat and the head's partition wall. He was determined not to sleep until he heard his first forecast. This was going to be a big moment in his life, another first. His very first fishermans' bulletin. No way was he going to let Fred and their new crew down.

Fred found him still sitting there at six-thirty fast asleep. He suggested unkindly, after roughly shaking him awake, that the next time it might be better if he switched the flaming set on!

'I stayed up all night,' Nigel protested, a little hurt at Fred's attitude, 'just to hear the weather forecast.'

'Great advances have been made in the last few hundred years,' Fred retorted through clinched teeth. 'If you care to check you'll find that alarm clocks have been invented and we have one on board.'

'I know that,' slurred Nigel defensively, pointing to the newly installed Sat. Nav. 'It went off twice already an I couldn't find the bluddy button to turn it off!'

Fred just shook his head in pained wonderment. This was something he had often seen Marge do. Like the time he suggested that they open a venison fast food restaurant and name it Bambi Burgers.

'I think it may be better if you go to your bed and sleep it off. I'll pick the lads up from the airport later.'

The crew were in good form on arrival at Faro airport and tumbled into the hired car, careful not to smash their clinking bottles of duty free booze, still laughing and joking. George, Pat, Kevin and Steve had found the flight memorable. They had entertained the flight staff with an endless repertoire of sea-shanty and rugby songs in an almost empty aircraft. They had been seated across from four giggly young women on a package holiday and had agreed to meet for a few drinks, 'or whatever' that evening. The 'or whatever' part was now taking up much of their conversation and Fred was getting a little annoyed as he felt that they should be asking questions about the boat and the proposed trip. They must leave Villamoura at six the next morning and no later. There was no time for gallivanting. They had a tight schedule to keep.

'The weather could change and we might get stuck in harbour for a few days because of a storm,' Fred fretted. 'These idiots are barely off the plane and already they are thinking of delaying our departure so as they could have some 'or whatevers'. Do they think this is a bloody package holiday, or what?' Fred wasn't going to stand for it.

To leave at daybreak the next morning they would all have to spend the evening moored to the customs dock fully cleared. Failing this, they would lose four daylight hours as the customs office didn't open early and it took hours to get through the paperwork. A demonstration of 'man overboard drill' was planned for that afternoon and Fred had invited Laura and a few of her friends and, of course, Jimmy for a last sail and a farewell drink. That evening only the crew were to have a meal on board, while being given a full briefing on their trip by none other than their captain.

Fred bit his tongue, deciding to say nothing until they were all settled on the boat.

First things first. He must take their passports, then their permanent guests must be shown to their quarters and settled in.

George and Kevin were to share the starboard cabin, Pat and Steve up front, while Fred shared the remaining cabin with Nigel. He would also use the sailing berth in the main cabin which was ahead of the galley. This offered an unobstructed view of the instruments at the navigator's table at night. From a lying position he could monitor wind speed, distance travelled, ship's speed, and the depth. More important still, he could keep an eye on those on watch through the open hatch entrance.

Fred took great pride in showing them around. He made a point of not awakening Nigel. He insisted that the main cabin was for the use of all and must not be littered with personal belongings. He showed them how to work the toilet and impressed on them to be sparing with the fresh water.

'If you need a wash, go for a swim, and don't put anything

down the toilet unless it's been eaten first with the exception of loo paper,' he advised severely. He showed them how to use the gas cooker and pointedly mentioned that a hot meal was a major requirement in keeping the crew's morale high during a protracted voyage.

'Each will have their turn at washing and cooking. No exceptions.'

'So far so good,' he thought. 'As soon as I mentioned the loo I thought there would be a stampede after all the drinking they'd done last night! Might as well bring the subject of drink up now.' This was going to be his last instruction and he knew it was going to be very unpopular.

He braced himself and took a deep breath. 'There will be no drinking on board while we're at sea.'

The crew were dumb-struck. Had the man gone insane?

'I will require you all to hand over your duty free, which will be kept in the drinks cabinet.' Fred pointed to the offending cabinet.

'Bloody hell!' swore Steve, in amazement, 'Has he got a lock on it! He'll need it!' Steve, coming from the land of exquisite fifteen-year-old malts could get seriously perturbed when it came to who was going to do what with his duty free.

'The bar will only be opened when we reach harbour. It's for your safety,' Fred continued.

'We'll have to think about this one, Fred,' Kevin interjected. 'I think you're asking too much of the lads. We should all hold on to our own booze.'

Nigel, who had been listening intently on his bunk to the latter part of Fred's preaching, thought he had better do something before things reached a stand-off. Jumping to his feet he opened his cabin door.

'Morning, lads,' he yawned, scratching his stubble. 'See you've all arrived safely.'

'What do you think about this drink restriction. It's a little Draconian, don't you think?' queried George.

'I know a good place to thrash this one out, guys,' giving them all a broad wink. 'Give me half a second and I'll be ready. I've found a cracking pub up the road.'

Nigel suggested to a gob-smacked Fred that he should come and join them once things were sorted out, but Fred already had his mind set. No, he would stay on board and tidy up.

'Sling your bags in your rooms, lads, and let's be off,' shouted Nigel, quickly getting dressed.

They left Fred wallowing in his pent up frustration. His martyrdom was only just beginning. He fiddled with the Sat. Nav. dejectedly, noticing that they still had only three fixes. One was U.S. – unserviceable – which he took to mean useless. This he confirmed easily as he plotted their position twenty miles inland and up a bloody mountain at that. To admit that there was something wrong with his only means of navigation, other than the compass, was unthinkable.

'It must surely sort itself out later,' he thought. 'Something's interfering with the reception. Must be local. Might be all the masts around here shielding the signal?' Worried as he was, Fred decided he couldn't abort the trip now.

Four hours had quickly slipped by since the crew had departed to the bar. Fearing the worst, Fred reluctantly went to look for them.

He found them doing a 'can can' routine in the middle of Wellies bar, helped by Jimmy and a few girls from the casino. They welcomed him like a long lost friend.

'Hey! Sputnik, good ole cap'n Sputnik,' shouted George, slapping Fred a little too hard on the shoulder. Fred was about to strike back when Nigel grabbed his hand.

'Now, now, Fred, there's no need to get physical, tsk tsk,' he reproved. 'I had to compromise on the drinks question, but I think it's fair,' he whispered, conspiratorially. 'They've agreed to a beer with each meal, or a glass of wine . . . and oh! Almost forgot . . .a sundowner.'

'Breakfast?' questioned Fred, sarcastically. 'Do they get a drink with breakfast as well?'

'Course not!' giggled Nigel.

Fred had to concur. 'The ignominy of it,' he thought, 'having to eat humble pie.' And it was his boat and his voyage. He had no choice, otherwise they would have started off on an even worse footing. Fred knew only too well that any discord at this early stage would be like a festering blister later and could easily ruin the trip.

Nigel called the crew together and explained the new terms so that there would be no confusion.

'And furthermore,' he continued, about to impart a piece of new and welcome news. 'Fred has suggested that we can each have a sundowner at dusk. How about that, eh?'

'Cunning basket,' thought Fred,

'Get's them on your side,' whispered Nigel.

'Good old Sput', knew he'd see sense. Give the auld bugger a beer,' cried George.

After many pats on the back, Jimmy and Fred slipped away without letting the others know where they were going. They moved Deceptive round to the customs jetty, where Jimmy filled her with diesel and Fred attended to the customs clearance papers. They would depart in the morning as planned, if the crew ever did managed to make it back from Wellies.

Fred made sardine sandwiches for himself and Jimmy. Fred liked sardines and this was his way of thanking Jimmy for his help. They would eat a lot of sardines on this trip as Fred had bought a whole case, assuming that everyone liked them as much as himself.

'Got anythin' else, Fred, can't stand sardines? Hey! how about a beer?'

Before Jimmy returned to Wellies, he assured Fred that he would tell the others where the boat was moored and would impress on them the need to return early, as they would definitely be leaving at first light.

'Don't worry, Fred, I'll get those bassers off their butts an back on board in plenny-a-time,' promised Jimmy. 'Kinda wish I was coming . You got one hell of a crew there.'

Fred also wished Jimmy was coming. His presence would have guarantied their safe arrival in Greece. At that moment he would have gladly swapped any three of them for one with Jimmy's experience.

'Don't forgit what I told you. Take it nice an easy an you'll get there. No problem, man,' were Jimmy's parting words.

Jimmy wasn't very successful at getting the others back on board early. At two in the morning Fred was awakened by bodies clambering on board. They brought four cases of beer, two of them Guinness stout, which they dumped on the deck. Nigel crashed out on the pilot couch and the others went to their cabins. All, were instantly asleep without undressing or unpacking.

Fred couldn't get back to sleep and was up at five making breakfast for everyone. He was going to make sure that they were on their way by daybreak. Nigel tuned in sleepily to the weather forecast. Jimmy was right, there was nothing to it. He wrote down the details in a brand new log book. The others looked rough but they were happy and now keen to start. Fred got the engine going after the third try.

'We will motor for the first few hours to get everyone familiar with the boat,' he informed them, gratuitously.

Just as the were about to cast off, Nigel remembered the hired car. If they left it where it was, it would continue to be charged to Fred's credit card which he could ill afford. And, to really set the cat among the pigeons, the car hire office wouldn't open until ten o'clock. They couldn't leave! Fred was furious with himself. He alone was responsible. Why hadn't he remembered it? As a result, they would now arrive in Gibraltar at least four hours later than anticipated and in the dark too. He had never sailed into a strange harbour before, let alone one in the dark. He inwardly baulked.

'Leading lights, lighthouses, sectored lights, channel buoys,' his brain was racing through a list of items requiring a lot more study on his part. It was no good. This trip was doomed to failure even before they had begun. He should call the whole thing off now while there was still time.

The crew went to their cabins to unpack and to sleep for another four hours. They all agreed that the first day had been terrific. Laura and the girls, they decided, were fun and they had tried to capture a few to smuggle on board, but to no avail. The boat was a real beauty and bigger than they had imagined. They would visit a dozen other towns like Villamoura on their way. Yes, it was going to turn out more or less as they had expected. It was going to be a nice relaxing holiday.

'A sort of boozing, cruising, and hooring affair' as George put it. 'Wasn't it?'. . .

4

Man Overboard

Taking a sharp left and heading Southeast after clearing Villamoura, Fred set a course to Gibraltar. They would have sight of land for the next four hours and, after that, would have to depend on Fred's ability to navigate without the aid of visual landmarks. The wind blew from the North at a steady eight knots. This was not enough to carry them along without the help of the engine, or changing the already hoisted self-tacking forcsail for the no1 genoa. Fred was in no mood to change up, so they were motor sailing.

In their enthusiasm to get involved, the new crew members made about every mistake possible. Trying to set the main and the self tacker they dragged his already stretched patience to its outer limit. He didn't feel in the mood to go through all that again, not yet anyway. He needed time to cool down. If their first efforts were anything to go by the trip was going to be a disaster. The main halyard was hoisted up the mast without anyone bothering to attach the shackle to the mainsail and had to be retrieved by Fred balancing precariously on the boom. The self tacking sail was hanked on upside down and then hauled up in full view of all and sundry on the nearby shore, much to Fred's acute embarrassment. He yelled for the bloody thing to be pulled down, breaking a personal resolve not to shout at his crew, and they'd barely left Villamoura.

On their way for more than two hours, Fred, now much calmer, decided it was time for the 'man-overboard' drill, postponed from the previous day. The conditions were excellent, he decided, after a calculated look around. The sea was calm and couldn't be better. With the help of the slightly bronchial engine, they were making a good six knots. Fred began to explain the exercise in a precise, matter of fact, manner.

'When you lose someone overboard,' he began, 'immediately throw out the lifebuoy and the Danford, that's the yellow pole with the light on top, at the back there. Do not, I repeat, do not take your eyes off the person in the water for an instant. The helmsman should immediately release the Autohelm, if it's engaged, take the wheel and start the engine. Have you got that?' he asked. They stared at him stony faced. They hadn't a clue what he was talking about. This was the first inkling they had that this was a serious business and they were amazed that they would actually have to do something if someone fell overboard. No one was going to be as stupid as that!

'Release the sheets,' Fred continued, unaware of the mental conflict he was causing. 'Remember to come through the wind and simply motor back. Stop, luff,' -he hoped that was the right word-, 'upwind of the person in the water and drift downwind towards them. Kill the engine, just in case it's accidentally left in gear. I would rather the person in the water kept his head, both in a figurative and a literal sense,' he joked.

Nobody laughed. It was double Dutch to them all, except Kevin, who recognised those instructions as a cop out and, in his opinion, a sure recipe for disaster.

Fred cleared his throat nervously and continued, now a little unsure. 'I think that, considering your lack of experience, this is probably the best method. Any questions?'

There were none. The lack of response was not surprising as there were only two crew members, besides Fred, who had ever sailed before, Nigel and Kevin. Kevin, even though he had never been on a cruising yacht before, had already decided that, in a real emergency, he would do it his way and wasn't listening to Fred anymore. Nigel had his mind on other things. Lost opportunities. All those beautiful women, a whole flaming chorus line, and he hadn't done anything. 'Must be slipping, boy!' he decided, 'going through a phase, need a tonic or something.'

'Okay,' said Fred, 'let's have a demonstration.' He thought he might get better attention with a little more humour. 'Steve, you jump in and we'll come and get you. If we haven't managed it in an hour, just swim to shore and get the bus to Gibraltar. Okay?'

There was a half-hearted response.

'I'll fling in a lifebuoy,' he continued, 'and we'll come back and pick it up. Kevin, you handle the sails. George, you're on the helm. Steve, watch the man in the water and direct us back.'

Without more ado, Fred threw the life buoy into the water and shouted, 'Man overboard!'

All Hell broke loose. George lost control at the helm and the boat zig-zagged from side to side. The boom swung backwards and forwards across the cockpit, causing Kevin to pop up and down like a jack-in-the-box. Kevin soon tired of bobbing up and weaving. Drawing on his dinghy sailing experience, he took over shouting instructions to the others while he pulled in the main. He then hardened the self-tacking sheet while ordering George to steer right or left. They came around and were about to tack back under sail, when Fred shouted, 'Let the sails fly.' He was annoyed at Kevin as he felt, rightly, that he was trying to show him up. Kevin did as he was told, shrugged his shoulders, not missing the chance to let the others know that he thought Fred's attitude a little infantile. They continued with the sails flapping wildly.

'Flogging themselves to bloody death,' muttered Kevin, loud enough for all to hear, including Fred.

Four passes were made before they managed to lift the life-buoy with the boat-hook. They forgot to put the engine off on the first try and this warranted a bellow from Fred. 'Get that friggin engine off.' When they remembered to put it off, the life-buoy drifted in unison with the boat, matching it perfectly, just slightly out of reach. They played the game for a full fifteen minutes before Fred gave up. 'Put that bloody engine back on,' he ordered, totally exasperated.

It was chaotic; the noise of the sails flapping was deafening. The mainsail sheets and slack reefing lines were lashing Kevin as he stood on the first step of the open hatchway, his arms up to protect his face.

'We'll drop the sails next time. It's obviously too difficult for you to do it the proper way,' Fred uttered, trying to hide the annoyance that he felt at his own ineptitude by blaming the others.

'Proper way my royal Welsh arse,' muttered Kevin, shaking his head pointedly.

With the sails down they perfected the manoeuvre and were able to pick up the life-buoy at every pass. At last Fred could relax a little. Now he felt sure they could rescue anyone who fell overboard without too much difficulty, but he would have to put them through one final test to make sure.

The top rung of the boarding ladder was flat and made an ideal seat directly above the life-raft. Fred had removed his shirt and was now dressed only in shorts. It looked as if he was trying to give his scrawny body a badly needed suntan. Everything had returned to normal and they were once again underway. At an opportune moment, when nobody was looking, he thrust himself over the stern and into the water, shouting, 'Man overboard.' The cold water took his breath away.

Coming to the surface, he saw Deceptive, under full sail, moving quickly into the distance, the life-buoy and Danford having hit the water almost as fast as himself. With swift even strokes Fred swam after the disappearing Deceptive and, grabbing the life-buoy, he firmly fastened the straps around his waist. If the training had been good enough they would pick him up in minutes. If not, he could be in the water for bloody hours, he thought. Glancing to his left he could clearly see the shoreline, a mere half-mile away, and not too far to swim if things went terribly wrong. 'Nigel was capable of handling the boat,' he consoled himself. 'Jimmy's careful tuition had seen to that.'

Fred wanted to see how fast they would react in a more realistic situation. He wouldn't have long to wait. Within minutes he saw Deceptive returning almost as fast as she had left. The sails were still up despite his instructions and he couldn't hear the engine.

'No engine? They've switched the bloody thing off!,' he exclaimed angrily. He could see Kevin at the helm giving orders and realised with a sinking feeling what was happening. A black, brooding, upsetting thought suddenly rattled round his brain like a pea in an empty bucket. Kevin was going to pick him up

'He could be in the water for bloody hours.'

without the assistance of the engine and, worse than that, under full sail. He was about to make Fred look a complete and utter fool and there wasn't a thing Fred could do about it.

A voice shouted for Fred to grab the boat-hook as they swept past. Deceptive was still plunging on at a good four knots and, as soon as Fred caught hold, his arms felt as if they were being dragged from their sockets. He had to let go, cursing loudly. Kevin brought Deceptive's nose into the wind, but he was now downwind of Fred and, instead of drifting toward him, she drifted further away. Kevin next went on a beat to get closer and almost ran Fred down. He made three more attempts and finally gave in. He dropped the sails, put the engine on and picked up, what appeared to be, an extremely angry Fred in a matter of seconds. Behind Fred's outward facade of unbridled rage there was a satisfyingly smug feeling. Kevin had botched the rescue.

'That'll teach the silly bastard,' he said to himself, much relieved.

Kevin had to follow Fred's initial instructions after all. If it had been a real emergency, and if someone had been injured, the extra time in the water could have made it a matter of life and death. Fred still couldn't let it pass without making an issue of it. He was the skipper. It was time to assert his authority,' he told himself.

'You deliberately went against my instructions and tried

to pick me up under sail,' he started. 'How could you do that?'

Kevin was ready for him. He was in no mood for a lecture as he knew he could outsail Fred and anyone else. He was the only real sailor on board. It hadn't worked because he didn't know the boat and he had become slightly flustered. The boat didn't respond as he expected. Everything was so slow compared with dinghy sailing and he couldn't get his timing right.

'Sorry, Fred,' Kevin began, disdainfully, 'but as you were in the water and, not knowing whether it was a real emergency or not, as First Mate I was in charge, so I decided to pick you up the way we do it in dinghy practice. And that's that!'

This wasn't the apology Fred was looking for, but he couldn't argue with the logic of it. So he decided to get rid of his frustration elsewhere.

'Take in those bloody fenders! We've been sailing for three hours and the bloody things are still out!' Fred was still peeved, but felt genuinely relieved that there was someone on board who could really sail, unlike himself and Nigel who had picked up the bare essentials and were liable to make mistakes.

Meanwhile George was busy stowing the recovered Danford. Nigel had gone below for a towel to dry off the shivering Fred.

'Didn't lose you for a second, Fred, had our eyes on you the whole way,' said George, reassuringly, justifiably proud of his efforts.

At last, order prevailed, man overboard drill was out of the way forever and now they could concentrate on other matters. It was time to start sailing in earnest. They cut the engine and Kevin hardened the sheets. Deceptive heeled over gently in the freshening wind. Kevin had never sailed anything as big before. He sensed her racing pedigree and knew he could get much more from her. He already longed for a chance to use some real sails, her spinnaker, a cruising chute, or her no 1 genoa. Then he would show them what sailing was all about.

Kevin decided Fred was unsure of the sails, and, furthermore, Kevin wasn't at all impressed by his attitude. He would have to take him down a peg. He also decided that, as he was best qualified, he should concentrate on the sailing elements of this trip and elected himself helmsman. There were plenty others who could clean and cook. It would give them something to do.

However, there were a few other things that Fred hadn't noticed on this, their first day out of Villamoura. The boarding ladder was still down with its end dragging in the water. The heavy locks securing the life-raft hadn't been released, and the rubber duck's oars hadn't been secured on deck and could easily be washed overboard. He also failed to notice one other pertinent fact. A crew member was missing from the cockpit. Pat was no longer with them.

The offshore wind had continued to freshen, making it a perfect afternoon for sailing. Everyone was exhilarated by Deceptive's increased speed, all except Pat, who had now retired to his bunk wishing he was dead.

As they headed far out into the bay of Cadiz, and away from shore, Fred knew that they would travel over one hundred miles before seeing land again and felt a little apprehensive. The Sat. Nav. hadn't worked since leaving harbour and he had no back-up system. But this was only a small part of Fred's worries. Steve and George were now referring to Kevin as 'Capt'n Kev.', because of the amount of time he was spending on the helm and his professed knowledge of sailing.

Nigel, watching the situation carefully, knew that there was only room for one captain on any ship, especially this one. Otherwise, the trip would be a disaster. He understood Fred's apprehension and his doubts of what the others thought of him. But Nigel already had seen him perform in the Atlantic, which the others hadn't. He knew that things would have to be pretty bad before Sputnik would give up. The others would have to think again if they thought Kevin should take over. Nigel knew who he would back in a crisis and decided that Fred needed some reassuring.

Fred, Nigel and Kevin could just about handle Deceptive, but what of the others? Pat looked a non-starter, George was keen, and Steve hadn't as yet shown any great interest. Time would tell.

As Pat hadn't been seen for some time, Fred went below and found him sprawled, face down, in his cabin wishing he were dead. His vomiting had stopped as there was nothing left in his stomach. He had swallowed some sea-sickness pills, but they hadn't remained in his stomach long enough to be of any use. He had come below to try to sleep, but all he could do was lie in misery and retch. Fred tried to cheer him up. He told him that Nigel had been just as sick on his first day out and suggested he eat something. Even a slice of dry bread might help his retching.

But, Pat was adamant. He just wanted to be left alone. He wanted to die in peace. Fred cleaned the sink as best he could before leaving. He was reluctant to leave Pat but there was nothing more he could do.

He closed Pat's cabin door behind him, trying to block out the nauseating odour of sickness, and went back to the chart table. It was now getting dark and he had to work out who was to be on what watch.

'Steve and me from nine till twelve, Nigel and George, or Kevin and George . . . from twelve until . . .' He was suddenly feeling very hot and nauseated. Vivid technicolour pictures of Pat's wash-hand basin flooded his mind.

'A breath of fresh air might do me the world of good,' he thought, drawing large mouthfuls into his lungs. He tried to continue with the rota. 'And then Kevin – and – and Pat if . . . if he's feeling any better . . .' Fred could no longer think clearly, but still continued at the chart table. 'They each must have, at least, six hours sleep, and a cabin to themselves.'

It was simple but Fred couldn't work it out. His brain no longer functioned and he could feel beads of perspiration flooding down his back. He felt awful. 'Can't let the others see me like this,' he decided, and climbed on deck, putting on a brave face. When he saw no one was looking, he quietly threw up over the side and immediately felt much better. He needed fresh air. He would have to stay on deck. He couldn't face going down again, not yet. Once his mind had cleared he decided to take the first shift with Steve and also the second with George. Kevin and Nigel could handle the remaining three hours.

At seven-thirty that evening they had their promised 'sundowner' and this seemed to raise flagging spirits. They discussed the journey so far and agreed that they had enjoyed the first day's sail. George was intrigued by it all and was keen to learn everything there was to know about sailing. Kevin was impressed by the boat's performance and told them that he couldn't wait until the big sails were up. Nigel had had a satisfying day, happy that once again the sea-sickness tablets were working for him, but secretly concerned that the already existing friction between Fred and Kevin might erupt into a no holds barred, royal battle. Fred was worried. He worried about the Sat. Nav, about Pat, about approaching Gibraltar in the dark, and about Kevin. In fact, there was little that he didn't worry about. It was an indisputable fact: Fred was happiest when troubled by something or other.

A friendly comradeship was already building up between them. Surprisingly, they had total faith in Fred's navigational ability. This was due to their total ignorance of the subject. They observed Fred's meticulous attention to the charts. He never seemed away from them, noting speed, distance travelled and marking off their estimated position. Unfortunately, Fred himself did not share their faith as he had no way of confirming his progress. The Sat. Nav. still hadn't given a solitary reassuring beep. They were making only five knots and he knew that there was a land mass to the north – the Iberian Peninsula. He comforted himself with the thought that all he had to do was turn left and eventfully they would hit land. 'Hit' being the operative word.

Nigel reassured Fred, after hearing his doubts, 'After all, Columbus had set out from Seville, sailed down the Guadalquivir for twenty miles, straight into this very bay on his way to discover the New World, five hundred years ago, and he, sure as hell, didn't have a Sat. Nav. on board!'

'If blind faith was a virtue Nigel would surely have the makings of the first Irish Pope,' Fred decided.

As it was getting cold, they put up the spray-hood and donned warm clothing. The cockpit, already damp from the night air, soaked the seats of their trousers and dowsed their high spirits. Lights were out below decks to avoid night blindness. Even though they hadn't seen a ship all day they had raised their radar reflector above the spreaders. This would not be removed again until the trip was over. It would warn other ships of their presence, or so they hoped. The navigation lights worked after a little coaxing – Fred tapping the deck connections with a spanner. He also handed out the six tiny torches he had purchased for those wishing to read in their cabins, hoping the message was clear.

The two harnesses were on deck and those on duty were safely clipped in. The only sound that could be heard was the strident whirr of the Autohelm and the rhythmical thumping of Deceptive's bow as she ploughed through the waves. They saw a coaster pass in the distance and then, once again, everything was black. No moon or stars lit the empty, daunting sea. Fred went below and set the wind alarm at twenty-five knots. His face reflected the dim red light of the instrument panel as he checked the Sat. Nav., but nothing. Still no fix. His frustrations with it had reached absurd proportions. He had believed in it, trusted it, and it had let him down. He would write to the company. He was going to tell them, in no uncertain manner, what they could do with their equipment. He wondered if he could sue them, demand enormous compensation for the worry, and make sure that they never sold another set again.

Later, he heard a plaintive beep beep coming from below decks and immediately checked the wind speed and the depth-gauge. Why he checked the depth-gauge was anybody's guess as they were so far from shore it couldn't sound the bottom, and was giving wild guesses, prefixed with a mark that indicated that even it was out of it's depth. The beep was the Sat. Nav.! It had aroused itself from its slumbers and they were getting their first fix at sea. Fred was ecstatic.

'Goody, goody!' he exclaimed, like a child getting a lollipop. He grabbed a pencil in anticipation. Soon he would know just how good his dead reckoning was. The L.E.D. read, *Computing*. Within seconds the whole crew crowded around the chart table watching Fred enter the position on the chart. A sneaking suspicion crossed Fred's mind. Maybe they weren't as confident of his navigational abilities as he had thought! His heart skipped a beat, it was going to be close. 'Eureka!' His last mark on the chart was within a half mile of the confirmed position.

'Ya wee beauty,' cried Steve.

'Good ol' Sputnik,' cheered Kevin.

'Magic! you done rightly there, Fred,' said George, giving him a another of his hard slaps on the back.

Fred offered a silent prayer to the saint of electronic gadgets. 'Please, please, please,' he pleaded, 'keep working and get us safely to Gibraltar.'

It was now past midnight and nobody wanted to bunk down for the night. The obvious excitement of their first night's sail was such that Fred changed his mind about taking a double watch as he thought it a little unfair. He was now feeling much better. Only two crew members were allowed on deck during the hours of darkness, so he decided to turn in and let Kevin and George take over. He would settle on the pilot bunk and keep a close watch on the instruments. Nigel would take over at three, joined by Steve, who volunteered to take Pat's place even though he had just come off duty at midnight. Pat still wanted to do his turn but Fred wouldn't hear of it. Fred was more tired than he realised and fell asleep as soon as his fully-clothed body hit the couch. His main worry was over. He had proved to himself that he really could navigate. His bookwork had paid off.

Two hours later, Fred was awakened by loud banging and heavy footfalls on deck. It took him a few minutes to realise where he was and then he noticed, from the instruments, that the wind had risen to twenty knots. Unaccountably, the boat's speed had dropped down to three knots.

'What on earth's going on?' he demanded, much gruffer than he'd intended. He stumbled on deck trying to keep his balance and changed places with George. Deceptive's speed was now down to two knots and she was wallowing badly. The din from the tins and bottles shifting about in the galley cupboards added to the drama. Everyone was up, wakened by the noise. Fred wanted an explanation. He could see that the sails were down.

'The wind was rising and we've taken some precautions. Better early than late, eh?' Kevin explained. 'I've dropped the working jib and taken two reefs in the main.'

Fred looked at him not believing what he had just heard. Here was the great white hope, their saviour, telling him that for twenty knots of wind they had dropped practically everything. All the bloody sails.

'Might as well put up a bloody handkerchief for all the good a fully reefed main was going to do by itself,' Fred uttered, a bit louder than he had intended. 'Well?'

Kevin glowered accusingly at Fred before continuing. 'You did say that we should reduce sail for night sailing and it's been gusting over twenty knots.'

He took exception to Fred's tone of voice, but was now fully aware that he had panicked needlessly. He got confused by the electronic gauges giving the wind speed and direction. Darkness, and the steadily worsening seas, didn't help either. Kevin had over-reacted, prompted by George's persistent references to minute increases in the wind's force. He had never worked with such complex instruments and found night sailing a more daunting experience than he'd expected. The boat had seemed to be gaining speed, going faster and faster. Faster than the log had been indicating. He had stupidly assumed that there must be a fault somewhere. Maybe a sliver of weed has caught in the spinner? The rough seas caused the Autohelm to work harder and as a result its whine was more strident than before. It had all added to his distraction and he had thrown a tizzy.

The significance of what happened was lost on Fred, but not so Nigel, he understood and took note.

'We've been on reduced sail all bloody day. At this rate we'll get to Greece by Christmas,' Fred growled. He was now facing the task of having to clamber along Deceptive's wildly bucking deck to re-attach the halyard, something he had wanted to avoid at night at all costs. 'We could ride out a bloody force ten storm with what that idiot's left up,' Fred complained to himself making his way, crab-like, along the deck. He was drenched from head to foot as Deceptive dug her nose, ever deeper, into the oncoming waves. He lost his footing frequently and once was thrown against the pulpit, bruising his side and causing him to swear loudly. To make matters worse George had crudely knotted the ties that held the sail to the guard-rail. Fred had to unpick these without light and with increasingly numb fingers. It seemed like hours before they were freed as the wind kept whipping the folded sail from his grip, time and time again, causing him to have to start all over once more. Worse still, the wind also brought with it lashing rain, and with that he was slithered all over the fore-deck, getting even wetter. Deceptive bucked and rolled. He was hardly on his knees for a second before he found himself sprawling on the deck again.

'Come hell or high water,' he promised himself, 'tomorrow I'll have those stupid so and so's tying knots until they can do them in their bloody sleep. It's far too risky playing Houdini with ropes which should open with a single bloody pull.'

They shook out one reef in the main and re-hoisted the self-tacking jib. Deceptive soon slashing through the waves, heeled over and did more than seven knots. The rattling had stopped down below. Spray was flying everywhere. Fred went down to change out of his wet clothes and slipped on an already wet floor, landing once again on his bruised side. He lay there trying to get his breath back. He noticed that the cabin sole was awash. How could that be? He had no idea how the water was getting in. He panicked for a moment, thinking the ship must be coming apart at the seams. They hadn't hit anything so they couldn't be holed. 'How could they be shipping water? Must be a stop-cock or something?' He at last worked out that the water wasn't flooding in. This was a relief.

He soon had the crew looking for the leak. All the lights were now on below decks to see better. Steve solved the problem, but not soon enough to stop Fred tasting the water to see if it might not be coming from the fresh water tanks.

'It's coming up through the bog Fred.'

The water was simply syphoning up through the toilet pan. Someone hadn't closed it off properly. Fred spat into the sink, trying to cleanse his mouth. He couldn't believe that he had just tasted toilet water.

Up on deck, Kevin was still smarting from what he thought was an unwarranted attack, and couldn't help sneering at Fred's predicament.

'It was only their first day at sea. What was the rest of the trip going to be like? It had looked really promising earlier that evening and now it was all going wrong again,' Fred moaned.

Deceptive was taking everything in her stride. There was nothing to fear but fear itself. Kevin's inexperience of night sailing had convinced him that the weather was worse than it actually was. Everything at night in the open sea looked different, more daunting. They would have to get used to that.

Twenty minutes later, everything was once again shipshape: peace had been restored, portholes had been firmly locked, sea cocks closed, and the shallow bilges over Deceptive's two and a half ton fin keel emptied of the toilet water with the help of a bucket and sponge. The wind was gusting to twenty-five knots, but the reefed mainsail kept her light on the helm. She positively thrashed and bucked her way through the white horsed seas, leaving behind a white, glimmering, phosphorescent wake. She would take almost anything the elements threw at her, unlike her crew who were already faltering. The voyage had hardly begun and they were slowly realising that this would not be a holiday at all.

6

Is There Anyone Out There?

The next morning was thankfully dry but, nevertheless, still heavily overcast. An empty steel grey sea stretched into the distance losing itself in an even greyer bank of distant cloud. The morning's weather forecast had advised of force four to five winds, slackening later. 'Was this good or bad news?' Nigel asked himself. He couldn't be sure. Anyway, they had no choice but to go on, too late for anything else.

Short, rough seas were making life very uncomfortable for the crew. They could now move about the boat freely, no longer like men blitzed out of their minds with drink, but more like large primates lurching from one handhold to another. Pat was the exception. His sea sickness had not abated for one minute. He no longer made an effort to come on deck, but lay staring through the fore hatch praying that his agony would soon be over. The reflection he glimpsed in the dressing mirror was that of a lukewarm corpse; skin pallid and eyes sunken beneath dark leaden rings.

Nigel worried about his condition and tried to cheer him up. 'A pint of Guinness is a sure cure for sea-sickness,' he said, pulling the tab on a cold can of the draught black stuff he had recently rescued from the ship's fridge and which now prompted this earth shattering revelation.'. . . in any bar as long as it's on dry land!' he added, smiling wickedly. He paused and took a long swig, waited for a reaction from the crumpled heap on the bunk, but there was none, just a muffled moan and then a long, 'Uuuubbbllllawwwwwagggghhhh.'

'No sense of humour,' Nigel decided, unkindly.

Pat realised that Nigel was trying to help but wished that he'd piss off and let him suffer in peace. The lurching of the boat seemed to coincide with his retching, leaving his stomach suspended in air long after his body had fallen back onto the bunk. Nigel left Pat, careful to hide the empty can from Fred's watchful eye.

Fred was exhausted after what seemed like an endless night with very little sleep. He blamed Kevin. Fred had tried to be polite but almost gagged with the effort. Kevin was also doing his best to control his dislike of Fred.

Later the wind moderated slightly and Deceptive, under full sail, trundled along at five and a half knots.

Breakfast, for those who could face it, consisted of cereal followed by boiled eggs, plain bread, butter and jam. The lot was washed down with mugs of steaming coffee.

Fred had tried to sleep again, after being aroused by Kevin's noisy lurching about on deck dropping the sails, but only succeeded in stealing a few short naps. His tiredness was now telling on him as he wearily tried to fix their position. He was unable to be precise as he had changed their point-of-sail a few times during the night to make it easier for those trying to sleep below decks. He knew he was close to his plotted position but needed urgent reassurance. The Sat. Nav. had returned to its slumbers and hadn't given any further updates.

He wondered, 'Was it the fridge or the V.H.F. radio that was blocking the signal?' He switched each off for long periods, but to no avail. Still nothing.

The V.H.F. was tuned to channel sixteen as it was the fridge's turn to be switched off. So far it too was remaining silent. Fred's sense of isolation was bordering on paranoia. 'Is there anyone out there?' he asked himself.

George, Nigel and Steve were up on deck while Kevin was in his bunk dreaming of his much loved Welsh valleys and of how he could make Fred look an even bigger fool.

The V.H.F suddenly crackled and then a South African voice, loud and clear, introduced his ship.

'This is the sailing vessel Transvaal Three calling the blue and white yacht on our port bow. Come in please. Over.'

Fred, working on the charts, immediately picked up their receiver's handset and returned the call.

'Hello, Transvaal Three, this is the sailing yacht Deceptive, We are reading you loud and clear. Over.' What good luck, he thought, now he would be able to find out exactly where they were. The South Africans must surely be able to confirm their position. However, Fred did feel a keen discomfiture in having to request the information. 'What would they think of a yacht's captain, miles from land, not knowing where the hell he was?' he wondered. Fred had never used the radio before and his voice seemed to catch in his throat.

'What did you say your boat was called?' asked the South African.

Fred was momentarily confused and started to spell the name Deceptive using recently learned code words.

'This is Decca, Echo, Charlie, Echo . . .' He was stuck . Embarrassed out of his mind, he shouted up to the cockpit for help. 'Anyone know what p is?' They didn't know either, but Nigel couldn't resist shouting down that he thought it was ninety-four percent uric acid, amid peals of laughter from the others.

Fred took a deep breath, re-pressed the handset button and repeated, 'This is Deceptive, Deceptive.'

They exchanged pleasantries for a few minutes and then Fred requested the information uppermost on his mind.

'What's your position?' he asked conversationally, doing his utmost to hide an annoying anticipatory squeak in his voice. Fred must have concealed his desperation well for his seemingly unimportant request confused Transvaal's captain.

He immediately answered in his deep South African accent, 'Benk Menager, retired.'

An inane smile crossed Fred's face. 'Was this guy real?'

'No, no. Have you got a fix?' Fred corrected, trying too hard to hide a bubble of mirth just about ready to burst from his throat. 'He'll probably answer that they don't do drugs on board,' he thought, apologising that his navigational equipment wasn't functioning properly and hence the request. He heard a loud guffaw immediately after he released the speak button. He remained unable to speak for a few moments despite urgent requests from the other yacht. Regaining his composure, Fred made his request again trying to keep his voice firm. A fix was supplied instantly. Fred could have sworn that he heard someone still laughing in the background. He looked through the hatch and saw his crew killing themselves laughing. The relay switch to the cockpit was switched on and they'd heard everything.

Transvaal's retired bank manager informed Fred that, on long voyages, they liked to call up any yachts that they passed, picking up pertinant information about local ports and conditions, but Fred was no longer interested and signed off as soon as politely possible.

Fred plotted the new position on his chart and found to his horror that it was a good twenty miles from his last estimation. 'How can I be so far off course?' he asked himself with a sinking feeling. 'I must be doing something drastically wrong.'

Popping his head out of the hatch, he couldn't see the other boat anywhere and realised, to his chagrin, that he had spoken to a yacht twenty miles distant which was passing someone else's bow at the time. He decided to keep this new information to himself fearing the others would tease him mercilessly. However, Fred couldn't help smiling, more in relief that anything else. His chart work had not been proven wrong after all.

In the afternoon they saw land. The Trafalgar lighthouse was almost where they'd expected to find it. 'Just a little too far to the right,' Fred announced.

'If it hadn't been there, we would have been up a gum tree without a paddle,' observed George, who got questionable satisfaction from his regular misquotes.

Fred was relieved but now his next worry had taken over. It was going to be dark before they arrived in harbour.

'Cape Trafalgar, won't be long until we see Africa then?' questioned Steve.

They never saw Africa, but Gibraltar was truly amazing. They hugged the coast from the cape lighthouse almost fearful of losing sight of land again. They didn't see the famous Rock until they rounded the last headland. Suddenly, there it was before them, only five miles distant, more awesome than they expected it to be. Its western approach was lit by the fast sinking sun. The tidal flood through the Straits was now against them. They would not be able to dock until much later.

The Rock appeared to grow to enormous proportions as night fell. It was more beautiful than they ever imagined. Its sheer sides rose straight out of the black water to tower majestically above them. They picked out the custom quay's leading lights. Fred had followed the many aircraft landing on the airstrip, which he knew to be close to his destination. They were soon tied up alongside the custom's office.

Once again Fred collected all their passports: the sealed plastic folder showing the bill of sale, and the sail number register. He jumped from the deck onto the quay more relieved than he could have imagined that their entry into harbour had been so effortless. But now a thought that had been bugging him since he first left Falmouth was prominent in his mind. The boat was not registered and he wondered if his papers were sufficient. Would they be allowed to continue?

The port official hardly looked up as Fred handed over his meagre documents and a neatly completed crew list.

'Is this yer lot?' said a gruff English voice.

'Do you need anything else?' asked Fred, who had learned a long time ago that the only way to deal with officialdom was to match their question with another question. He didn't get an answer. Deceptive's name, dimensions and tonnage were noted, as were the crew's passport numbers and it looked as if he was free to go. Fred almost bounded for the door but was stopped in his tracks by the gruff voice.

'Where are you going?'

Fred's heart almost missed a beat. It had been too easy. His crew would have to fly home while he spent endless weeks trying to sort out the problem of his ship's registration.

The official came around his desk and faced the now panic stricken Fred, who, in the past, couldn't even bring himself to smuggle an extra bottle of booze through the duty free, much to Marge's annoyance.

'Which marina are you going to use for the night?' he asked, 'I had better show you the way. It's not easy in the dark and we don't want you tying up to the runway, now do we?'

Fred, relieved, overreacted to the customs officer's attempt at humour and cackled louder than was necessary. The officer looked at him suspiciously.

'Whichever is the handiest,' answered Fred, sensing the change in the official's attitude.

Back aboard Deceptive, Nigel asked Fred how he'd fared.

'No problem,' he answered, and couldn't help adding, complacently, 'After all, this is a British port and this is an English boat.'

The flag, which the official clearly saw in the light of his open door, fluttering at the rear of Deceptive as she pulled away from the quay, said something entirely different. He went back to his desk and, picking up the recently completed papers, double checked his entry, and then made a phone call.

The crew motored Deceptive to the adjacent marina where they were shown to a vacant berth. They tied up for the night happy in the knowledge that they were secure and after an evening meal they could sleep until – What was it Fred had said? – six the next morning. Fred noted, after yet another aircraft roared into the night sky, that sleep might not be as easy as anticipated.

Pat decided he had enough. He was banjaxed, caput, finished and decided to jump ship. He had given it his best, so there was no honour lost. He was going home. The fifteen minutes he'd spent, head down, trapped between the cabin door and his bunk, had settled it for him the night before. No one had heard his cries for help as Deceptive pounded through the rough seas. It had seemed like an eternity until he had gained enough reserve strength to push himself back onto his bunk. The sea sickness had a debilitating effect on him and now he felt weak, drained out.

Once on the jetty, he was surprised by his recovery. It was truly remarkable. Falling on his hands and knees he kissed the ground, not once but three times.

Nigel joined Pat on his knees. 'Al Akbarr, Al Akbarr,' he intoned as he too kissed the ground. 'I think we should be facing due East, don't you?' They both faced East and did a few more.

'Bloody idiots,' thought Fred, unkindly. 'They look like ducks in a pond, arses in the air, ducking for worms.' He tried to convince Pat to give it a few more days, just to see if he could get his sea legs.

Pat was adamant. He was leaving and that was that. The idea of spending a few days on a beach getting a tan appealed to him, and then heading back to Villamoura to use the return half of his charter flight ticket. He would have been surprised if he had known how the same notion had sprung to a few other minds. Long distance sailing was not what they had expected at all.

'I might even renew my acquaintance with Laura, the dancers, and American Jimmy,' he mentioned, as they were having their well-earned evening meal at a nearby restaurant.

'Hold on a minute!!' piped up Nigel. 'Does one smell a rat, something that deserts sinking ships? Could this be a ploy? Is Pat really leaving his friends because of his persistent puking and mewling, to quote the bard, or is it something more sinister? No, of course not! It must be his illness. Who in his right mind would leave a voyage such as this to return to seven of the most gorgeous, sexy, ravishing women, ever to have had the good fortune to walk on this earth? We will never know the truth, will we Pat?' The silence from the others was indicative of their mood. If they could only trade places!

'Nigel, performing again,' thought Fred. 'It looks as if Pat is going to have a difficult evening.'

'Deserters are not treated kindly,' continued Nigel, 'I think he should pay for the meal.'

'Make him pay forra meal, or be keel hauled,' suggested Steve.

However, they did not make Pat pay, but he had to buy each of them a drink as a token punishment for his desertion. And Nigel was right; a Guinness in a bar was a sure cure for seasickness, he even had a few himself to prove the point.

7

Short Back and Sides

Next morning Fred was up bright and early. Far, far too early.

'It's already six and we should be on our way by now,' Fred shouted into each cabin in an effort to raise the others, but it was no use. They told him, in no uncertain terms, that they didn't want to be bothered and advised him to go back to bed. Fred climbed on deck, with a face as long as a fiddle, a sadder but also much wiser man. It was hopeless; black ominous clouds were gathering in the far recesses of his mind. The trip was doomed to failure. They would never make it to Greece at this rate.

As Fred popped his head out of the main hatch he noticed a dark shadowy figure taking more than a passing interest in their boat. Fred waved to the sinister man on the quay. He seemed taken aback, immediately turned on his heels and walked away at a brisk pace.

Kevin was first to appear. It was now 9:30 a.m. He greeted Fred with the question, 'What did we drink last night?' Fred didn't speak as he thought the question would be easier answered if phrased differently, like, 'What didn't we drink last night!

Kevin said he was desperate for a hair cut. 'It will only take a few minutes, okay, Fred?' Fred let him go but asked him please to hurry as he didn't want to hang about all day. He didn't mention that if they left sharpish, they might get away without paying berthing fees. Kevin set off on his mission. This was to be the first of his many fruitless attempts to find a hairdresser.

The others got up and had a shower on the quay, came back and had breakfast. They too seemed keen to get underway, but still Kevin had not returned. Steve went to look for him but he also didn't return. Pat had packed his bags and he left with Nigel to find Steve and Kevin. They didn't return. George left to find Steve, Kevin, Nigel and Pat. George didn't return either. 'What on earth's going on?' Fred wondered.

The sinister man from that morning's visit came back to find Fred. He asked him who they were, who owned the boat, where they were going and where they'd come from. Fred decided that this man was not a sailor, despite his uniform, as he didn't mention the weather once. He inquired about each member of the crew, individually, asking how long he had known them and asked to see their passports. He examined the ship's papers and casually mentioned smugglers, gun runners and Libya in what appeared to Fred to be an off handed, humourless manner. Fred thanked him for the chat, remembering only too well that Gibraltar had its share of terrorist activity in which three IRA members had been shot dead. It was only after he left that Fred noticed the green, white and orange Irish tricolour hanging limp on Deceptive's transom.

'I hope he doesn't think we're . . . naw, naw he couldn't.' He'd told the custom's officer last night that his was a British boat. Suddenly, Fred felt the hairs rise in the back of his neck. It would look to them as if he'd made a false declaration, and to her Majesty's Customs and Excise at that! 'Oh hell!' He would have to do something about that flag, but then he saw the others returning. 'What in heaven's name have they been doing?' he thought, fearing the worst.

It was now 11:30 a.m. Kevin had had four beers, Steve three, Nigel and Pat two and George one.

'Well! Each lot was ready to return, then the next one arrived, and we couldn't leave until he had one too, and so on. So we had to have another. It was really perfectly simple. If you hadn't sent the others looking for the others, the others wouldn't have had all that extra beer,' Nigel explained, burping loudly.

'El . . . hic . . . elementary, my dear Watshun,' burped Kevin, 'ha, ha, ha.'

It made sense, Fred couldn't deny that. So it was his fault!

'If we're late leaving Gibraltar it's all my fault.' Fred shook his head in disbelief. 'And did laughing boy get his haircut?' Fred asked himself. 'Too bloody right he didn't!'

They bade their farewells to Pat and cast off. An aircraft took off on the adjacent runway, almost deafening them as it roared into the midday sun. They waved to Pat and were genuinely sorry that he was unable to continue with them.

They would arrive at their next port six hours late.

'In the middle of the bloody night again,' Fred muttered, to no one in particular. As far as he was concerned they were all to blame. He was doing his level best to stop blowing a fuse.

An hour and a half later, as they pushed around Gibraltar

The pilot was trying to tell them something.

point, a helicopter positioned itself directly above their mast, the down draft causing circular ripples to appear around Deceptive. The pilot was trying to tell them something. It looked to Fred as if he wanted them to return to harbour. He kept pointing and gesticulating.

'Shouldn't we put the radio on?' queried Steve.

'If anyone touches that flaming radio, I'll cut their flaming hands off,' Fred threatened. It was obvious that they were required to return to harbour, but as they'd already lost so much time Fred was disinclined to oblige. Going back now would mean a further loss of three hours. Nevertheless, the helicopter continued to hover. Fred was decidedly ruffled by the pilot's antics, but wouldn't give in. Going by the chart, he knew they must be almost outside the three-mile limit. 'Or was it twelve now?' he asked himself. 'Must be three,' he decided. Once there, that bloody flyboy could gesticulate as much he wanted and they wouldn't be obliged to do anything.

Fred brought out his bearing compass and took three sightings on the famous Rock. Great battles had been fought and won off these shores and Fred wasn't going to lose this one. He checked his chart and found that he was almost outside the limit.

'Once I'm three miles off they can whistle,' he told the crew. Coming back on deck he pushed the throttle full forward. The down draught from the helicopter was causing Deceptive to dance about a little. Fred searched among the many tankers at anchor for any sign of a fast moving launch. There was none. He was going to make it.

Beer has been known to stimulate conversation and create a feeling of mateyness, but this was not the case aboard Deceptive. There was only a brooding, glum silence. Their captain had gone stark raving mad. They wanted Fred to head back to Gibraltar. Nigel suggested that perhaps the limit was ten miles, but Fred wouldn't be swayed. Damn the consequences, he was going on and that was final. They would have to send a gun-boat after him to make him change his mind. The others sat frozen to the spot, amazed by Fred's pig-headedness. Steve muttered to George that he thought they'd get ten years for this.

Fred was adamant. He'd spent the whole morning, as far as he was concerned, being questioned, and now this. A Norwegian boat had left at the same time as them, so why couldn't they go and bother it instead?

'Wave to him, pretend we're friendly,' suggested George.

Fred waved alright, but the sign he gave was distinctly unfriendly, followed by three fingers held in the air to point out that they were beyond the three-mile limit. He noticed that they were still flying Nigel's flag. This wouldn't do, so he changed it for the 'red duster'. Protocol was satisfied. Now a British boat flew a British flag. Much to their bemused looks the helicopter noticeably dipped and moved away heading, to their surprise, for a large naval carrier in the distance.

'I wouldn't argue with that if I was you,' said Nigel, breaking the ice. They all laughed.

They motored for the next five hours due to lack of wind, heading up the coast of Spain, past Marbella, Malaga, Motril and Almeria. Cartagena was to be their next stop and it was going to take them at least two and a half days to get there. Fred noticed the fenders and ropes had been neatly stowed by George who had adopted this as one of his permanent tasks.

They were getting used to the motion of the boat at each passing hour and life on board was not too unpleasant. Now that they were well away from Gibraltar, they began to admire Fred for his stand.

'Damn right, Fred,' said Steve, 'Don't let the bastards grind you down.'

'Drunken pillocks,' thought Fred. If it hadn't been for their drinking we'd have been away before anyone knew the difference, and we wouldn't have had to pay those bloody mooring charges either.

The sea now shimmered like wet glass and Deceptive slid peacefully over its unbroken surface. Some read, others slept as the hours passed slowly by. Navigation was not a problem as they could identify the various landmarks on their port side. As long as they pin-pointed each town, headland or highest mountain peak, they wouldn't get lost. Fred and Nigel practiced 'distances off' and soon had it down to a fine art. They no longer had any problem sighting through the hand-bearing compass and were now able to pick up difficult points for their reverse readings.

Late in the afternoon they were buzzed by a couple of low-flying jets. The pilots dipping their wings from side to side in salutation before flying off. 'Low altitude training,' said George, but Fred was once again deep in brooding, guilt laden thoughts. He would have to return sometime in the future to Gibraltar. What if they were waiting for him? Were those fighters checking on their progress? He now fervently wished that he hadn't been so mulishly resolute. Had the helicopter pilot been trying to contact them because there had been a tragedy at home? Could he ever forgive himself if this were true?

The wind came off shore at about seven that evening and they were able to hoist the main and working jib. They cut the engine and made a steady five knots.

George, now christened 'the fender bender,' offered to make dinner. It was to be their first full hot meal on board and a box of tagliatelli was opened. He patiently simmered the pasta and mixed in gently cooked red and green peppers, carrots, onions and liberal amount of spices and seasoning. He opened a bottle of wine and set the saloon table properly. The crew then sat down to one of the worst meals they had ever eaten in their lives. George had accidentally dropped the contents of a small container of sweeteners into the pot. He tried to pick them out but obviously missed quite a few. He didn't tell anyone and nobody mentioned the sickly sweet taste. But, some rather unkind comments were made behind his back.

Later that evening, the sea reverted to short crossing waves and became very choppy and uncomfortable. Once again, Fred was sea-sick as were the rest, with the exception of Kevin. But now they were able to cope with the illness. They ate dry bread or drank some liquid all of which would be ejected, but there was no desperate retching any more. They openly blamed it on George's cooking and someone suggested that perhaps he shouldn't cook again. George smiled to himself, the secret of the sweeteners wasn't about to be revealed just yet.

In the dark, Fred found it much easier to navigate than he had expected. The lighthouses could be identified from miles off. He would count one hundred, two hundred between flashes and was surprised at the distance at which they could be seen. Some lights could be identified over twenty miles away. He had difficulty, however, accepting that they were further from shore than they imagined.

Fred also practiced identifying a ship's type and direction

from its lights as they passed silently in the dark. The Sat. Nav. had only worked once during the night, fixing their position a few miles further back than where the crew thought they were. Fred now considered it virtually useless and decided it should be forgotten about. They picked out the reassuring lights of Calahonda, Cala Moral and Fuengirola before losing sight of land again. Fred began to fear that the seas they were experiencing at night were, perhaps, normal. If this was the case, they were in for three weeks of abject misery.

At daybreak they were well past Malaga and seventeen miles out to sea. They wouldn't see land again for eight hours or so. During the day the wind changed to the West and they had their first *run*. The No.1 genoa was up and they goose-winged most of the day with Kevin at the helm, keeping both sails full without any apparent effort. Fred rigged a boom-preventer in case of an involuntary gybe and later used the spinnaker pole to pole-out the genoa. Kevin's sailing was instinctive and excellent. He handled each change of wind, calmly and intelligently picking his way over the rough seas. He would gladly stand at the helm for twenty-four hours if asked, but would not cook or wash a dish.

Below decks things were not so calm. George asked Fred if he could move into Pat's vacated bunk. George was a meticulously neat person. His clothes and shoes were always the very best that money could buy and were treated as such.

'It's an unbelievable mess in there,' he complained to Fred, pointing to the cabin he shared with Kevin, 'Its like sleeping in a tumble dryer. Everything's scattered all over the flipping place. I can't find anything, let alone a place to sleep!' When Fred inspected Kevin's cabin, he quickly realised why George wanted so badly to move out. It was as if a hurricane had passed through. Socks, underpants and shirts were strewn everywhere. Cupboard doors were open and the contents spilling out. A plastic cover had come off a bulkhead light and was lying on the floor waiting to be trodden on and crushed. The sink still had the residue of that morning's shave and a dirty soup mug lay amongst the bedclothes. Fred was furious, but refrained from creating further friction between Kevin and himself. He had said that their cabins were their own special places where they could withdraw in peace and where their privacy would never be invaded. The cabin may be a tip but he still would say nothing.

Both Fred and Nigel understood George's wish to move in

with Steve. But they wondered if Kevin would resent George's desire to move out? Kevin was, obviously, unaware of the problems he caused George. Ashore they were the closest of friends and had been drinking buddies for years. Nigel wondered if moving George would cause a rift between them.

All the crew, baring Fred, had known Kevin for years and knew that he was untidy, but Nigel hadn't expected him to be so inconsiderate. He would speak to Steve rather than have Fred talk to him. It would be better coming from him. He didn't think Steve would mind sharing now that Pat had left.

That night George shared with Steve. Kevin wasn't in the least put out. Now he had a cabin to himself and he was delighted. He could crash out whenever he wanted without fear of being disturbed. He had resented George moving his things about. Every time he missed a sock or a shoe he knew who to blame. George had hidden it somewhere. He was already bored with the trip anyway. Being cooped up on a boat for days on end was no longer his idea of a holiday. What seemed like only five minutes in a town wasn't enough for him. He needed time to immerse himself in its atmosphere, to breathe in its smells and to get the feel of a place, time to have a few beers at leisure, without darting from country to country.

Meanwhile, irksome, jealous thoughts were running through Fred's mind: Kevin was the better sailor and now he had a cabin to himself, something he, the owner, didn't have. He even had Steve and George calling him captain. He had them eating out of his hand, but not for long. Fred was going to show them who was the better man.

They reduced sail as usual that night. Their passage was rough and uncomfortable, once again. As they were now running close to land, they had a multitude of lights to take bearings from. Capo Scratif had been in their wake since seven the previous evening and by daybreak Capo da Gata was directly ahead.

Here they saw the most beautiful dawn imaginable. The sea was absolutely still, coloured by the sun which climbed over the horizon as a massive glowing ball, diminishing in size as it gained height. The nearby cliff changed from black to grey to cream as its rays searched out its sheer face. Unlike mornings on land, with its cacophony of bird-song, here everything was perfectly quiet. All the crew were on deck as they motored towards the rocky headland, cameras at the ready. The only other soul to share the sunrise was a lone fisherman moving in and out of the rocks in a tiny boat, completely oblivious to the surrounding beauty.

Later that day they once again motored close to shore and stopped for a swim, trailing a long mooring line in case the boat drifted too fast for the less able swimmers.

There was plenty of horse play. They hung on to a halyard and, pushing themselves out from the pulpit, tried to swing in as wide an arc as possible to land on deck. Most ended up in the water. Steve was thrown back in every time he managed to dry himself off, much to his shipmates' amusement and his annoyance. It was really becoming a holiday. They were having a great time, all except Fred, who had far more important things to do.

'Grown up men behaving like little children. Maybe that was how they should be treated,' he mumped. 'Might get better results.'

Lunch was eaten on deck and consisted of salad and cold meats.

'Your fridge is working well, Fred. This beer is really cold,' observed George, taking a deep appreciative gulp.

'There is nothing like a chilled beer on a hot day, or a hot woman on a chilly day. Cheers,' said Nigel.

'You speak for yourself, I'd prefer a cold beer and a hot woman any day,' added George. 'Of course she'd have to be from Belfast and not one of your namby-pamby women from Dublin who keep their mouths open and their knees tightly shut.'

'Give me a Guinness anytime! To hell with the women,' retorted Nigel.

'Naw, I'm afraid it has to be raw sex with me or nothing,?' added Steve. 'I remember . . .'

'This was going to be good,' Nigel thought.

'I remember having it off seventeen times in one night.'

'Hang on a minute there, Steve, we've all heard about your sexual prowess,' said Nigel, 'but seventeen times in one night? Never. Need to be a bloody Meccano set. Do you remember that party at Kevin's when you fell madly in love with that tall skinny one that had been ignored all night?'

'Was that the one with the runny nose, who kept asking people for a Kleenex?' asked George, winking at Nigel, 'She ended up with a toilet roll in her hand, tearing off bits and honking into them.'

'Yeah, the very one. She could have been anyone's,' added Nigel, 'Even though I felt sorry for her I had to knock her back a few times myself.'

'She was begging for it. Like a bitch on heat,' said Kevin.

'Steve was eying her up all night waiting for the right moment to pounce,' continued George.

'But even she had some pride left. She gave Steve the knock back. Didn't she, Steve?' said Nigel, hoping that Steve hadn't seen the trap.

'Naw, she didn't,' said Steve, too quickly.

'Ah! ha, so you admit you tried to get your leg over, you dirty bugger.' Broad smiles greeted Steve's discomfiture.

Steve was often the butt of their humour as he invariably boasted about his latest conquest, many of which they suspected as being mere figments of his vivid imagination.

They lost sight of land again that afternoon and later, after dark, returned to a poorly beaconed area of the coast which caused endless confusion. They saw a multitude of lights ahead and hidden somewhere in that glittering midst was the marker-buoy leading the way into Cartagena harbour. George, who was showing an interest in navigation, estimated that they should arrive in harbour about two in the morning. He was very apprehensive because he could clearly see the darkened headland and it seemed dangerously near. To make him even more nervous, the chart showed rocks and small islands quite close to their route. Fred took bearings and put their course right in line with the obscured entrance some six miles distant. George also tried taking bearings and convinced himself that they would be on the rocks in minutes if they didn't head out to sea.

This was becoming too much for Fred. George confused him. He had to go below and point out George's mistakes.

'There is no doubt about it, George, you've got it wrong. You've mixed up one of your sightings on shore,' Fred declared. But the seeds of doubt had been planted and Fred wasted the next fifteen minutes proving to himself that he had been right all along. By George's reckoning they should have been on the rocks already. Fred had to fight a desire to head out to sea just to be doubly sure. Nevertheless, he held his course, keeping a watchful eye on the depth sounder which was also helping to confirming his position. The depth showing was exactly what it should be for his present position. George persisted in his belief that they would run aground at any second and continued to get on Fred's, already raw, nerves.

'Look! George, damn it! The only thing that's going to get hit here is you, if you don't stop laying eggs all over the place. Will you piss off below and check the chart again?' Fred pointed to the dark shore and picked out some features for George to use as reference points. Use that headland and that bloody lighthouse and that other headland there, which you'll find is the tip of that bloody island you've misplaced!'

A mass of lights ahead was getting nearer and suggested a large town. Cartagena was in an enclosed harbour surrounded by cliffs. But, there it was, straight ahead. How could that be? Fred checked the pilot again and again, but the town should not have been visible from their present position. George, noting Fred's confusion, was even more terrified of going aground. They still had to pass on the inside of the island, three miles off the entrance and there was no visible way through yet. Fred sent George below once more to re-check his bearings, but really so he could get some peace to concentrate on the job ahead.

'There it is!' Fred found what he had been looking for. He had picked up the port entrance buoy as the channel between the mainland and the island opened up to his view. It was the only flashing red light, and its sequence was correct. Fred called for George to come back on deck.

George now in a panic, shouted back, 'You told me to re-plot our flaming position and I'm not coming up until I've done just that!'

Fred smiled to himself. 'But, George,' he called sweetly, 'I've found the entrance, you don't have to plot any more.'

George was angry. 'I don't care,' he retorted, 'I'm just going to finish what you sent me down to do and . . . wha?!'

'Don't be silly, George,' said Fred even sweeter.

The lights that had confused Fred and George were from an industrial complex of some magnitude partly hidden by the island at the entrance to Cartagena's large harbour. It was either an oil refinery or chemical plant, Fred thought. It looked massive in the dark. As they turned and headed into Cartegena, he saw that the industrial complex even had its own large jetty.

It was time to awaken the others. Fenders had to be put out and mooring lines prepared.

It was two in the morning when Fred brought Deceptive alongside the visitor's quay. A stiff breeze blew from shore as Kevin, a mooring line in each hand, leapt onto the dock. He had not moored a yacht before and was trying to hold Deceptive side on to the wind without making a quick turn with the mooring line round a bollard, or anything solid. With his heels gaining little purchase on the concrete, he was being dragged to the edge shouting for help. Already the others were too far off to jump to his assistance. The windage causing by Deceptive's high freeboard was too much for Kevin to hold by himself.

'What do I do now? he yelled?'

'Aaaagh . . .' Was the last sound heard on board before Kevin tripped and somersaulted into the water. Fred was in a quandary. He couldn't use the engine because of Kevin's presence in the water and the newly released mooring lines might foul the propeller. All he could do was let Deceptive drift, while the ropes were pulled back on board. He would attempt to turn her before she bounced off the nearest yacht.

Someone on shore was jumping up and down and waving his hands in the air.

'Who's that ijit dancing over there?' Nigel asked Fred.

'Looks as if he wants us to use the mooring buoy at our stern and tie up bows to the quay,' observed Nigel.

'Bloody typical! He could have told us that sooner, the stupid berk,' exclaimed Fred, who was keeping a watchful eye on Kevin in the oily water.

'Can he swim?' asked Steve. They all knew that Kevin was a good swimmer and the question caused a few smiles to light up tired faces.

Fred looked at the immense mooring buoy. How were they going to get a line onto that monster? he asked himself.

'George, you'll have to do it.'

George was startled by Fred's new found faith in him and asked, 'Do what?' uttered in a voice just a little too edgy for Fred's liking.

'I'll back up as close as possible while you put a mooring line through the ring, but be fast about it. I don't think I can hold her head into this wind for any length of time.'

Fred went astern beautifully and stopped, much to his

pleasure, inches from the buoy. George, on the boarding ladder, put one foot on the buoy and managed to slip the warp through the ring. There was no one to take up the slack and Deceptive slowly moved away. George's legs were opening wide. He tried to jump back on board, misjudged, and joined Kevin in the water.

'Two down, three to go,' shouted Steve.

'What a performance. Doing the splits like that George could get a job in that chorus line in Villamoura,' Nigel added, thankful that it wasn't him in the water. Fred wasn't amused by George's demonstration. Now there were two idiots in the water to worry about.

'Can he swim?' asked Steve, overcome with laughter.

At least the stern was now held. All that remained was to get the bows around, head towards shore, and get a line to the watchman.

'Oi! What about me?' George shouted.

Fred waited while he climbed up the boarding ladder and then, as Nigel slowly let out the stern mooring line, he motored slowly towards the quay. Steve had now picked up the forward warp and was standing in the pulpit ready to jump. Deceptive inched forward, Fred just giving enough throttle so that she wouldn't veer off. They were within three metres of the pier when Fred shouted to Steve to throw the line. It was no longer attached. The newly coiled mooring line wheeled through the night air and rained on the watchman who was desperately shielding his face. Steve consoled himself. Fred had shouted to throw it and he'd done just that. It wasn't his fault that the end was loose. Was it!

Fred gave an almighty roar. 'Tie the effing thing on next time!'

The watchman looked at the boat, then at the rope and then Steve. It was one of those slow calculating looks that say it all. He tied the rope around a bollard and handed an end to Steve, who had climbed outside the pulpit and was hanging on with one hand. Steve shouted urgently, 'Reverse! Reverse!,' Their bow was going to damage this nice gentlemen's quay. Steve still holding the line, was pulled out over the water as Fred went into an emergency reverse.

'Stop! stop!' screamed Steve whose arms felt as if they were being pulled out of their sockets.

Down the Hatch

It was one of those slow calculating looks that say it all.

Kevin, who had just dragged his dripping form back on board wondered what would have happened to him if he had been in the water an instant longer. He looked at Fred suspiciously. 'That old goat would have reversed right over me,' he thought. Both Kevin and George were, hopefully, anticipating Steve's gasp as he too hit the water.

'Well, it was his turn,' George thought, 'and then Fred and Nigel's. Might as well make a proper exhibition of ourselves.'

Kevin also made a silent prayer. 'Can he swim?' he uttered, poignantly mimicking Steve's earlier comments, his teeth chattering from the cold. 'Hope that smart bastard falls in and stays under.'

Nigel couldn't hide his amusement at this unexpected banter from Kevin. Obviously Kevin was not impressed by Steve's earlier remark, which he'd overheard in the water.

Fred quickly motored forward and Steve was able to pull himself back on board without suffering the fate of his dripping companions. He tied the mooring line to the forward port cleat, but instead of putting it under the rail he left it lying on top. The watchman shook his head and walked away. Nothing could surprise him any more . He'd seen it all before. Now it was starting again, and the season hardly begun. He would resign. He couldn't take another summer of such stupidity, amateur sailors defiling his harbour. Fred could almost hear him tut-tutting as he walked slowly away, still shaking his head.

8

The Case of the Missing Fender

Cartagena is a really quaint town. This was the considered opinion of Kevin, Nigel, Steve and George as they enjoyed yet another beer in yet another tree shaded garden cafe, overlooking yet another part of the town's main square! Fred hadn't formed his opinion yet, although it was already noon, because he hadn't left the boat. He was in another blazing mood and found little solace in his own company.

'I suppose they think the water and diesel tanks will miraculously fill themselves!' he fumed silently. 'I'm left to do every blasted thing on this flaming boat myself, while they're topping up their tanks!' Playing the martyr was one of life's few free experiences and Fred made the most of it when frustrated and angry as he now felt.

That morning's breakfast had been a tight-lipped affair. Petulant stares were returned with an equally testy challenge. Each daring the other to say something. Even the breakfast cereal seemed afraid to crackle and pop, in case the snap might be sharper than usual.

On awakening, Fred found a fender missing and launched the dinghy while the others slept on. No one offered to give him a helping hand even though he was sure they must have heard him heaving and puffing as he wrestled to get the non-compliant, rubber monster into the water. After a fruitless hour searching among the moored yachts, he rowed over to the commercial area and nosed his way around the few cargo ships that were unloading there. When he returned empty handed his mood was even fouler than it had been in the early hours of the morning, after the unmitigated fiasco they'd created on arrival.

'Fenders don't grow on bloody trees,' he ranted. 'They cost money. Twenty-eight pounds down the flaming drain because one of you couldn't be bothered to tie the damn thing on properly!' They regarded him steely-eyed and sullen-faced. He would hurt them where it hurt most, their pockets. 'And . . .,' he paused for emphasis, 'the same goes for the winch handles. Twenty pounds if one is lost overboard.'

After the initial shock of being scolded, Nigel told him that he was becoming a real pain in the arse and was ruining the trip for everyone. Kevin followed Nigel's lead with the most brutal comment of all.

'If you wanted a proper crew Fred, you should have hired one. I'm saving you an effing fortune! You'd have to pay through the nose for a skipper and, on top of that, you'd have air fares and food to think about.' Kevin was going to say his piece regardless of the consequences and had continued with his diatribe building up to a final ultimatum.

'No effing way, Fred! If you continue like this we're going to piss off home. You don't know when you're well off,' he snapped angrily, 'The only reason we're still on board is because Nigel's our mate. The sooner this effing trip is over the better, maybe then we can all have a real holiday.'

Kevin retired to his ramshackle, unkempt cabin loudly banging the door. The others looked on speechless, feeling that Kevin had gone too far this time and suspecting that Fred would tell him to pack his bags and give him his marching orders.

Later, the chance of a reconciliation had been flatly refused by Fred. Nigel had suggested that he join them on their journey to the town centre but Fred hadn't quite cooled down enough yet.

At one o'clock Nigel returned with a fender tucked under his arm. At first, Fred thought the crew had bought a replacement and was a little taken aback but then recognised it as the missing one.

'You'll never believe where I found this!' he offered by way of explanation, passing the fender over the bows to Fred. 'One of the stevedores had seen an old geezer walking off with it under his arm first thing this morning. He fished it out of the water further up the quay. Must have known it belonged to one of the boats tied up here.' Nigel continued, 'We found out where he lived and, sure enough, there it was hanging on a clothesline with a freshly painted name on it. I recognised it as ours by the braided rope. The paint was still wet so he didn't have a leg to stand on.' He pointed to the blotch he had made when he first drew his finger through the paint. 'Some neck, eh?'

Fred couldn't help but join Nigel in a broad toothy grin. He was relieved they had recovered the fender and now thought it time to make his peace with the crew.

'Are the lads a bit upset?' he inquired guiltily. 'And Kevin . . . ?'

'They were, a little, but they're all right now. All except Steve, he's leaving us and Kevin, well, Kevin is Kevin, all bark and no bite.'

Fred smarted from an inner spasm of guilt. Nigel, noticing his concern, tried to make light of it.

'Look! It's not your fault that Steve's leaving, it's a whole lot of things. Steve really feels that he is not cut out for this type of holiday and could still return to Villamoura in time to catch the return flight home. He wanted to leave in Gibraltar, but Pat beat him to it.'

'Should I talk to him?'

'No,' Nigel answered, quickly. He was not going to let Fred off the hook that easily. 'I think you've done enough harm already!' Nigel's intended barb did hit its mark. Fred winced noticeably and averted his gaze. Nigel knew it wouldn't make any difference anyway, as Steve's mind was firmly made up. He would leave the boat the next morning, just before they set off for the distant island of Ibiza.

That afternoon Fred, Nigel and George replenished the water tanks from an adjacent stand-pipe and ferried six jerry-cans of diesel by taxi from the nearest garage almost a kilometre away. Kevin went hunting for a barber once again, and Steve bought some presents to take home. 'Forra few of the birds!' he informed them with a decidedly smug look on his face, unable to hide his relief that this trial was ending.

Fred secretly wished that Kevin was leaving and not Steve. He was going to miss Steve as he genuinely liked his company. His raw Glasgow humour had amused them all and Fred couldn't fault his behaviour on board.

As Deceptive made her way out of Cartagena harbour, at first light the next morning, they gave a final wave to the small dark figure left ashore and turned to the more immediate tasks at hand. As they motored along the headland they passed close to the industrial complex which had so confused Fred and George with its lights the previous night. Still they couldn't decide exactly what it was. They were down to four crew members, but this would be a bonus as each could have some privacy now.

By midday the coast was lost, the wind was on their port quarter. Kevin let the sails fully out. They averaged five and a half knots in a hitch of a sea. This point of sail didn't suit Deceptive and it was very uncomfortable for the crew. The Autohelm had been switched off and each took turns at the wheel. The No.1 genoa emptied and filled with loud reports as she see-sawed her way through the irregular waves, causing Fred to consider dropping the main entirely.

Fred had taken Jimmy's advice and rigged a boom preventer on the main in case they accidentally gybed. Kevin noticed Fred's unease at the thought of controlled gybing.

'Putting your tail through the wind is normal in dinghy racing,' he mentioned to Nigel more than once and loud enough for Fred to overhear. He was desperate to demonstrate the procedures to the others. It would be another notch in the stick he used to beat Fred's back. It would show them who was the better yachtsman. Kevin had noticed that everything happened much slower on a sailing yacht than on a dinghy and thought it would be a very simple exercise. He discussed sailing at length with George and Nigel querying every decision made by Fred. Fred found this irksome as he had hoped that, with a smaller crew, attitudes might have improved somewhat. Later, Fred decided to defer to Kevin's superior knowledge as a means to breaking the ice between them and suggested that they should give gybing a try. It was time to shake hands and make up.

As the boom would sweep the cockpit, Fred requested that everyone stay low. George was to pull in the main sheet as fast as he could and Kevin would take the helm. Fred went forward to release the boom preventer. He was not entirely convinced of

Kevin's ability to complete the exercise without mishap so he kept a half turn on the midships cleat. He felt that, at a pinch, he may be able to reduce the velocity of the boom's swing should it be necessary.

Without warning, Kevin turned the wheel, shouting, 'gybe-ho,' a little too late, and George was unable to even begin to pull in the sheet as Deceptive's stern came through the wind. To make matters even worse, the wind, now gusting to twenty-five knots, added more force than expected to the gybe and the boom hit the opposite shrouds with a resounding twang which shook the boat from stem to stern. There was a yelp of pain from Fred followed by profuse swearing. Unable to hold the boom restraining rope, it had run through his hands badly burning both palms and breaking the skin.

'We could have lost the mast, you stupid bastard! You know nothing about yachts,' shouted Fred, both hands now tucked firmly under his arms to try to relieve the searing pain.

Kevin was instantly contrite and blabbed an apology. He really hadn't expected the wind to whip the sail round so fast. George also felt guilty because he had been busy ducking when he should have been pulling for all his worth. Nigel hoped that Fred and Kevin had both learned a lesson from the episode, but this was not to be. He helped bandage Fred's hands assuring him that they would be alright.

'Rope burns are sore things, but they don't kill you.'

'I know who I bloody want to kill,' Fred spat, glaring daggers at Kevin.

Early that afternoon a small aeroplane appeared from the South and, coming closer, circled twice for a better look at Deceptive. They waved to the pilot and he waved back before heading off towards Ibiza.

'Nosey basket,' observed Nigel, and thought no more about it, but Fred wasn't so easily satisfied. He wondered why it had circled twice and assumed that they were being identified for some reason. He had convinced himself that they hadn't heard the last of their experience in Gibraltar.

Later, the wind changed round and, once more, they were plunging headlong into troubled seas. They were on a beat and their progress was very uncomfortable. The No.1 and the main were up and they were making a good seven knots. Their starboard rubbing strake was permanently buried in Deceptive's white bow wave. Below decks, everything was secure. The portholes were firmly closed and the sea-cocks shut. They were in no mood to cook and settled instead for bread and jam. The sky was very black and the weather worsening ahead, but there was a feeling of exhilaration on board. The waves were soon over two metres high and the sea was breaking regularly over the decks. They put up the spray-hood and this, at least, gave the crew nearest the hatch some shelter. Deceptive started climbing and crashing with such force and frequency that it was impossible to stand without hanging on to something.

The No.1 genoa should have been dropped when Fred first thought of it, a full twenty minutes before. Now it was going to be difficult. To their horror they saw frequent flashes of lightning in the sky ahead and were particularly worried by an ominous, mushroom-shaped cloud which seemed to rise straight from the sea directly in their path. Fred and Nigel had seen enough of those coming through Biscay to know that they could spell real trouble. They were in for a squall. Gusts of wind of forty knots or more should be expected. Already Deceptive was launching herself off each crest to crash into the foam streaked hollows, before slowly lifting her head again with spray showering off her flooded deck. Fred considered it too dangerous to clamber forward to get the sail down and, taking the helm, shouted instructions for Kevin to release the halyard and for George to go forward once they were on a run. He brought Deceptive round until the wind was on her quarter. They were now heading back the way they had come. What had been bedlam a few moments ago eased to relative calm and they managed to replace the genoa with the working jib without getting any wetter. George couldn't believe his eyes and yelled back to Nigel.

'One minute like a fecking bucking bronco and the next as docile as a pet pony.'

Nigel recalled the many times in Villamoura when they were beating down the coast of Portugal, hanging on for dear life, when they would pass a yacht on a run, heading towards them with the crew relaxed, having elevenses on deck. Fred brought Deceptive back around once they had reefed in the main. She had lost some headway, but was ready when the squall hit. She simply heeled over slightly and continued in her stride. Fred handed the helm to Nigel as his hands were now too sore to continue.

'At least, the salt water's keeping the wounds clean,' he thought. They were now effectively down to three helmsmen until his hands mended.

Kevin, surprisingly, complimented Fred on the manoeuvre and suggested that the next time they felt hungry they should do the same thing and have a decent meal. Nigel, George and Fred exchanged knowing glances and couldn't help smiling. They had all noticed Kevin's reluctance to get involved in the galley and that he hadn't even made so much as a cup of coffee since their trip began. It was obvious that he had only complimented Fred to try and make up for the earlier accident.

That night the lightning lit up the sky spectacularly, followed by deafening thunder which seemed to shake the boat. It was so fierce that each crew member was terrified that Deceptive might be hit. They had never seen anything like this in England. Each flash back-lit the clouds, outlining their edges as sparks shot out in all directions like giant colourless fireworks. Fred didn't know what action to take. George had expressed his fear of the mast acting as a giant conductor and asked what should be done.

Fred had read about instruments being destroyed in lightning storms and switched everything off including their log. Even though he was frightened himself he had to do something to calm the others. He eventually crawled forward and draped the anchor chain around the mast, dropping a bight over the side to trail in the water. Every moment he spent on the exposed deck he expected to be his last. He was going to be struck down by a flash from the heavens. The job was done in a hurry. They had never seen Fred work with such purpose and speed and gave him a rousing reception when he clambered back into the cockpit.

'It will conduct the electricity directly into the sea,' he reassured them with more confidence than he felt. In reality, he didn't know whether in fact the chain might attract the lightening instead of conducting it into the sea. The object was to ease the apprehension of the others and he had succeeded, but it did absolutely nothing to allay his own fear.

'The arse had been blown out of boats before by a direct hit and it could, too easily, happen to us, Kevin thought,' checking, stupidly, to see if the life raft was still in its place and if, at a run, he could be first in it.

Steve watched the display from the safety of his hotel balcony and thanked God he wasn't on board.

They made their way safely through the lightning storm. Fred and George were on the second watch that night and at about one o'clock encountered their first fishing fleet. No matter which way they headed there always seemed to be some trawler on a collision course. He suspected that they couldn't be seen by the fishermen. He put on every light he had. He even shone the ship's torch onto the sail, feeling that this large white area must surely be visible from a distance. He knew the fishermen would be blinded by their own floodlights, unable to see outside the bright ring created around their ships. After an hour of playing cat and mouse he noticed two large trawlers following them and gaining fast. He couldn't see anyone on their brightly lit decks. They had searchlights illuminating the sea between them and it looked as if they were trawling. Nets stretched from one boat to the other. He steered to port and then to starboard, but they were still gaining. It was like having a nightmare. He put the engine on for extra speed and tried to edge away to their left. They were still faster than he was and eventually overtook Deceptive, at the last minute altering course and heading rapidly away. A figure came out on deck and waved a greeting. Fred waved back, muttering profanities under his breath.

The thunder and lightning passed, leaving behind strong wind and heavy breaking seas. Their efforts to avoid the trawlers and the fact that his log had been switched off for hours caused Fred some further worry. He was back on their original heading, but was not sure how far they had run off course. Where he should have seen the Rotja light there was only empty blackness. Fred kept popping his head through the hatch to see if he could see the light and then dashing down to check the chart, much to the consternation of George. George was well-versed in using his sharp Ulster wit and surpassed himself, in what was probably the most astute remark of the trip, much to Kevin's amusement who was just getting ready for his watch. Fred had bobbed up yet again, this time with the ships binoculars and was scanning the horizon.

'Fred, you've been up and down there for the past hour like knickers at a whore's convention and you haven't spotted anything yet,' he said. 'Tell us what you're looking for and we might be able to help.'

Kevin couldn't resist a whelp of laughter.

For days afterwards, if anyone asked where Fred was,

the answer was bound to be. 'Well! He's up and down like . . . !'

Nigel had been feeling a little squeamish earlier, so Fred decided to let him sleep on. He would keep watch with Kevin until they saw the coast of Formentera which should be in view shortly. With the aid of the binoculars Fred could see a dim outline, not too far distant, and running parallel to their course.

'It couldn't be Formentera?' he observed, questioning his own judgement . 'It's just a low cloud on the horizon, we haven't even seen the Rotja lighthouse yet.'

Kevin was unimpressed by Fred's musing. He was buried deep in his own troublesome thoughts.

'Formentera is shaped like a lady's shoe,' Fred explained. 'We are following the heel, whereas, the light we're looking for is on the more distant toe.'

Fred realised, a little too late, that they had missed it completely, due to the thunderstorm, and were now well up the coast. He scanned the horizon, searching for any clues that would lead them to the small pass between the island of Espalmador and its large neighbours Ibiza and Formentera.

Later, and much to Fred's relief, they identified some lights on the western approaches to Ibiza and changed course to head directly for the gap which they knew to be marked by danger beacons.

Kevin voiced his apprehension. 'It will be too dangerous to attempt to enter the channel in the dark. We might run aground.'

Fred had to agree and held back for an hour in miserable, wallowing conditions, waiting for daylight to show them a clear path through the danger that lay ahead. This was enough to make both Kevin and Fred seasick. Their large scale chart of the area was missing. Fred knew that he had one, but where was it? It was not easy to check for it in his condition. Any more than three minutes below deck and he wanted to throw up. They would have to round the bottom of Ibiza and head north to the town and there were rocks in their path. Fred had enough, he couldn't stomach any more, he was going to go for it,- daybreak or no daybreak-, to hell with the danger.

A mile to starboard a fishing trawler was sweeping the sea in large circles dragging her nets along the sea bed, happily killing plant and fish alike, working steadily along the coast. Round and round it went, showing red then green then white and then red again, its crew unaffected by the grim weather and heavy seas that were making life such a misery for Fred and his crew.

The sails were dropped and Deceptive motored toward what looked like a very narrow channel marked by a flashing light on a pinnacle of rock to starboard. This was off a dark outline that Fred took to be the island of Expalmador. Ibiza, he knew, was the other dark mass of land to port. There, another light, on yet another small island, flashed a welcoming, or warning light, depending on the observers frame of mind. Now he desperately needed the missing chart, but still couldn't find it. He pulled everything out of the chart-table, much of it spilling onto the floor. Deceptive pitched and rolled getting closer and closer to the flashing beacons. But it wasn't to be found. Kevin panicked and shouted to Fred to get up on deck, fast.

As they closed, the gap between the two small islands grew wider and wider: Again, darkness was playing havoc with their perspective.

'There's room for a large battleship to pass through here,' Fred couldn't help mentioning to Kevin in a loud, 'I told you so', tone of voice They motored through without incident. Fred couldn't help but notice that Kevin had been scared.

'He's scared shitless! No wonder he's been such a prick!' he thought, unsympathetically. He was surprised that he hadn't noticed Kevin's fear before now.

But, the danger wasn't over yet. As they changed course and headed directly for Ibiza town, the first grey light from a heavily overcast sky illuminated more large pinnacles of rock rising from the sea. They were like black ragged daggers waiting to impale the unwary. 'Probably would have seen them in the dark,' Fred affirmed to Kevin's unspoken reprimand. Fred was glad that they had held back earlier, although he would never admit this to Kevin. They were on the leeward side of the islands now and the sea was suddenly calm. The debilitating lurching was over and Fred already felt much better, his queasy stomach almost immediately settling.

On entering a marina near Ibiza town, two hours later, they had completed an estimated one-third of their journey. They were worn out, spent; broken by the endless energy of the sea and lack of experience. Hardened sailors would not have found that last stage particularly difficult, but not so Fred and his crew. Kevin hoped he would never have to go through anything like it again.

Here they would take a full day's break to take stock of their situation and have a well-earned rest. Uppermost in Fred's mind was the troubling fact that he couldn't afford to lose any further crew members. They were effectively down to three until his lacerated hands healed. He would have to be careful, watch his temper and be more patient with Kevin. Especially now that he realised that it was all a front on Kevin's part.

'Scared bloody shitless!' he confided to Nigel, 'and it never crossed my mind.'

But, it had already crossed Nigel's mind, among other things. He thought he finally knew what the real problem with Kevin was. He reflected on the old adage: If you put a group of people on a sailing boat for a week, natural leaders will emerge. 'Separates the men from the boys,' he thought. Nigel felt well protected by his own, chosen, non-competitive position. He felt his talents would be better used in keeping the peace. Nevertheless, the question still intrigued him: who would stand revealed as the natural leader, Kevin or Fred? And what about George, how was he coping? He was learning fast. He made few mistakes and those he did make, he never made again. He was helpful, and could already take over in an emergency without anyone worrying about his capabilities. Furthermore, he was becoming more sure of himself as time passed. Even now, he appeared in better shape than Kevin or Fred, despite the difficult crossing. Nigel was as sure of one thing as it was possible to be sure of anything: Fred and Kevin would have to grow up and start acting like men rather than spoiled brats, otherwise the trip would end in disaster.

9

Another Bloody Documentary

Fred almost fainted when he heard what the mooring charges were to be.

'Bloody highway robbery,' he muttered angrily, 'I don't think we'll come back here in a hurry. Twenty flaming quid!' He was angrier still when he found out later that if they had used another marina it would have cost them less than half that price. He still hadn't caught on to the to the notion that owning a boat was like shovelling money into a bottomless pit. Piracy was no longer restricted to the high seas, it was also firmly established on shore in the guise of marina charges and inflated equipment prices.

'Aw! what the hell. They would have a relaxing day. A leisurely stroll into Ibiza for lunch and perhaps a few drinks . . . and why not?' Fred decided. They certainly felt as if they had earned it. Fred was to join his crew for a few beers for the first time on their arrival in a strange port.

'Things are looking up,' thought Nigel, 'and anyway he couldn't do much on the boat with his hands in that condition. It might be nice for a change to have Fred wet his whistle with the boys. Might make us more of a team.'

A small solitary figure with dark glasses stood next to an old, worn out, sailer-cruiser watching their every move. Fred had seen him and taken note. All was not as it seemed. Were they being watched?' he wondered, not wishing, yet, to pass on his worries to the others. The incident in Gibraltar had really rattled Fred. He felt that, perhaps, they hadn't heard the end of it yet.

In Ibiza town that afternoon after a pleasant lunch, they purchased fresh vegetables, eggs and fruit. The fruit consisted of oranges, apples, bananas and, most important of all, a few lemons.

'Anyone who knows a baggywrinkle from a can of worms, will wax lyrical on how lemons and limes were the saviour of many an old tar,' began Nigel, who had recently found out that a baggywrinkle was not a close relation of a baggy-minnow, but the pen-name of a nautical illustrator who had a sarcastic, cynical, cutting view of his fellow sailors, and who he imagined to be both baggy and wrinkled.

Fred thought he should explain the real meaning of the term, but as Nigel was still calling fenders bumpers, he decided it would be a waste of breath.

'He's making another bloody documentary,' muttered George to Kevin.

'Scurvy,' continued Nigel ignoring George, ' – scurvy was responsible for more deaths than a total combination of storms, sea battles, ship-wreckings and piracy, all lumped together. Did you know that?' he asked, switching the bag of groceries from one hand to the other.'

George adopted an interviewer's stance. Pulling a banana from the bunch in Nigel's bag, he placed it in front of his mouth.

'Is there anything else the British viewing public should know about this awful disease. Do you think that a cure will be found in our life time?' he asked, mimicking Nigel's voice.

Nigel grabbed the offending fruit and rammed it down George's trousers. 'And that'll possibly cure your particular affliction.

'Boys oh boys! Aren't we all having such fun,' Fred thought, sarcastically, not in the mood to voice his opinion.

Nigel's purchase of lemons had nothing whatsoever to do with preventing scurvy. He just liked the odd slice in his gin and tonics.

'A gin and tonic without a slice of lemon is like sex without marriage,' he informed them, engrossed in a new vein of thought. 'They both work perfectly without the other, but you miss that . . . underlying . . . bitterness, that biting acidity, . . . the sourness.' He laughed, amused by his own cleverness.

Nigel had a reporter's jaundiced view of life, especially marriage, since his wife ran off with an undertaker, or so he said, but nobody really took him seriously.

'Ah! the poor old biddy found living with me too boring,' he began, breaking into his usual routine. 'She wanted a bit of life, excitement, bright lights. Life with me was a dead end for her, boring. So she ran of with a bloody stiffs' parker, an undertaker!' He examined their faces. They were sufficiently amused. You know, I'm happy for her. I'm sure he'll be the last man to let her down!' He waited for their response. They finally got it, and laughed. 'The auld sundowners will taste so much the better now, eh? D'ya think we could pick up a block of ice somewhere? A lump of ice would finish things off nicely.' When it came to matters of drink, Nigel could be a little pernickety. He claimed to be the inventor of a lethal concoction which he named Screaming Orgasm. This consisted of equal parts Baileys, Tia Maria and Vodka. In trying to promote this cocktail he would ask young women if they wanted a screaming orgasm. He had found this to be a boon to his sexual proclivity, for some said yes without realising that he had meant a drink and those that knew better, after two or three, were decidedly more responsive.

The restaurant they selected for that evening's meal had the reputation of being the best in Ibiza and they would have to dress accordingly.

'If we're paying big bucks, we might as well look the part,' suggested George, who liked to do things properly.

After the regulatory 'sundowner', suitably enhanced with Nigel's lemon, they set off once again for the distant town of Ibiza. To Fred's acute embarrassment they were now all neatly dressed and had even donned collars and ties for the occasion. Fred was the only exception.

'Scruff bag!' George teased.

'Wouldn't be seen dead in that gear,' he told them. 'Oh, no!' He wasn't going to become the laughing stock of the marina. He had pretended he didn't have a tie with him, even though Marge had packed two. He could imagine, only too well, how the real yachtsmen in the marina would react to a boat-load of so called sailors leaving their sailing yacht in gin-palace garb. 'Stink-pot crews could dress as they pleased,' he thought. The casual, slept in look he had adopted for himself, after many months of careful contemplation, suited him perfectly. Sure as hell, he wasn't about to make a fool of himself by dressing up like a stuffed dummy. However, in view of the occasion, he had made one concession. He changed his underwear!

Fred still looked and played the part that he felt he was born for to the full, that of yacht-skipper, boat-owner. 'Capt'n Fred,' he liked the sound of that. Well, he was still the owner, he told himself, even if Nigel's share was gradually increasing. Fred allowed the others to get a good head start before venturing out on deck. After a furtive glance to left and right to make sure the others had not been observed, he hurriedly left Deceptive

He felt as heady as a newly kissed Roger Rabbit.

and caught up with them as they passed through the marina gates.

As they crowded around the small restaurant bar for pre-dinner drinks, Nigel noticed a pretty girl come in. She was also dressed for the occasion and sported a cute, off the shoulder, number, which left little to the imagination. She seemed to be alone. 'Probably waiting for someone,' he thought. He was instantly attracted and flashed her one of his deadlier smiles. She averted her gaze and suddenly seemed keenly interested in inspecting the tip of one of her patent leather, slip-on shoes. This was Nigel's cue to play it cool. He stood unconcernedly talking to the others for some time, slowly sipping his drink. He pretended he hadn't noticed her coming to the bar. She stood next to him trying to attract the barman's attention. 'Still by herself, can this be possible? Must be,' Nigel thought. He waited for a chance to make his move. The age-old hunt was about to commence. 'Desire's red hot ingot was on the anvil, ready to be shaped and moulded, or doused in a bucket of ice cool water,' he thought. He waited until she was about to leave and then, turned awkwardly, almost knocking the newly replaced gin and tonic from her hand. He was unable to stop the contents splashing her pelmet of a dress. With deft, experienced dabbing movements of his handkerchief he quickly brushed droplets from her dress and bare shoulder. Apologising, he offered to buy her another drink. She smiled.

'Love, fifteen,' he thought. He found her ready smile breathtaking and was even more intoxicated by her beauty. Having hardly spoken to her, he was already in love.

'Can I get you a re-fill?' he asked, 'Name's Nigel,' offering her his hand.

'Sandy,' she answered coyly. Their hands collided awkwardly in mid-air before meeting and holding firm. She giggled with flushed embarrassment, like a teenager playing forfeits. Their grasp held, neither wishing to withdraw.

'This is pure animal magnetism,' Nigel decided. 'Was it her openness, her odour, her dress, her nearness?' he wondered. He couldn't tell, but he already felt eager manly stirrings in his white and green, medium sized best cotton, Marks & Spencer boxer shorts. He blushed.

She told him that she worked as an auditor for a large international firm of accountants. She was tired of hotel food, she explained, and decided to go out for a meal as it was her last night before returning to London.

'Brains as well as everything else, and she is alone . . . and hungry!' he thought. 'What beautiful teeth, and that cleavage and . . . and . . . those slender legs and tight . . .'

'He's got such a cute dimple on his chin. I really hope he's not married,' she thought.

Nigel informed her that he was Irish and sometimes a television announcer. She replied that she was English, had never seen him on television, and hoped he wouldn't hold it against her. For a fearful moment he wondered what it was she didn't want him to hold against her.

'Gawd! he's Oirish,' she gave an involuntary shiver. 'Maybe my mother was wrong? What the hell! I still want to hold him in my arms, take care of him, cuddle him, kiss him. Oooo, he's so cute and he blushes too.' Her head was spinning, things were going too fast. 'I don't care if he is married,' she decided, her heart pounding in anticipation of their impending liaison. She was already as sure of this as she was of the insurmountable loss she had confirmed in the holiday company's accounts she had just audited. She wondered if he would be gentle with her and if he would do to her what she had just done to the travel company!

'What would you like?' he asked, interrupting her flow of thought.

'I'm not sure,' she replied.

'How about a Screaming Orgasm?' he suggested.

Endless seconds passed before she realised that he meant a drink.

'Maybe I'll try one then,' she replied, amused.

'It's the name of a drink,' he explained unnecessarily. 'Equal parts Baileys, Tia Maria and vodka,' he added, to cover a sudden acute and unexpected embarrassment. He found himself blushing again.

'I guessed that,' she answered. 'Pity.' She giggled.

Bong! He felt as heady as a newly kissed Roger Rabbit, steam shooting out of his ears, heels clicking, eyes spinning, and hurtling into space.

He introduced her to the crew. 'These are my shipmates, Kevin, Fred our skip., and this is George. Meet Sandra.'

'Call me Sandy,' she offered coyly, fully aware of the effect her dress was having on them too. She shook hands with each one in turn.

Kevin, Fred, and George were captivated by her beauty, each requesting that she join them for dinner as she seemed to be alone. She accepted Nigel's unspoken invitation with a questioning nod of her pretty head.

During dinner they found her spellbinding. They answered every question about themselves: how they had come together, where they were from, where they were going to, and how long the remainder of their journey would take.

Fred, who was drinking a little more than usual, had heard those self same questions before, asked in the same manner, and was becoming a little uneasy. 'Naw,' he thought. 'It's just a coincidence, there can't be a connection.'

The dinner was excellent. The three bottles of wine were even more excellent. The bill was a disaster. They each clamoured to pay, trying to impress Sandy, knowing full well that they would be reimbursed from the kitty. Sandy offered to pay her share but they wouldn't have that.

After the meal they visited another bar and spent another two hours 'chewing the fat', recounting their experiences so far.

'God!' she exclaimed, 'It must be a dream, sailing from Portugal all the way to Greece in a yacht. I would do anything for a trip like that,' she said more than once.

Fred silently recalled the helicopter incident, the two jets that had buzzed them off the Spanish coast and the tiny spotter plane. He also remembered the little rowing boat that had been on their tail for a mile after they left Cartagena harbour the other morning, Was he really going fishing? And then that other plane? This was all Nigel's fault, insisting on flying his Irish flag. No wonder they were suspicious, whoever they were. The drink was getting to Fred; it was time to call it a day.

Nigel and Sandy excused themselves from the company. He had offered to see her to her hotel and she had accepted. This was going to be their first and last night together. 'Lovers thrown together by fate,' he romanticised. They walked slowly, arms entwined, her head on his shoulder, along the beach. Clouds flitted across the bright moonlit sky, wave followed after wave, slowly rolling in. But all Nigel or Sandy could see or feel was each other and they quickened their impassioned steps heading straight for her hotel room.

The next morning was windy, far too windy to risk the long journey to Cagliari. Sardinia would have to wait for their presence one more day. Nigel hadn't returned. Fred had already taken three headache pills by ten o'clock, but still the violent throbbing in his temples wouldn't go away. This was another reason why they certainly weren't going anywhere today. Fred decided to walk into Ibiza to try and find someone to fix the Sat. Nav., hoping that the long walk might clear his pounding, blinding headache. He remembered his bizarre thoughts of the previous evening and decided he must pull himself together. Was he becoming paranoid? Of course not, just letting his imagination run riot, that's all. He resisted the temptation to look over his shoulder to see if he was being followed.

The dealer Fred found couldn't have been more helpful. He

phoned the maker in England and explained the situation as fully as possible.

Yes, he had earthed the set. Yes! Yes, the connection to the battery was direct. In fact Fred answered yes to every question the manufacturer asked concerning the set's installation. He even mentioned to them that when the antenna wasn't connected, the set still showed *Aerial O.K.* He thought, wrongly, that this news might be invaluable in diagnosing the problem. They seemed unimpressed and ignored his comment.

The set was still under guarantee. Fred expected a replacement and, of course, he wouldn't have to pay for the engineer's time, or would he? Yes, unfortunately he would. It was his fault. Obviously he was doing something wrong and this was going to cost money to be rectified. This didn't seem fair to Fred. He had to accept, assuming that the charges would be nominal, especially considering the rapport he was building up with the engineer. He had just given Fred a computer enhanced colour replication of The Turin Shroud.

'What a saintly man,' he thought, meaning the engineer, and admiring the brightly coloured Christ that seemed to stare back reproachfully from the print.

They replaced the aerial and the cable and re-tested the set. It went through its usual self analysis: *Aerial O.K. Battery O.K.* etc. The dealer was satisfied and asked Fred for the Spanish equivalent of ninety pounds. Fred thought this excessive for one hour's work and offered twenty, but had to settle for sixty as this was all they had in the kitty.

'If it works, it'll be well worth it,' Fred thought, casting an enquiring glance at the Turin image which he was about to place in the chart table. Were those eyes following him too!

As the day progressed, Fred's headache lifted as did his depression. He was his old self again. That was until Nigel returned to the boat with Sandy in tow. She had a large suitcase which they placed next to the dining table and which Fred decided to ignore; that is if you can ignore something you have to climb over every time you want to sit down or go to the loo. They talked about the weather, which Nigel gave as his reason for not returning earlier. 'Lying berk!' Fred thought. They discussed the yacht's navigation system. They had a few gin and tonics with lemon slices, but the subject of the suitcase wasn't broached despite the inordinate amount of room it took up on the saloon floor. Throughout the afternoon there were lulls in the conversation Fred would look at the suitcase for long moments, and then the Sat. Nav. to see if it had given up its lone stand for the liberation of digital machines. He couldn't work out which he disliked most, the suitcase or the Sat. Nav. The Sat. Nav.'s conscience, unlike Nigel's, was definitely bothering it. There was no doubt about that. Every so often a little red light came on and shortly after the first star would appear. Four were needed for a fix. It would get to three and retire exhausted.

Fred decided to go to look for the dealer while Sandy unpacked her things in the forward cabin.

George and Kevin had, in the meantime, been renewing their acquaintance with the local bars. Kevin had wanted to get his hair cut, but the original urgency in the matter had diminished the more beer he consumed.

Fred returned to the boat two hours later. He had been unable to locate the dealer as, not surprisingly, his shop was shut. 'Obviously off on a bloody holiday with my sixty pounds,' Fred thought. However, he did find George and Kevin who hadn't considered themselves at all lost. On their way back, Fred gave some consideration to the new sleeping arrangements aboard Deceptive. He wasn't pleased, but kept his thoughts to himself. Nigel was a part owner after all, with a large investment in the boat. He could hardly object in the circumstances, as a further sixty pounds had been added that afternoon. Kevin and George didn't seem perturbed. Privately, George welcomed Sandy's inclusion, hoping that it would diffuse what he saw as an inevitable clash between Fred and Kevin. He also fancied Sandy, fondly remembering the little sexy number she had been poured into the previous evening. 'It was as if somebody had forgotten to say when!' he thought.

When they arrived back on Deceptive they found that Sandy had prepared dinner. It was the best hot meal they had on board but, as there had only been one previously, the comparison wasn't fair. This time there were no added sweeteners! There was no doubt about it, Sandy was an excellent cook. The soup was followed with an exquisite casserole. Then a simple fresh fruit desert rounded things off. A good notch was knocked off the flagon of wine from Cartegena. Sandy was ceremoniously elected chief cook and bottlewasher and welcomed as a fully fledged crew member.

The Sat. Nav's. plaintive alarm did beep three times before they settled down for an early night. Fred looked once again at the image on the Turin shroud and remembered the Bible quotation, 'The cock shall crow thrice . . .' It seemed to be working at last, but would it betray him again?

George was now sharing a cabin with Fred, but only for the cupboard spaces as Fred was firmly ensconced in the pilot bunk. They would leave at first light. The weather forecast predicted good sailing conditions for the next few days. Customs had been cleared and marina fees paid. All that was required was to cast off and be away.

'Sandy's huge case might come in handy after all,' observed George. 'We could tow it behind Deceptive. Spare life raft? Dinghy?'

Fred put his foot down.

'Ditch it,' he ordered uncompromisingly.

10

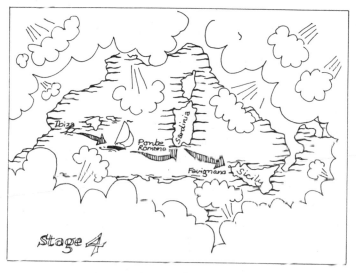

Ibiza · Sardinia · Ponte Romano · Favignana · Sicily

Stage 4

Trial and Terror

Fred got up next morning with a strong feeling of apprehension.
The next leg would be the longest by far and, with bad luck,
could easily stretch to four days. It would depend on the wind
and seas. Their next stop was to be Cagliari in Sardinia.
Originally, they had agreed to leave at first light, but Fred had
reconsidered. He felt that, as there was at last someone on
board who could throw more than a sandwich together, some
serious provisioning should be done as soon as the first shops
opened. Kevin, who was once again dreading the thought of a
long journey, offered to go. Fred, fearing that he might have yet
another urge to go in search for a haircut, nominated George
instead, and suggested that Kevin should get the sails ready.
Nigel shouted after George to bring back some sweets and
Sandy added yogurt, tomato puree and real potatoes to her list
She wasn't at all enamoured with all the 'instant crap', as she
called it, which seemed to stare out of every cupboard she
explored.
    They had filled the water tanks the day before and had plenty
of diesel left as very little had been used between Cartagena and

Ibiza. Their fuel tank wasn't nearly big enough to give them the range they now required. For the first time, they would have to concentrate on canvas only, using the engine as a back-up.

Sandy spent endless minutes in the toilet that morning. It had seemed like hours to Fred. He could get very tetchy on the subject. Especially when needing to 'go-a-place'. When she had finally emerged she looked immaculate but the toilet shelves were littered with various bottles containing hair sprays, make-up and shampoos. All would have to be re-stowed before departure. Fred took Nigel aside and suggested that he should explain to Sandy how things work on a boat, and be fast about it. Otherwise he might not be responsible for his actions.

'Things might disappear through a handy porthole if found lying about,' he threatened. 'I'm not going to risk my flaming neck every time I go to the loo. Could break your bloody neck if you stood on something. Start with the wash-hand basin in your cabin. She can put her stuff in there. That is if you can find it. Then the rest of us can have a pee whenever we want.' Nigel agreed that perhaps Fred had a point and cautiously broke the news to Sandy, She took it in good form, gathering all her bits and pieces together which now cluttered the sink and shelves in Nigel's cabin.

George soon returned with provisions and they were on their way once again. This time everything worked like clockwork as they left the marina. The fenders were taken in, the mooring lines stowed, log entered and courses set. At last they were getting the hang of it. George darted about, checking to make sure everything was put away properly and any loose deck objects firmly tied down.

With more than just a little regret they watched Ibiza disappear into their rippling wake. The No.1 genoa was hoisted to take advantage of the light winds. They were on a dead run. The feeble breeze was barely strong enough to push them unassisted, over a coarse, lumpy sea. The boom was let out until the starboard aft shroud was clearly outlined in the mainsail's fabric. They were 'goose-winging'. This meant that the helm would have to be manned throughout the day. Preferably by Kevin who had proved his ability to maintain a compass course while keeping both sails full. It was ideal weather for the spinnaker, but Fred felt they were not yet ready. Kevin, of course, thought differently.

Sandy prepared all the meals and snacks throughout the day, whilst the others took turns at washing up. Kevin however, still hadn't rid himself of his aversion to any chore other than actually sailing the boat.

Their progress was slow and Fred was tempted to use the engine, but resisted. Everything was going as planned, except for one annoying, recurring problem.

'The blasted Sat. Nav. still doesn't work. Sixty quid down the flaming drain,' Fred moaned to Nigel, even though it wasn't his sixty pounds that had been lost. This was a major worry for Fred. The distance they were about to travel out of sight of land, was now very considerable. He decided that the signal was being interrupted by the swaying movement of the boat. There could be no other plausible answer as it had worked, once again, while in harbour.

'Three hundred and eighty flaming miles and all we have is the flaming compass. If I ever go back to Ibiza, I'll have that incompetent bastard, I really will,' he threatened.

Nigel thought it better to say nothing. At night they would pass within thirty miles of Majorca. He doubted if they would see its lights or even that of the nearer island of Carbrera, if they had any. Fred still hadn't found their detailed chart of the area. He had to rely on the only one he had on board which showed the Balearic Islands. This encompassed the Mediterranean from Ibiza to Italy and was useless for coastal work.

Fred had every reason to fret. A few degrees too far South and they would miss Sardinia altogether. The prevailing wind and the currents could also push them further South than intended. Fred would also have to make allowances for this. The bugging question was, 'by how many degrees?' How much allowance should he make? Another niggling consideration was the compass. It hadn't been swung since he purchased the boat and he was assuming that the deviation card stuck under the chart table lid was correct. Fred made his mind up, deciding to play safe. After all, Sardinia was a big island. He would head further North, for the Isolo di S. Pietro, further up the coast. From there, he would set a course for Sardinia's southern headland.

'It might add a few hours to our journey. What of it? In the circumstances that can't be helped,' he told, a very impressed, Nigel.

Nigel had his own worries to contend with. He noticed that the barometer had been plummeting out of control, since early morning. He feared that there may be bad weather ahead even though the forecast had been favourable. 'Possibly some freak condition,' he decided, tapping the glass with a bent index finger. 'No need to worry the others yet.'

Later in the day, Fred decided to run the engine to top-up the batteries. The fridge had been running continuously, and they would probably need a boost. Nigel pressed the starter button in the cockpit, but the engine failed to start. Nigel hit the button again and again, at first in anger then in fear, but it still didn't fire. Fred tried squirting W.D.40 into the air intake. The engine coughed into life for an instant then wheezed with a last asthmatic gasp and died. Something serious was wrong but Fred couldn't figure it out. He even bled the air from the fuel lines as American Jimmy had shown him, but still it failed. He cleaned all the filters carefully and once again expressed all the air with the finger pump, but still no joy.

'What's wrong with the frigging thing?' he blurted out, frustration getting the better of him. He squirted more W.D. 40 into the air intake while Nigel once again pressed the starter button in the cockpit, but it still wouldn't take. The separate engine battery was now dangerously low. He would have to use the domestic batteries. If he did, the fridge, which had an inbuilt safety monitor, would switch off when they discharged to a pre-determined level. This was a safety feature which insured that the fridge, which consumed more power than anything else, could never drain the batteries completely. Fred, deciding to give it a rest, glowered threateningly at the recalcitrant engine.

'Think you'll ever get it going?' Sandy inquired, looking over his shoulder.

'Typical, isn't it?' Fred fumed. 'Just as the wind is dying and we need the engine, the frigging thing packs up on us. We'll never get to Sardinia at this rate.'

'Is it really dangerous without an engine? I thought sailboats were meant to sail, that the engine was an extra,' added Sandy, unable to hide the nervousness in her question.

'You're right,' Fred agreed reassuringly. 'There's no need to panic, Sandy. Until recently, boats like this had very small auxiliaries. Really just enough to help them in and out of harbour. It's the thought of hanging around waiting for a breeze that bothers me.'

'Why don't we use the spinnaker? queried Kevin, who had been listening to the conversation. 'The winds are light and it'll give us the chance to get used to it. We'll be able to handle her without any bother. Piece of cake really.'

Fred had no option. He had to agree. Everything Kevin said was true. They really should fly the spinnaker.

'It would be interesting to see how it will pull us along,' added George, getting excited at the prospect. 'Even in this wind we might get four or five knots, right Kev.?'

Fred replaced the cover over the inert motor. He mentally conceded defeat. 'Kevin, you take charge. We've never used the sail before.'

Kevin swung into action immediately, shouting orders to left and right. 'Fred, you help up front.'

Fred almost gagged on the instruction, but complied just the same. There was no point in doing otherwise.

The spinnaker was brought on deck in its special bag and placed next to the forestay. The spinnaker pole was hoisted into place and a sheet taken through one end, then round the front of the forestay to the bag. Fred tied the end of the bag to a lanyard on the guard-rail as he imagined it flying overboard as the sail was hoisted.

The silk-like material used for the spinnaker was so light that even the smallest puff of wind would cause it to fill and billow. It was essential that it remained secure until the last moment when it would be raised straight from the its tub-like bag.

Both sheets were attached and led back to the cockpit. Once the second sheet was secured and the halyard attached, Kevin took his place at the helm. 'This was more like it,' he thought, hoping that everything would run according to plan. He took a line in each hand. They fed through blocks on each of Deceptive's quarters, right behind his position at the helm. He would have to steer as well as balance the ends of the huge sail. The No.1 was dropped and secured to the guard-rail.

After checking, from his position at the helm that all was well, Kevin shouted to George. 'Pull her up fast.'

George answered, 'Right Capt'n Kev.,' and pulled with all his strength, and as fast as he could.

The spinnaker blossomed beautifully, forming a massive,

radial cut, blue and white scoop ahead of Deceptive. The bottom corners seemed to be too close together and not opening as expected. Fred immediately understood the reason. The starboard sheet, inexplicably, ran through the port bowline knot. It held both ends of the sail close together. There was no more than an arm's stretch between them. Fred had read the book, studied the drawing, the only thing he hadn't done was set the sail. Any fool could see what was happening, he thought. He wondered why Kevin wasn't dropping the sail and why he had used the genoa lines instead of the special spinnaker sheets with the fitted snap shackles. Fred had brought them on deck especially for the purpose, thinking that Kevin must surely use them. He hadn't wanted to interfere, having given Kevin full rein. Now, he had to do something. He shouted to Nigel to pull the whole bloody thing down.

Kevin hadn't worked with a sixty square metre sail before and was surprised at the tug on the sheets. Even with the blocks he wasn't going to be able to hold her. He would have to get the ends round a winch, but he would also have to steer. He couldn't do both. He realised his mistake too late. It just couldn't be done. He needed help and fast.

'George, get those ends round a winch while I steer,' he shouted in desperation.

'Drop the spinnaker. Drop it! ' Fred shouted from up front. George was confused by the two different orders and hesitated before making a jump for the sheets as Kevin's shouted instruction seemed the most urgent.

The wind had also picked up, gusting to twenty knots and over.

The spinnaker filled even more, taking Kevin completely by surprise and whipping the lines from his hands. Nigel lunged forward and grabbed the bowline knots at each corner of the sail.

'For heaven's sake don't let go!' was the last instruction he heard from Fred, who saw the sheets running out and imagined the sail being carried upward to wrap itself around the top of the mast. Nigel was whisked over the pulpit and into the air by the un-tethered sail. He hung on for dear life, not wanting to end up in the cold uninviting sea. He was surprised at the ease with which he was been carried upward. Already he was twenty feet in the air and wondering why the others weren't pulling him

Nigel was going up and up, higher and higher.

down. George thought the whole thing remarkably funny and doubled up with laughter. Kevin was dumb-struck, everything had gone terribly wrong again. 'What was it about this boat?' he wondered. Sandy was apprehensive that Nigel might get hurt when he hit the water.

Nigel was going up and up, higher and higher. Something had to be done fast. He had climbed another ten feet before Fred managed to jam a sheet as it sped through the guide at the end of the spinnaker pole. Immediately, the air spilled from the sail. It tilted drunkenly to one side and Nigel hurtled back towards the sea.

'Let go!' shouted Fred.

'Aw shit, nooooo! ' screamed Nigel, bracing himself in anticipation of a very unwelcome cold dip.

Fred pulled in the sheet and just managed to guide the

97

collapsed spinnaker behind the shelter of the mainsail. He shouted to the still amused George to let the halyard go. George released the mainsail halyard by mistake and it began to drop.

'Not that bloody rope,' Fred shouted furiously, as the spinnaker filled and wrapped itself around the forestay.

Nigel was already swimming towards the stalled Deceptive. 'This is one for the flaming book,' he muttered, spitting out an unwanted mouthful of water. He liked the experience of being lifted into the air and wouldn't mind trying it again sometime, but the water was too bloody cold for his liking.

'The view was great from up there,' he reflected, now swimming in earnest to catch up with the drifting Deceptive. He had been able to see for miles all around and there was not a solitary, single, boat anywhere. They were all alone. Really, all alone. The thought stuck in his mind.

He clambered aboard shivering, to be comforted by a much relieved Sandy.

Fred was throwing a fit. If they couldn't untangle the spinnaker they wouldn't be able to hoist the No.1, or any foresail for that matter. With no engine their progress would be minimal. He steered left and right to try to untangle the mess in the upper forestay. It took fifteen minutes to unwind the spinnaker as they only had the mainsail to gain headway. As it was freed it was roughly pushed down through the forward hatch by George and a crest-fallen Kevin. They were making sure that it didn't escape again.

* * *

Later that evening Nigel helped Sandy cook the evening meal. It was already dark when they all sat down to dinner. The wind had veered to the North and the No.1 was, once again, giving them good speed. The Autohelm was coping well with the seas despite its mournful wailing. Fred had rigged a boom preventer in case of an accidental gybe. He hadn't suggested changing down to the working jib, which was his rule for night sailing as there wasn't enough of a breeze. He was now more confident of his ability to control Deceptive. If the weather should change he would be able to handle it.

George was on watch but, as they hadn't seen a ship all day, Fred suggested he join them for the meal.

'Take care to go on deck every few minutes or so,' he ordered. 'Just in case.'

Once again Sandy's cooking was superb. She had made a pasta dish with a potent wine sauce followed by fresh fruit sprinkled with a little brandy she'd found in the drinks cupboard. Fred remembered it as the remnants of the bottles he'd bought for Bert in Falmouth. He wished Bert was here. It had all seemed so easy on the way down to Villamoura. It was only now that he realised how competent Bert had really been.

They enjoyed an extra few glasses of wine and relaxed, all except Fred. He worried about the engine and whether or not he could get it going again. They couldn't turn back earlier because they were on a dead run. The wind was then directly behind them. Had they retraced their path, they would have hit it head on. They could have headed for Majorca, but the missing chart posed other problems for Fred. Now was the time to decide. The wind had turned just enough to allow them to return close hauled. They were still only nine hours out. What was he to do? Go on, or return?

George had noticed Fred's brooding consternation and tried to make light of matters.

'There's one good thing about a sailing boat,' he started.

Fred knew what was coming next and tried to get away. He wasn't in the mood for George tonight.

'If the engine fails at least you've still got the sails to fall back on,' George continued, unaware of the turmoil he was causing in Fred's aching head.'

Fred was astonished by this revelation and wanted to say so, but bit his tongue, realising that George was just trying to be kind. George, unlike Fred, was in the mood for a chat and turned his attention to Nigel, who was usually more receptive

'I must say, Nigel, I thought we had lost you back there,' he began. 'Funniest thing I've ever seen. Why didn't you let go?'

'Why didn't you let go?' echoed Fred, who had been intrigued by Nigel's acrobatics.

'Because you told me to effing hold on, if you remember correctly, and when the captain gives an order . . .,' Nigel answered, good humouredly. 'D'you think for one minute I enjoyed being whisked off the deck and carried into space like that? Before I knew it I was fifty feet in the air.'

'But not without a parachute,' added George, laughing again at the memory.

'Actually, lads, you know, it really wasn't a bad experience at all,' continued Nigel, reflecting on his astonishing feat. 'Maybe, just maybe, this could be the start of a new sport altogether.'

'Been done before,' Kevin added, sourly. 'I remember reading about it somewhere.'

'You would, wouldn't you,' retorted Nigel.

They finished the meal and washed up. Sandy put on a Van Morrison tape and snuggled closer to Nigel on the couch. George attended to the drinks.

'Whatch'a want?' he asked Nigel.

George liked Nigel but, despite their friendship, couldn't help being attracted to Sandy's very obvious charms. Chasing a mate's girlfriend was not his usual form but he couldn't help himself. He found her company invigorating and as a result was paying even more attention to his appearance than usual.

'If you hadn't made it, I would have looked after Sandy for you. Eh! Sandy?' he said, giving her a knowing wink, which she chose to ignore.

'Guinness. A cold draught Guinness please and if you can't supply that, mister barman, how about a gin?' interrupted Nigel.

'There are three kinds of gin, sir, oxy . . . gin, hydro . . . gin, nitro . . . gin, which one do you require, sir?' asked George, in his best, jocular, Savoy accent.

'Just give me an effing gin, will you, and less of the chat,' retorted Nigel, pretending to be annoyed.

'Certainly, sir. And did you also know that there are three kinds of turd, sir? Mus . . . turd, cus . . . turd and you, you . . .'

'That's enough of that,' interjected Sandy, highly amused at George's off-the-mark wit. This pleased George no end.

He continued to entertain, making Nigel and Kevin the butt of his jokes. He started to hum a tune and then sang; 'He flies through the air with the greatest of ease, that daring young man on the flying . . . , Your gin, sir, . . . trapeze. Is it a bird? Is it a plane? No its Super Nigel,' he continued with a strong nasal American accent. 'During the day he works as a broadcaster and then at . . . .'

'For Pete' sake, will you shut up, George, and let us have a little peace,' interjected Kevin, rudely.

'The fourth turd!' added George, nodding towards Kevin.

Even Kevin's rudeness couldn't make a dent in George's high

spirits. He was so high from the day's sailing that he was floating way above cloud nine. Sailing was fast becoming his dream thing, whereas Kevin was having serious misgivings about his ability to sail a yacht at all. He was not enjoying the long hauls one little bit. In future he was going to stick to dingy sailing, he reflected. A few hours out and then a few more in the pub was more in line with his present mood. This was pure, utter boredom. 'Ten minutes of excitement and then what?' he asked himself, not caring at all for the answer, which had for some time been causing him so much heartache.

In the course of the day's sailing Nigel couldn't help but notice that Kevin was once again in serious mental decline. He was troublesome and abrupt and took little interest in anything other than the helm. He went out of his way to antagonize Fred, leaving his personal belongings strewn about the saloon. Fred gathered them up and just slung them onto Kevin's bunk not caring how they landed. Since getting the cabin to himself Kevin had become even untidier. Now little piles of discarded, dirty clothes lay everywhere. Fred couldn't resist passing an odd comment and Kevin retorted by challenging every instruction given by Fred. Nigel thought it was going to take more than he could offer to keep those two apart. Sooner or later things were going to erupt and get even nastier. The lid was off, the powder was dry, and the slow burning fuse was already lit. He feared that they might even come to blows. Fred had made a mistake in trying to appease Kevin by allowing an inexperienced crew to try to fly the spinnaker. Nigel would try to see that this didn't happen again.

'There are plenty other ways of relieving boredom, without putting people at risk,' he decided.

The barometric pressure continued to fall. Nigel had noticed rows of small dappled clouds in the sky before dark, remembering the old sailors saying, '*A mackerel sky with mares tails, means tall ships carry low sails*'. Was it a mackerel sky? It looked very like the photograph in the cruising guide which he had checked time and again. All the signs were there, but they must be wrong. At the moment they had barely enough wind to keep them underway.

Throughout the day Nigel and Sandy had hardly left each other's side. They touched and kissed frequently. Fred was still suspicious of her. He couldn't understand how two grown-ups could behave like love-sick sixteen year olds. Fred wondered if Marge and himself had ever been like that. He didn't think so. His present all consuming love was Deceptive. He had never felt that kind of love for his wife, but they must have had something. 'Probably . . .,' he played with the notion, 'animal magnetism,' and chuckled to himself with the thought.

Later Nigel called Fred on deck to express his fears.

'I'm not too happy about the weather,' he began gravely.

'Me too,' admitted Fred, who had also been watching the barometer. 'I really can't imagine a storm. Not when the forecast was so specific. Are you sure you had the right sea area?'

'Yeah, of course, I'm certain,' answered Nigel, a little annoyed at the suggestion.

'If a storm, hit with no engine we'll have to keep some canvas up,' Fred informed him. He had always intended to motor out of difficulties, but now was being forced to think again. They had a storm jib on board which they could use if the going got really tough.

The little wind they had, changed back to its former direction. The No.1 wasn't really doing very much except billowing and emptying as it peeked from behind the shelter of the main. Fred pulled both sails in and moved Deceptive ten degrees to windward, making a mental note of the time and the new heading. If the weather did turn nasty they would have to change the head-sail, he thought, but now they needed as much canvas as possible to maintain headway.

From the deck all looked peaceful. They could see a faint glow in the sky to the North and assumed that it was Palma. Not another light, signifying that other boats were abroad, could be seen. Fred decided to have another go at the engine despite the fact that it was now past eleven and Kevin was in the adjacent cabin trying to sleep.

The wind hit one hour later without warning. Fred was halfway through bleeding the fuel pipe again. The engine cover boards, which also formed the steps to the cockpit, were strewn around the saloon. Anyone trying to come up on deck had to clamber dangerously over an exposed engine. Within minutes it was gusting to over forty knots. Nigel quickly dug out waterproofs and life jackets, but there wasn't time to put them on. Their single most pressing objective was to reef the mainsail and drop the genoa. Deceptive lurched forward at an alarming rate and Fred, who had quickly clambered to the helm, found it impossible to hold her on course. She tried to come up into the wind in strong, overpowered turns, her starboard rail almost under. A more experienced sailor would have been able to hold her on a run until the crew were ready to sweep into action, but Fred had already lost control.

At a critical moment, with a sweeping turn, Deceptive came right through the wind, the boom preventer causing the main to back. The genoa also backed. As a result Deceptive started to spin slowly.

George clipped his harness to a lifeline and started to crawl along the deck followed by a still sleepy Kevin.

'Get the genoa down! Drop the flaming thing!' Fred shouted to his semi-dazed crew who seemed unable to interpret any of his many instructions. Spray blinded those on deck once more.

'Release the boom preventer and reef the bloody main.'

They could hardly stand let alone work. Fred's orders were fast and furious, but little seemed to be happening. He had Deceptive back on track again, but another gust overwhelmed the helm and the carousel started all over again. The spinning action caused Sandy to fall across the saloon, showered by un-stowed books, cutlery and wine glasses. What moments ago had been perfect order, was now complete chaos.

'One of you release the flaming halyard!' Fred roared, in desperation.' He was tempted to leave the helm and do it himself, but Deceptive healed over even further, completely out of control, and building up even more speed. The sea was boiling. Deceptive was pivoting on her side one moment and in the next rushing madly ahead. Something had to give. There was no way she could withstand this pressure. Fred glanced fearfully at the wind-speed indicator. It registered forty-five knots and they were still under full sail.

Sandy was still below, panicking. She didn't know what was going to happen next. Nigel was trying to calm her down, by calling to her, while fighting his way on deck. He was thrown sidewards against the exposed engine with each of Deceptive's twisting lurches. He felt as if he was bruising from head to foot.

'Stay where you are and sit down,' he advised Sandy roughly. 'You're safer down here.'

Sandy had trouble believing him but, nevertheless, slid

Deceptive healed over even further, completely out of control.

around the couch and jammed herself behind the dining table.

The wind was still rising and Fred was worried that they would broach or that the mast might go before they got the sails down.

Deceptive came around again, her sails filling with a loud report and water sluicing along her lower deck. Fred hoped all the portholes were firmly closed otherwise they would ship water. The rudder was partly out of the sea and now useless. Fred was becoming frantic.

'For chrissake get the sails down!' he shouted, tempted, once again, to rush forward and let everything go.

The rubber duck, which they carried inflated on the starboard quarter gunwale, tied to the guard-rail, had its lower edge in the sea. It was been dragged away from Deceptive by the force of their erratic headlong rushes. Any minute now she was liable to break free. Fred was also trying to lob the painter outside, to act as an extra tie, and still steer at the same time. If they lost their dinghy they would never find it again.

Kevin and George, up front, were being bounced around, unable to keep their feet as sheets of blinding spray obliterated them from Fred's view. They were already shivering with the cold, their soaked clothes no barrier to the ferociously bitter wind.

George tried to release the boom preventer but a trapping turn had been made on the cleat which was jammed by the extreme pull on the rope. He could use only one hand as he needed the other to hang on. He could feel the water gurgling over his feet and then, as the sails backed, he was upright once more. Deceptive levelled off for her next turn. 'If he could only get the main, or the genny down,'

Fred managed to hold Deceptive into the wind for a few seconds until she lost way and veered off again. He swore loudly. If he only had that damn engine he could have held her, allowing the others to complete their jobs safely.

As Nigel emerged, bruised and battered through the hatch, Fred shouted to him to release both halyards. Nigel jumped to it. Fred once more brought Deceptive into the wind and Kevin managed to pull down the foresail as George wrestled with the main.

Kevin worked with the fury of a dervish. He was in panic and thought that, any moment now, he must be swept into the sea and lost.

Immediately the sails were slackened, Deceptive stopped her crazy waltzing and adopted a new bucking motion. Kevin, with glum intensity, dragged the soaking genoa out of the sea and over the guard-rail, securing it to the ties along the starboard side. He had a lot on his mind. Decisions would have to be made. He wasn't going to get into a situation like this again if he could help it. There was no question about it, in his opinion, Fred was incompetent. He had got them into this, who was going to get them out?

George managed to release the boom preventer and Nigel pulled in the main sheet. They then rolled the main into itself and tied it as best they could, regularly losing their balance and being forced sharply to their knees. Icy pellets of rain still stung their arms and faces. They were soaked from head to foot, but were relieved that their ordeal was over. Sheet lightening once again lit up the sky in a continuous barrage of sound and light.

Nigel hurried below decks, almost breaking his neck as he tumbled over the exposed engine. He wanted to try and calm Sandy down. She was still huddled behind the dining table unable to move, oblivious to the water coming through the partly open saloon hatch. It was now, thankfully, mostly rain.

Fred and a tight-lipped Kevin put up the spray hood and inserted the lower duck board into place.

Fred returned to the helm. He tried to anticipate the run of the waves to steady the boat, but to no avail. They were impossible to avoid before breaking over the deck with shuddering intensity. The sea looked like a boiling mass of white, effervescent suds emphasized by a foreboding backdrop of pitch blackness. Visibility had become very restricted. The deafening noise, as the wind tore through the rigging, was far more frightening than the roar of the waves. Fred checked the compass. They were being pushed well off course and, even without sails, were making considerable headway.

Fred was furious with himself. He couldn't understand why the engine didn't start. He would now be forced to use the sails in conditions which he would prefer to use the engine alone. Deceptive, doing five knots under bare poles, was almost out of control. He decided to do something fast. Otherwise, the continual battering and stomach heaving wallowing would have an even more demoralising effect on his crew. One thing is certain, he told himself, he'd have to remain at the helm until the weather abated. Kevin didn't look in too good shape, and he couldn't trust anyone else to maintain any sort of headway.

Having changed into dry clothes, George and Kevin huddled in each corner of the spray-hood, which offered little protection from the driving force of the wind, as it propelled Deceptive miles off course.

Nigel had cleared the floor, put the engine cover back on, and was now sitting comforting Sandy. Below decks, once again, everything was in order. The boat's pitching didn't seem so intense and the soft red glow from the instruments panel had a reassuring effect.

'These boats are built to withstand conditions far worse than this,' Nigel offered quietly, giving Sandy a firm hug. She smiled back at him, appreciating his efforts to re-assure her and tried to kiss him softly on the cheek. He felt her soft breath moments before their heads collided with a smart crack. Suitably chastened, she withdrew smiling to herself. There would be time later, she hoped. When the wind had abated. Then she would have another stab at it.

Fred decided to hoist the working jib and raise the mainsail, but leave it fully reefed. George was in agreement, but Kevin suggested they leave things as they were and ride the storm out. Fred didn't think it prudent to mention that if they didn't get back on course soon they might have a lot more to worry about than just the wind alone. 'It might be handy to know where you are when approaching land,' he thought.

The decision was made to hoist the sails, they would have to move fast. There was no way Fred could hold Deceptive into the wind for long without the engine. The main couldn't be raised as the runners on the mast had a habit of jamming if not straight out. He would have to get the working jib up first. It was going to be wet and dangerous working up front, but it had to be done. George went forward and changed the foresail. Kevin tugged the halyard and very soon full control returned to the helm. George got to work on the main leaving the soaking No. 1 where it was, tied to the rail.

'Winch her up if necessary, but get the flaming mainsail up as fast as you can. Once I've got some headway from the jib, I'll turn her into the wind. Right!'

As Fred feared, the mainsail jammed. Then too much pressure on a winch handle caused the sail to tear right next to the twisted clip. They would have to risk it. It looked as if the sail wouldn't rip any further. So up it went.

Once the sails were set, Deceptive steadied noticeably, her speed increasing. They were once again heading in the right direction. The working jib had changed the trim of the boat, lifting her stern and pushing the bow further into the waves. They were on course and Fred, happily, made a mental note of the time. There was now little chance of the sea swamping the cockpit. But Deceptive did seem to shudder more viciously every time she struck a rogue wave. This terrified Deceptive's least brave occupant. Sandy expected the hull to crack like an egg at any moment. She had missed the previous occasions when the crew thought the hull couldn't take any more, but she was catching up fast. The others hardly noticed it any more.

A little later, the wind eased and blew at a steady thirty-five knots, sometimes gusting to forty-five. Most yachtsmen would never venture out in these conditions. But Fred's crew were happy. This was a whole lot better than what they'd just come through. It seemed as if the whole episode had taken hours, days even, but in fact, they had only been pushed, flattened and spun for less than forty minutes. It had taken less than five minutes to get the sails down. It was like those seconds before a car crash, when time stands still.

Fred, now that order reigned once more aboard Deceptive, decided to give the engine another go. He lifted the hinged lid seat section which sheltered the cockpit engine dials, turned on the ignition, and pressed the starter button, whilst still maintaining an awkward position at the helm. The throttle was full forward, but she still didn't catch. He was just about to give up when he noticed in the glow of the instrument panel, that the stop lever was full out. He couldn't believe his eyes.

The flaming engine hadn't started simply because it was starved of air. He couldn't believe he'd been so stupid.

'If I'd come on deck instead of fiddling around below,' he thought, 'I'd have noticed it immediately. What bloody idiot didn't push the lever home the last time the engine was stopped?' he wondered, angrily, aloud. The others hadn't heard him, which was just as well for Fred. It had been none other than one Frederick Alexander McNaught, occasionally known as Sputnik, who had last switched off the engine. 'There is even a sign right next to the starter button,' he remembered, punishing himself even further. 'Push home stop before removing key,' it said. 'What a dilly, what an asshole,' he told himself. 'If anyone asks . . . !'

Fred hit the starter button. The engine fired immediately and caught.

'See you got it going then?' Kevin asked in his, at this moment, very unwelcome Welsh accent.

Fred knew it would have to be Kevin. What other smart arse would ask such an obvious question?

'Must have been some dirt in the diesel, sounds alright now,' Fred blustered. 'We'll let her run for a while, give the batteries a bit of a boost. Put the fridge back on, will you,' he added, giving a nervous cough.

'Do you want the sails dropped now that the engine is on?' asked Kevin, hopefully.

'Naw! we'll let her go as she is. The sails seem to be steadying her,' replied Fred.

'Why don't you go down and get out of those wet clothes. I'll take over here for a bit,' Kevin offered. If they couldn't just motor he would feel safer if he were in charge.

All the others had changed into dry clothes long ago, but Fred was still reluctant to leave the helm. He had enjoyed the recent excitement and wanted to savour the taste a little longer. His adrenalin was in full flow and he hadn't felt the cold even though his clothes were saturated. The working jib was doing its job nicely and he felt sure that an even bigger sail could be used safely, despite the severe wind. Fred was at last getting to know his own boat. He released the helm and went below to change, but first he decided he must try to establish their position on the chart.

Sandy had calmed down thanks to Nigel's careful attention. She was still a little apprehensive, fully expecting the drama to start all over again. The brute force of the wind and sea was still new to her. Earlier she'd felt like a Ping-pong ball being bounced around the cabin. She was still feeling a little squeamish but thankfully wouldn't be seasick. Sandy was one of the ten percent of seafarers who can help themselves to fried egg, bacon and sausage while all others about them are trying hard not to think of food at all.

Nigel had remained firmly on the couch next to her, pretending to read, but really keeping a watchful eye.

George had the kettle on the wildly swinging, gimbaled cooker and was standing, legs apart, supported by a special restraining strap around his buttocks, putting heaped spoons of coffee into huge mugs nestling safely in the sink.

He welcomed a dripping Fred with, 'Got your name on one of these. You did a grand job back there, skipper. Sorry I couldn't get that damned rope off before we had our little twirl. Should be plain sailing from here on though, if the sail holds. I sure learned a helluva lot back there. One spoon or two?'

Fred was inwardly delighted. This was the first time anyone had called him skipper without saying it for effect. He knew that he had earned George's respect the hard way. George was not given to passing indulgent compliments. Fred supposed that this was George's way of saying that he had faith in his judgement after all was said and done. He began to relax and felt that now they were really going to make it. Little did he know that it would take only a few confused minutes before George had altered his newly formed opinion.

Fred dripping wet clothes were creating little puddles on the saloon floor. He pulled out the navigator's pinion seat and, on the instant he was about to sit down, Deceptive struck a wave hard which threw her roughly to one side. The force of the shock threw Fred heavily onto the leather-covered chair. It snapped with the impact and he landed on the wet slippery floor, sliding head first between George's open legs, to be struck with the outward swing of the cooker. He lay there dazed, blood gushing from a superficial wound on his forehead. George was knocked off balance and fell over the restraining strap spilling the entire jar of coffee over the very wet Fred. He began to turn a dark shade of brown. The coffee justly earned its instant tag. George and Fred spent endless minutes disentangling themselves. The dark brown mess spread along the floor, and over the newly dried George, ruining one of his best pullovers. Fred in his moment of triumph had fallen as only the proud can. Vanquished, he lay there looking at a fuming, coffee coloured George.

Nigel and Sandy couldn't believe their eyes. This was vintage slapstick. Hal Roach in his hey day couldn't have produced silent comedy as good as this.

'You stupid bloody eejit! Look at my clothes! They're ruined!' George yelled, as he unhitched the restraining strap which still held his legs suspended in air. Then he noticed the broken seat and the gash on Fred's head.

'Are you alright , ya daft bugger?' he asked contritely.

Fred remained on the floor motionless; bleeding and dazed. Sandy regarded him with a long questioning look. She tugged Nigel's arm, concerned that maybe Fred was badly hurt.

Fred's shoulders began to move rhythmically. He snorted coffee from his nose and his ingrained face burst into an instant, broad grin.

'Must look a bloody sight,' he interjected between sobs of laughter. 'Bloody black and white minstrels. First we spin round in circles, then this.'

Nigel began to worry. Was it hysteria? He'd never seen Fred like this before.

George forgot his ruined clothes and helped Fred to his feet, beginning to see the funny side of the episode as well.

'I think we should invite Fred to join our team as scrum half. I haven't seen a tackle like thon for years. What do you think, Nigel?'

Sandy and Nigel couldn't resist any longer and ended up helpless with laughter as well.

Fred killed them totally with a few bars of 'Mammy'.

'The sun shines east, the sun shines west . . .' sang Fred, arms extended.

Tears of laughter were streaming down Sandy's face as George and Nigel laughed uproariously.

Meantime, Kevin could hear the cackling down below and wondered what on earth there was to laugh at. He was not amused. He found nothing at all in his present position even remotely amusing. He was determined to save this ship and get them to port. His years of dingy sailing had not prepared him for this. He suspected, hoped, that the others were just as scared as he was. He alone could get them to Cagliari and once there, they wouldn't move again until he was sure the weather was okay. He could rely on Nigel or George to back him up. There was no real reason for being out here, in the middle of bleddy nowhere, in this weather. He wasn't about to risk his life any longer so that Sputnik, 'and that . . . that other space traveller and his fancy bit could get to Greece. No way!'

Clearing up the coffee was a real chore. As the brown granules and their magic missing component met, the resultant brown sticky mess seemed to spread out of all proportion to the amount spilled. Fred was reluctant to use too much fresh water. He had to set an example after all. Later they would notice brown streaky patches where they had never suspected coffee could have reached.

Sandy cleaned Fred's wound carefully.

'You won't die this time Fred. How are your hands healing from your last episode?' she asked.

'Who told you about that?'

'Nigel did. You're a bit of a walking disaster aren't you?'

Fred's clothes were dispatched into the ship's bucket to be washed in salt water. George rinsed his out with hot water and left them to soak in the sink, much to the Fred's annoyance. Fred couldn't say anything. He was responsible for dirtying George's freshly changed clothes. However, he did make a mental note to bring up the subject whenever a suitable moment arose. The thought had struck him, 'If we used sea water for washing the dishes we could save quite a few gallons of fresh water every day.'

The remainder of the night was going to be difficult. Each crew member would be required on deck, some time or other, if the wind kept up. Fred dispatched Sandy and Nigel to their cabin. George, before joining Kevin in the cockpit, mentioned to Nigel that he hoped the heaving and bumping in the fore cabin wouldn't be too much for Sandy. Nigel didn't miss the point, but thought it better to say nothing. He did, however, make a rather rude two fingered sign as he closed his cabin door. This left little reason for doubt as to what he thought of George's comments.

Fred still looked a little shaken after the bump on the head and George suggested he lie down for a few hours. The cabin lights were doused, even though the engine was still running. The batteries needed to be recharged. Fred didn't think he could sleep, but with the comforting sound of the engine and a few pain killers, he was soon drowsy, and then he was dead to the world.

An hour later the engine was switched off, but still Fred didn't awake. The bang on his head had hurt much worse than he had admitted to the others. Nature was taking its course.

Two hours later George shook Fred awake. He had made some soup which Fred took gladly. George and Kevin's spell on deck had been uneventful. The wind had dropped to thirty knots. A mountainous sea had built up, which Kevin was mastering with some skill. Deceptive rolled down the back of each huge wave to be picked up and carried surfing along the next ridge, only to slide back down again. It looked as if the seas were higher than the masthead. Kevin had remained at the helm for the full shift and had not allowed George to take over.

'Not even for a frigging second,' George complained to Fred. 'Not even while he was piddling over the cockpit gratings, the dirty scut.' This last act had really disgusted George as much as he maintained. He was feeling a little put out by Kevin's insensitivity.

'The spray will soon wash it off,' Fred assured George, seeing the look of disquiet on his face. 'You do know that more people are lost overboard while having a 'Jimmy Riddle' in bad weather than at any other time, don't you?'

George was really miffed. He felt that he had earned his place on Deceptive. He had already proven to the others that he could handle her but Kevin still hadn't allowed him to take the helm. 'Isn't Kevin supposed to be my mate?' thought George.

Each time they had surfed along a wave's ridge he had to

correct their heading at exactly the right moment to let her fall back, stern to the following wave. Otherwise, Deceptive could have slid sideways, and possibly broached. On the crest of each wave Deceptive picked up momentum, rapidly surfing along the top, and sometimes attaining speeds of eleven knots or more over ground. This was exhilarating sailing indeed. Deceptive was light for her class, but didn't seem in any danger of being pooped by the following wave. It just picked her up and carried her along the summit, until she couldn't go any faster and fell back to start the cycle all over again.

Fred took the helm from Kevin, taking care to match his now well established rhythm. Kevin was glad to be relieved and immediately went below. He stretched out on his bunk, still in his wet gear, and was instantly asleep.

George convinced Fred that he wasn't tired and suggested that they let Nigel sleep on. Fred saw right through his ploy. His intent was not terribly well disguised. George desperately wanted a chance at the helm to see if he could match Kevin's mastery of the waves. Fred saw no reason why George shouldn't take a turn at the helm. He decided to play him along for a while though, until he finally came out with it and asked to take the helm. Fred, unlike Kevin, had no objection. Fred was also not sure how long his partly healed hands could take the tremendous strain, even though he had taken the added precaution of putting on a pair of gloves.

Much of the mundane work on board was willingly attended to by George. He had scrubbed the decks in harbour without being asked. He had polished the chrome and whenever in the cockpit had coiled the loose ropes and halyards, stowing them neatly in their proper places. He prided himself in being able to tie a bowline faster than anyone else.

Fred knew that George had indeed earned his right to time on the helm. Kevin did tend to hog it a bit. Fred wasn't too worried by the huge waves. At least they had long troughs, giving plenty of warning of an approaching ridge. He was confident that Deceptive could take those seas in her stride. She would only flounder if silly mistakes were made by her crew.

Now, she rose with each wave, and suspended on its crest, Fred had an unrestricted view for miles around. Not a light could be seen, signifying some other crew battling their way through the troubled night. This was the most difficult watch of all. In calm weather it was impossible to stay awake. One had to busy oneself with endless chores to remain alert. Tonight was a nail-biting affair. In spite of his still aching head and sore hands, he wanted to go on. He used every muscle in his body to retain his balance. With feet wide apart, one knee bent, then the other, his legs acted as powerful shock absorbers, cushioning the swaying movements of the yacht. He hauled the wheel to port and starboard maintaining their course through the towering seas. One minute he was skimming along on top of the world, the next enclosed in a foaming green abyss, surrounded by mountains of glistening, translucent, water. It had a motion all of its own. 'Like poetry,' Fred fancied.

An hour passed. The still hopeful George made some coffee, precariously bringing a mug on deck for Fred. Though Fred was reluctant to hand over, he felt it would be selfish not to give George a chance at the helm. He directed George to stand beside him, with a nod of his head. He took the proffered coffee from George's grasp, still holding the helm with one hand.

'Put both you hands on the wheel and match the rhythm. Get the feel of the helm,' Fred instructed. He knew that it would take a little practice before George became familiar with the twists and turns necessary to guide Deceptive safely over this towering, helter-skelter of a sea. Once he felt sure that George could handle it alone, he stepped aside.

George wasn't ready. Deceptive had just finished her surfing motion, and begun her sideways slide down the back of a wave. He had to turn hard to port to bring her head around, but he spun the wheel too slow and then was unable to correct his mistake as Deceptive stalled and began to lean over awkwardly.

Deceptive slid down the wave sidewards causing her centre of gravity to change abruptly. Her two and a half ton ballast wasn't enough to keep her upright and with the help of the strong wind she was soon over on her side, the mast falling towards the oncoming wave. It all happened so quick. Fred was amazed to see the seas break over its upper reaches and then cascade towards the reefed main. The inclinometer in the cabin registered 45 degrees then 55 . . . 65 . . . 75 . . . and 90. She was going to capsize!

Fred and George had their harness on, but what of the others? Fred shouted a late warning wondering if this was the end. Deceptive was on her side and there was ever chance he would tumble into the water. He made a last ditch effort to right matters. Holding on for grim death with one hand to a winch, he furiously tried to release the sheets with the other. The coffee cup was long gone. They were so far over that the rubber duck was fully submerged beneath the gunwale and, luckily, added much needed extra buoyancy. The cockpit was awash but the spray hood and duckboards were enough to curtail the ingress of water below decks.

Nigel and Sandy were slung onto the carpeted wall of the fore-cabin, not knowing what was happening. Half awake, unable to move, they feared Deceptive would go over the whole way, capsize. Sandy was the first to realise what was happening. A scream of terror, which silently built up deep down in her throat, burst from her lips and could clearly be heard by Fred above the fury of the sea. She clung tightly to Nigel, horrified.

Seconds became hours as Deceptive slowly righted herself. The top of the mast reappeared through the crest of the wave with a cataract of water cascading from its uppermost portions. George swung the wheel to bring her head round. The two inch scuppers were quickly draining the water from the cockpit, even before she was fully erect. Fred's instinctive reaction in releasing the sheets saved Deceptive from serious damage. He wondered if they might have lost the mast, or drowned. This must be how American Mike had lost his mast, he imagined.

George regained control as soon as the rudder got a grip on the water. Fred was resetting the sails to get back their earlier stability, when Kevin stormed out of the hatch demanding an explanation. Fred had had enough of Kevin. He told him to shut up and go back to bed as everything was under control. Kevin, demanded satisfaction, realising that George had been at the wheel. He wanted to know why Fred had so endangered their lives? How had he let someone so inexperienced take over?

'You must be out of you effing mind letting George take the helm!' he shouted, almost spitting the words. Fred tried to appease him, but to no avail. Sandy and Nigel regarded the scene with some trepidation from below.

'It was obvious from the start that this trip was going to be a disaster,' continued Kevin, now hysterical. 'Nobody knows what the hell they're supposed to be doing around here.'

Kevin struggled to the helm and tried to wrench the wheel from George's grasp. Fred was sick to the teeth of Kevin's tantrums and warned that, if he didn't let go immediately, he would shut him up good and proper with a belt in the gob. Kevin took a swing at Fred and missed. Nigel clambered over the duckboards and grabbed Fred, before he could reciprocate. He shouted at them both, telling Kevin to get back to his bunk and Fred, for everyones' safety, to watch George on the helm. Nigel was disgusted with both of them and couldn't understand how two grown men could start a fight at a time like this.

'Right slap bang, in the middle of a flaming storm,' he complained to Sandy, 'and all they can think of is having a go at each other. What next?'

Fred needed a strong pain killer to overcome the searing throb in his temple. He went below to search among the strewn contents of the saloon. Books, along with cushions, charts, pencils, navigational aids, mugs were scattered all over the cabin floor. He found the missing chart of the Balearics and threw it disgustedly onto the chart table.

'Wouldn't you know it!' he uttered out loud.

Sandy began to help Nigel to tidy up, while Fred checked the masthead lights and the V.H.F. for damage. Thankfully everything was working. He was still inwardly shaking, not from the near disaster, but from what he felt was an unprovoked onslaught from Kevin. He badly needed something to calm his nerves. He took three tablets before returning to sit with George. His head still throbbed and he could feel the bile rising in his throat. He felt nauseated, but knew he must stave off the sickness until the pills had time to do their work.

Shortly after, Fred fell into a troubled sleep, huddled in the corner of the spray-hood. He was awakened by Nigel, coming on deck to relieve George.

It was a already dawn and the sky was clear. The waves were now tamer than earlier. The wind was down to a steady twenty five knots. Fred had suggested they shake out the reefs in the main, but keep the working jib set in case the weather worsened again.

They had made remarkable progress throughout the night and now, with the main fully up, were doing well over six knots. Everything seemed so changed in the light of day. The pounding no longer worried Sandy. She made scrambled eggs and coffee precariously keeping her balance on the damp floor. She had long since regained her composure, but black tell-tale marks still remained around the eyes from when she had been crying. Now she was putting a brave face on the new day's proceedings.

Fred, pale and drawn, decided to put his head down and get a another few hours sleep. Hopefully he would wake up refreshed. He felt jaded.

George, even though he had been up all night wanted to go on but Nigel wouldn't hear of it. Sandy joined them for breakfast in the cockpit. The Autohelm took over the job of keeping their path constant and true, better than any helmsman could. It whined continually as it worked flat out. How would they have coped without it. The thought never struck them, although it soon would.

Everything today looked bright, clear and peaceful, but the maelstrom of the night before wouldn't be easily forgotten.

'At least the knock-down washed the cockpit clean,' George reasoned, reminded of Kevin's urinary baptism. He wouldn't have to fling buckets of sea water over it to clean it any more. Nigel, cushioning a hot cup of coffee in his hand, remarked that in daylight things did look much calmer.

'It must have something to do with our dark and murky past,' he added talkatively. George agreed with him good humouredly.

'Last night, that was really something else,' said Sandy shovelling a fork full of scrambled eggs into her mouth.

'Were things really as bad as they seemed or was it just because it was night-time? If they had been knocked down during the day, would it have seemed so horrific?' George wondered.

'From light to darkness, from joy to woe,' quoted Nigel, who was in one of his more reflective bents.

They all agreed that it probably wouldn't seem as bad, deciding that a lot of their worries were caused by an inbuilt fear of the dark. Kevin, who could hear the conversation clearly in his cabin, turned over in disgust, burying his head deep in his pillow.

'What a load of wankers,' he muttered aloud, deciding that he could no longer face breakfast.

* * *

When on duty, each crew member was to make an entry in the ship's log book. Each day had two facing pages. The left hand page was for practical purposed: time (G.M.T.), barometer readings, log , speed, compass heading, and wind direction etc. The page on the right had spaces at the top for the weather forecast, leaving the remainder blank under the heading *Comment*.

As it didn't specify what type of comment, it was left to the imagination of the compiler. Without success, Fred had tried to point out that the 'Ships Log' was a legal document and, as such, must be treated with respect. Anything written on it should be pertinant and to the point. Suffice to say entries were rarely relevant and were mostly unsigned.

One entry read; 'Passed a trawler at 01.00 hours G.M.T. Don't think I will be able to sit down for a week.'

Various night sightings were noted such as, 'Saw our first iceberg tonight. Can we still trust Fred's navigation to get us to Greece safely?'

More poignant ones were; ' If you hang in there, you to can go up in the world – like Nigel.'

'My name is Steve,' another read. 'I did it only seventeen times last night, must try harder. My name is Steve I did it only seventeen times last night , must try harder. My name is Steve . . .'

Or, 'Kevin almost washed a cup today, stopped himself just in time.' This entry had been written by Fred in a heavily disguised hand. Everyone knew that it was his handiwork, including Kevin.

Now, George half stood, half sat on the fractured, chart table, seat and made the latest entry under 'Comment:'

'Almost lost the boat last night in a fierce storm. Waves of up to twenty feet, winds force nine plus. But for the swift action of our captain we would never have made it. Good old Sputnik!

11

Danger Dead Ahead

Throughout the day, the ragged uneven seas made life unpleasant for the crew. Cooking was nearly impossible. Nobody really cared any more. They didn't feel like eating. Their appetites lost somewhere in their turbulent wake. Sandy prepared, as best she could, coffee and sandwiches, but only enough to stave off their hunger.

Deceptive's erratic waltzing movements had a deleterious effect on morale as she pounded and yawed her way ever nearer to Sardinia.

Kevin, in order to avoid Fred, was now spending more and more time reading, surrounded by the strewn contents of his disordered cabin. He was thoroughly ashamed of his behaviour of the previous night and was searching for a means to right matters, without having to apologise. He withdrew further into his sleeping niche beneath the row of cupboards, their open doors banging in unison with Deceptive's swaying passage. The glow from the reading lamp beneath the bulkhead competed feebly with the daylight filtering through the two side portholes. Kevin had no interest in conserving battery power. Here, his life was bearable. He could bury himself in his novel and forget everything else.

The wind was on Deceptive's port quarter for most of the day. They maintained an efficient broad reach.

Fred spent considerable time at the chart table trying to re-establish their position. He hoped to get at least one fix from the Sat. Nav., which was regularly picking up satellites as they arched unseen above Deceptive. There was the familiar glimmer of red signifying that they had a lock and then the flicker of one star, then two, but, as always, it failed before confirming where they were. He sat watching it, mentally coaxing it to relent, but it always fell at the last hurdle. He moved the aerial from the port to the starboard guard-rail, but to no avail. The antenna and the cable had been replaced by the computer assisted Christian in Ibiza, so what was the problem? It had to be the set itself. There could be no other explanation.

Fred admitted to himself that he didn't really know how far

they had been blown off course the night before. This candour, however, didn't quite include telling the others. 'What they don't know won't bother them,' he decided, firmly closing the option to come clean and discuss the problem. He worried whether or not he had over-corrected today's heading. He marked up the log and noticed the latest entry in the comment column. He read and re-read George's footnote about his efforts of the previous night and couldn't hide the heady rush of pure satisfaction. But, he knew, deep down, that luck had played a big part in what had happened. He chastened himself by remembering that it was probably his inexperience that had put the boat in danger in the first place.

He was tired, felt drained, worn out, and tried to grab a few minutes sleep whenever possible, but he always awoke exhausted. He felt as if he could no longer control his mind, as his thoughts darted from one imaginary crisis to another. He'd had enough of night sailing. The wind inevitably freshened and, with only two safety harnesses between five, he was worried that someone would be lost overboard. He had taken to tying the tail of any unused halyard or sheet around his waist to secure himself, rather than use a harness which might be of more use to a less sure footed member of his crew. He knew that if someone did go overboard at night, they would never be found. The rough seas would see to that. His weariness played havoc with his nerves. If he didn't get a restful sleep soon he felt he would crack up. His responsibility for all on board and the continual bickering with Kevin was beginning to take its toll.

As he had anticipated, the weather worsened again that night. The tightly stacked isobars caused further high winds and flurries, but nowhere near as bad as the previous night.

Fred had worked out the rotas. Deceptive was on a reach and the Autohelm could cope perfectly with this point of sail if the ratio between wind and canvas was maintained. Too much of either and the machine couldn't cope. Only one person need be on watch at any time. The working jib was once again hanked on and hauled up the forestay. The others could now grab enough sleep to make up for what had been lost.

'Kevin will have the eleven until one watch,' Fred began. 'George from one until three, myself from three to five, and then Nigel for the last few hours before daybreak. Sandy will make breakfast at about eight. I will sleep in the saloon, as usual.' He paused to make his point felt. 'Make sure you wake me up if any of you need any help. Okay? If we have to go back to manual steering, we will need two crew members on deck, one on the helm, and the other to watch the sails and keep the log. If we have to we will return to last night's rota and extend the watches by one hour.'

Fred made up his mind to get as much sleep as possible. He knew that the others would awaken him, but only if it was in an emergency. He remembered his exhaustion on his arrival in Portugal and knew that he must not allow himself to deteriorate to that level again. They settled down for the night. Fred crawled into his snug sleeping bag and fell fast asleep.

On deck, Kevin pushed himself into the corner of the spray-hood. Through the ever-changing water rivulets on the perspex windshield, he could see what was going on ahead and to his left. The sails effectively blocked his view to starboard. But, as he had an unrestricted view behind him, he could practically search the sea all round without having to get wet or cold.

The continuous whine of the Autohelm had a strangely soothing effect on Kevin as Deceptive climbed the equally spaced waves and then dropped, shuddering as she hit the troughs with her full weight. The rhythmical movement added to the lulling effect and before long Kevin was fast asleep.

*   *   *

The container ship Barak had come through Suez that morning and was heading for Barcelona to pick up some cargo. First she had to make a drop in Palma for their sponsor in Dubai, who was a wealthy sheik.

'The container probably contains his custom built Mercedes again,' Barak's first officer guessed. 'Needs it to swan around in Majorca.' He browsed through the manifest for the umpteenth time. His guess hadn't been pure chance. This was a ritual undertaken every summer as the sheik had an elaborate villa on the island. The container ship was usually empty on its return journey from the Middle East and so offered special concessions for return cargo, especially to its patrons.

Barak was classed as a medium-sized trader and had the advantage of being able to unload containers in ports restricted to larger vessels. In this instance, that flexibility had been seized upon, much to the annoyance of the captain, who would have preferred to continue straight on to his original destination.

They were far from the shipping lanes tonight and the watch could relax a little. The sonic sweep of the ships radar showed all clear for fifteen miles ahead. The first officer also found the night black and gloomy. On his ship there was little evidence of the uncontrolled pitching experienced on Deceptive. He had, luckily, missed the previous night's storm. That definitely would have hindered their progress. He sipped a large cup of steaming coffee which he had laced with a stiff brandy. He was an experienced seaman, having already served this company twenty of his twenty five years at sea. The weather fax had, just that minute, been updated and was showing a progressive worsening of the weather ahead. This was nothing new to him as he always encountered bad weather around this time of the year in the Med. He pushed the square of paper carelessly to one side and peered through the bridge windows for a few moments, then turned away disinterested. He glanced at the log.

Barak was doing eighteen knots and closing fast on the, as yet unseen, small sailing yacht directly in her path. He played with the chart plotter, circling imaginary obstacles ahead and trying to out guess the computers time to contact.

*   *   *

Kevin was sound asleep, his head resting on his folded arms. Deceptive continued to pound her way East making about four and a half knots, showing only her separately filament tricolour masthead light, which Fred had put on to save the batteries. He wasn't aware that they weren't complying with accepted procedures. He didn't have the correct lights switched on, even though Deceptive had a full array to conform with maritime law.

Kevin woke with a feeling of impending doom. He instantly saw both the container ship's port and starboard lights, her black mass eating up the short distance between them. They were going to be run down! He leapt out of his seat towards the helm feeling cold sweat on his brow as the flow of adrenalin constricted his arteries. His face was sheet white and he began to tremble uncontrollably. His knuckles stretched tight, he clung desperately to the wheel, not knowing which way to turn. Barak's green light winked and disappeared. The only way he could turn without gybing was to port and that would take him directly under her bow. He had no choice. He had to start the engine quickly and try motoring away, leaving the sails to their own devices. The engine didn't start at the first touch. He had to press the starter twice more while giving her more gas. Kevin, now frantic, had just got the engine going and was forcing the wheel round without disengaging the Autohelm, as Fred staggered on deck. Fred had to duck quickly to avoid being struck by the boom as Deceptive raced forward, due to Kevin's too fierce use of the throttle, white smoke belching from her exhaust. Kevin was turning away from what he still thought was certain death. Already Barak was upon them, towering above them, her outline blending with the night sky.

'What the hell's going on?' shouted Fred.

Kevin pointed to the other ship. Fred still couldn't make her out. All that was visible was a black wall, indistinguishable from night, which was Barak's sheer port side.

'There! there!' Kevin shouted, desperately pointing up through Deceptive's spreaders.

Fred looked up and saw Barak's port light. He let out an involuntary oath, grabbing the wheel roughly from Kevin and, releasing the Autohelm's belt. He tried to bring Deceptive further around, but the helm was over as far as it would go.

There was hardly any noise from the other ship, just a deep throb from the disengaged engine deep in Barak's bowels, and the whish of her bow slicing through the waves as she drifted past. A face appeared on the deck way above them and watched until they were well clear.

Kevin was shaking with fright. They were now heading away from Barak's wake, going in the wrong direction, but neither Fred nor Kevin made a move to get back on course. The Autohelm had not been discharged fully and was now whining out of control, trying to bring Deceptive back to heel.

The container ship re-engaged her engine and her powerful prop began to push her forward again. She then gave a long toot of her horn and continued into the night, her name clearly displayed on her stern. Her wake hit them shortly after, throwing Kevin off balance and pitching him against the sprayhood rim. Fred was flung against the wheel, but used it to remain upright.

Fred was raving. 'Didn't you see it?' he bawled at Kevin.

'Yes I saw it,' Kevin lied. 'It turned at the last minute.'

'Turned at the last minute!' Fred echoed.

He dived down the steps in his hurry to get to the radio. He was going to call the ship on the radio and demand an explanation. Switching to channel sixteen, he called the now fast disappearing Barak, all sense of protocol long gone out of the window.

'This is Deceptive calling the bastard that almost ran us down,' Fred screamed at the handset. Instantly there was an answer.

'This is Barak calling Deceptive. Do you receive? Over,' called a calm American voice.

'Yeah, I receive you . . . you bastard,' shouted Fred, 'What's the big effing idea, eh?' You almost killed us!

'Look, feller,' said the patient voice. 'Next time you keep your eyes open, or there won't be a next time. Right? It's hard for us to pick you guys up on our radar. If we hadn't turned when we did, you'd have had it.'

'But it was us that turned,' retorted Fred indignantly.

'Have it your way, feller,' said the patient voice. 'You must have heard our engines kicking in. We were coasting for a quarter of a mile before we passed you guys. If you had kept on your course we would still have missed you by plenty.'

'You looked bloody close to me,' faltered Fred, suddenly realising what probably had happened.

There was no doubt about it, they were clearly in the wrong, sails or no sails. Fred apologised and asked for confirmation of their position and also a weather check. He wrote the details straight into the log and thanked the American for his help, wished him good luck, to which the American suggested that they needed it more than him.

Fred couldn't understand why Kevin hadn't seen the approaching ship and Kevin was not about to tell Fred that he had fallen asleep on watch. Fred had his suspicions, but kept them to himself. There was little to be gained from another slanging match with Kevin. The latest entry in the log would say it all.

Fred plotted their new position on his chart. He couldn't believe it, they were only two miles off course! There was nothing to this navigation game, he decided. Only two miles off in thirty six hours and in a storm as well. Child's play!.

Twenty minutes later they got their first satellite fix. 'Typical,' thought Fred, 'Just when you least need it, there it is! Like a spare prick at a bloody wedding.'

There was more bad weather on the way. Fred wondered if it would ever clear. He couldn't believe their bad luck. They had now been on their way for a week and a half and he could barely remember two good days so far. If it continued much longer the rest of the crew would become as shattered as himself. If the weather didn't ease off he would have to abort the trip. It was as simple as that. There had already been too many near misses. By the law of averages, they should have run out of second chances by now.

Kevin had also had enough and was just about to throw in the towel. Falling asleep on watch was inexcusable.

The others had slept on unaware of the near tragedy. Sandy and Nigel lay snug and warm in the lea side of the fore cabin, their arms entwined, her head on his chest, their bodies moving in unison with Deceptive's pitch and fall. Nigel had had a new lease of life since Sandy appeared. She had been the morale boost he had needed as he had been getting a little stale. Nigel thrived on social intercourse, meeting new people.

It was time to wake George for his shift. If the weather was to worsen, they should reef the main now, rather than later. Fred worked out that, even if it did slow them down a bit, they still had a few hours in hand. If a squall did hit as Barak's first officer had predicted, they would be ready. He'd had quite enough frights, not just for one night, but a whole lifetime, he decided. It was still six hours until daybreak and he was going to make sure that there were no further problems. The wind was now veering further to the East and Kevin had sheeted in the sails. Even though their speed hadn't changed, Deceptive's passage seemed more determined than before. The yawing had stopped but now the pounding of the bow as it smashed down into each gully was more intense, more urgent. It seemed as if she, too, wished to get this section of the journey over and done with. If they could maintain this progress they would arrive in Cagliari much earlier than expected.

The night passed without further incident. George let Fred sleep on and handed over directly to Nigel for the last few hours. Sandy joined him on deck to keep him company, and to get away from the fearful impacting sound in her cabin of Deceptive hitting the waves.

Fred awoke, much rested, to the smell of bacon and eggs. Sandy once again had won the day with her cooking and they all huddled in the cockpit eating greedily. Fred couldn't believe it. The expected storm hadn't arrived. 'Typical, bloody typical,' he mumped. Nigel looked at Sandy and gave a broad wink.

*   *   *

Fred decided to head for the nearest port. Cagliari as a destination was now of little importance. They just wanted relief from the continual battering they had taken for the last three days. They might resume their voyage tomorrow, but today they had to get their feet firmly on dry land. Directly ahead was the island of S. Pietro and, beyond that there had to be a safe haven where they could rest for a while.

12

The Big Entrance

They were approaching the port of Ponte Romano in what Fred considered to be a very proper manner indeed. 'Ship shape and Bristol fashion,' he muttered, through his shaggy, untrimmed, grey beard. The fenders were secured to the guard-rail and the mooring lines made ready, even though they were still a long way off. The halyards and sheets lay neatly coiled on either side of the hatch. The mainsail was wrapped in the special cover that protected the seams from the pernicious ultra violet rays of the newly emerged sun. Everything was perfectly organised. Fred's critical eyes proudly surveyed the scene. This was how things should be done, he thought, remembering their previous ramshackle entries into harbour. His crew were really getting the hang of things. They no longer had to be asked, they just went ahead and did their bit. Fred couldn't be happier. Here he was heading into port, after three days of pure hell, and everything was absolutely perfect.

At that precise moment the engine failed. It had run for twenty minutes, then hiccuped once or twice, spluttered and died.

His fragile mood was instantly shattered. The warm glowing feeling he had experienced was replaced by cold apprehension.

'What's wrong with the frigging thing now?' His frustrated question caused little surprise among his fellow sailors, they were now used to his muttered expletives and took them for granted.

Deceptive was drifting, gently making her own way to shore, but not where they had intended. Nobody was paying a blind bit of notice. Fred was already up to his elbows in grease and diesel fuel. Nigel sat at the helm staring at nothing in particular, but ready to push the starter button on Fred's command. Sandy and George lolled in the cockpit in quiet conversation, gazing at the scenery in much the same way as a cow looks over a hedge, unseeing and uncaring, happily regurgitating grass for another chew of the cud. Kevin lay stretched out on the deck, enjoying the warmth of the unexpected sunshine, thankful that their ordeal was over.

They were now completely sheltered from the winds that still raged outside the bay. To put the sails up would have been a waste of time. Nobody thought of readying the anchor.

More W.D. 40 was sprayed into the engine's air intake, but the thirty-horse power Yanmar failed to catch. Fred went through the usual checks while the others continued with their musings. It was hard to believe that, only a short time ago, they were forcing their way through tortuous waves, and now it was all over, so calm, so peaceful. They gazed out past the headland where they could see the boiling sea and yet, here, it was so smooth, so perfect, so blissful . . .

The jolt as Deceptive's keel hit the stone bottom shook them from their lethargy. It was like being doused by an ice cold bucket of water on a hot day. Pandemonium broke loose on deck. Fred scrambled out over the exposed engine and made a run for the anchor.

'We've bloody run aground', he shouted needlessly. 'What the hell were you bloody doing up here? Daydreaming?'

'It was truly amazing how astute Fred can be in times of emergency,' George thought, perhaps a little unkindly.

Roused from his shallow contemplations, Nigel peered into the equally shallow sea and could clearly see the rock strewn bottom. He glanced at the depth gauge. It was showing one and a half metres. There was nothing to do but jump in and fend her off. Nigel hit the water in the instant Fred dropped the anchor. The anchor hit bottom, but Nigel was out of his depth. The read-out from the depth sounder was from under Deceptive's bilges and not the surface as Nigel had assumed.

Deceptive was still afloat. Nigel could clearly see the rocky ledge which they had just collided with, and from which they were now swinging slowly away. Nigel passed on the good news to Fred who tied off the anchor and returned to his work on the engine.

Nigel climbed back on board shivering. Sandy went below and returned with a towel to help dry him off.

'This is more like it,' he exclaimed, enjoying the luxury of being towelled by Sandy, He spoiled the mood completely with his next remark. 'Hurry up, woman, I'm freezing,' he ordered. He had hardly uttered the words when he was hurtling back into the water again from a playful push by Sandy.

This time he didn't break surface. Sandy peered in, but

couldn't see him anywhere. The others also waited, but Nigel didn't reappear.

'My God! he's hit himself on the ledge,' she exclaimed, fearing the worst. She jumped in fully clothed and made frantic dives to the bottom, but she couldn't find him. Nigel came out from behind the rudder with a smug, satisfied look on his face, his teeth bared in a broad smile. Sandy also bared her teeth, much as a pit-bull terrier bares his, before leaping for the jugular. Nigel was in deep trouble.

'You're an idiot,' she exclaimed, showering him with a sharp slap of spray which temporarily blinded him. Rubbing his eyes, he saw the well-defined outline of her rigid breasts through her now transparent blouse. He reached out and grabbed her, pulling her towards him and then hungrily searched for her mouth with his. Still annoyed, she returned his kiss like a mollusc trying to gain a grip on a slime-covered rock. They held in a long embrace until she felt his body responding, then, pushed him away. She mounted the boarding ladder knowing that it would take a little while before he could join her on deck.

'That'll teach him for scaring me half to death' she thought. She looked coyly over her shoulder at the still perplexed Nigel. 'Serves you right for being such a pig!'

George couldn't help but notice Sandy's cover-girl appearance as she climbed on board.

'With a body like that she could make the centrefold in Playboy. The jammy basket!' he thought jealously, envious of Nigel's success. Why couldn't he get a woman like that?

Sandy saw the look in his eye and thought of another way of getting her own back on Nigel, but decided that he had been punished enough.

Fred came back on deck and pulled in a few metres of anchor chain. He couldn't allow Deceptive to drift any closer to the shore. He calculated that, if there wasn't any wind, they would be alright for a while. What could he do next? he wondered. One thing was certain, they couldn't stay here for long without rowing the anchor to deeper water and pulling themselves out. Any moment they could swing and hit that ledge again.

Fred looked around for inspiration and noticed a small fishing boat chugging past in the distance. Fred waved and the fisherman waved back, not at all surprised by the friendly wave he had just received, and continued on his way. Fred thought of the ship's radio. He could put out a mayday call, but decided that the risk of salvage was too great. He realised that he knew little about marine law and felt that he would really like to hang onto his boat for just a little longer.

Their engine was knackered. They would have to tow Deceptive into harbour themselves.

Fred and Nigel launched the rubber duck and mounted the tiny, two-horse power engine on its transom. Fred didn't know yet if it could shift Deceptive, but was willing to give it a go.

'If it can't,' he announced, 'there are enough strong men on board capable of handling an oar. We could scull the remaining mile. That was how they did it with the long ships in the past. Might not be the most dignified way of entering harbour, but enter harbour we will.' Fred ignored the incredulous stares his words were met with and ordered George into the rubber duck with Nigel.

They lifted the anchor and placed it between them in the inflatable. The weight of the chain kept pulling them back, regardless of how much Nigel strained on the oars. George got the outboard going after a dozen hefty pulls on the cord and a shouted instruction from Fred to open the air intake screw on the fuel cap.

The outboard's controls were simple: there was fast and slow, but no neutral.

'This baby is no idler,' George remarked, working out that to get reverse you would need to swivel the whole engine one hundred and ninety degrees.

They set off at a snail's pace and then gave her full throttle, using the anchor chain as a tow rope. They were certainly moving, but not forward. They were swinging from left to right barely shifting Deceptive at all.

'What do we do now?' Nigel shouted to a seriously baffled Fred.

'Shorten the towing chain.'

They tried every possible permutation, but Deceptive didn't move fast enough.

'She's got her heels well dug in, Fred We're not going to be able to tow her like this without running out of petrol. That's for sure.' yelled Nigel, conceding defeat.

Fred had a sudden brain-wave. ' Bring the boat around to the back and we'll attach the outboard to the boarding ladder,' he pronounced, with just the right level of optimism to convince the others that he knew what he was doing.

Fred felt disposed to take a bright view of things as the sea was still calm and he could clearly see their destination only a bare mile away. They had travelled over three hundred miles non-stop. This little hop and skip wasn't going to beat them. Why not experiment a little? The small engine was placed on an appropriate rung on the boarding ladder and the holding brackets tightened. The head of the motor fitted snugly between two rungs and held perfectly. There was only one minor, niggling, trivial detail that worried Fred and the others. The controls couldn't be reached. Once the starter cord was pulled, the little engine would run on full throttle, with no evident way of stopping it.

'I don't think we'll have any worries,' Fred reassured them, willing to take a gamble without knowing the odds. 'We'll be going so slowly that it won't matter. I can control our direction with the ship's rudder.'

The anchor was stowed and the outboard yanked into life. They began to move, slowly at first, and then gradually building up speed as Deceptive gained momentum. Fred found the helm responsive and steered in a broad arc to avoid any further nasties lurking in the shallows.

'This is more like it. Just what the doctor ordered,' Nigel reflected, making himself comfortable in the dinghy, now being towed behind Deceptive. In the mile long passage to the harbour they had to refill the little engine once, more fuel ending in the sea than in its awkwardly placed tank. They set off once again, leaving a rainbow of oily colours in their wake. Deceptive slowly built up speed as before. Fred could clearly see the harbour wall and headed straight for an opening between two large fishing trawlers. He glanced at the log. They were charging along at three knots and all that he really had to worry about was how on earth he was going to stop Deceptive before crashing into the quay.

San Antico is a quiet sleepy little place. It is rare that anything of significance happens in the town and, when it does, news travels fast. The locals had already seen Deceptive near the shore. They knew there were submerged rocks there, and had assumed that she had gone aground. They hadn't helped because it was the lifeboat crew's duty and they weren't due back until next day week as they were attending yet another 'Festival De Mare' somewhere else on the island.

Everything was someone else's job hereabouts. This explained why little was ever done. All would be attended to 'A domani' which had a similar meaning to the Spanish 'Manyana' but it didn't have quite the same urgency! Now, here was the spectacle of an expensive 'barka' coming into harbour. Was it being pushed by a couple of idiots in a dinghy, rowing like mad? they asked themselves. It looked very like that from the quay. It was obviously out of control if one could judge by the antics of the other 'idiota' on the helm, the one with the white beard and the blue cap perched precariously on the back of his head, obviously the captano, no!

The onlookers on the quay almost had it right. George and Nigel were rowing like mad alright, but not pushing Deceptive towards the shore as it seemed. They were pulling in the opposite direction. Trying to reduce Deceptive's headlong rush for the harbour wall. Fred had no choice. He was going too fast and would have to head out to sea again.

Fred tried the same manoeuvre a few times more, hoping that their fuel would run out, and they could simply coast in. He knew this was a long shot and was desperately racking his brains for inspiration.

The crowd on the quay was getting larger and more animated. The circus wasn't due 'till next week, was it?. Anyone selling tickets around here?

'D'you think there's much fuel left?' Fred shouted down to George and Nigel. George leaned forward precariously, hanging on to the ladder with one hand, while trying to balance on the bow of the dinghy. Still managing to keep clear of the propeller, he opened the fuel cap and took a quick glimpse inside.

'Enough here to get you to Greece and back, Fred.'

Fred was tempted to drop the outboard into the sea if only he could loosen the bracket. This was only a fleeting thought brought on by the ridiculousness of his predicament. He wondered if a prayer might help. In reflection, he thought not. Help from that department hadn't been forthcoming in the past.

In a blinding, but now far too late, flash of inspiration, the answer came to him. All they should have done was tie the dinghy firmly to the side of Deceptive, with the little engine on that, it would have done the same job and they would have had full control.

The locals could tell this was a foreign boat, Not by the yellow flag beneath the spreaders, which stated, to the informed, that customs had not been cleared, or to the uninformed, that there was either a party or yellow fever on board! It was the total lack of gesticulation. If this had been a local boat, a well-known pattern of vigorous gestures would have been established by now. The Sardinians on the quay decided that they should give the newcomers a few lessons, fearing that their boats were going to be damaged by one of Fred's more erratic turns. They started to wave their hands in a very complicated pattern, completely alien to Fred. Being a gentleman he refrained from using one of the few simpler signs he had perfected over the years. Comments were also being made which didn't require a degree in linguistics to interpret.

Up to that moment the locals were enjoying themselves. The threat to their livelihood so far had been a minor one, but now

'Now!' shouted Fred to George in the dinghy.

Deceptive was heading straight for them after another of Fred's aborted dockings. Things were looking serious.

A lull that one feels rather than hears, just before the blade sinks into the tortured bull's heart in the Spanish bullring, descended on the small crowd.

Il silencio . . . They were holding their breaths.

Deceptive was heading at full belt for the quay. Fred had devised a devilishly cunning way to curtail Deceptive's headlong rush towards disaster. He couldn't get at the throttle or the stop button. To dismount the engine further out, would have meant cruising around close to shore until the fuel had run out, never knowing where he was going to stop, and then having to anchor there.

How then was he going to stop Deceptive? Was he going to throw a rope around the prop?

No!

'Now!' shouted Fred to George in the dinghy.

George simply leaned forward and pulled the lead off the outboards single plug and the engine immediately spluttered and died.

'Easy peasy,' thought Fred. He couldn't resist a few seconds of stolen glory. He wallowed in a momentary glow of self-conceit. Conceit quickly turns to defeat. Fred was like a hippo in heat in a muddy pool, cool and hopeful. But his feet were on quicksand as their speed merely slackened a little. He no longer had the option of turning. He had to go for it. He suddenly noticed that, even though the fenders had been tied on, they had not been thrown overboard.

'Get the fenders out and the lines fixed,' he shouted.

Kevin and Sandy sprang into action in an instant.

Fred continued to aim for the gap between the two fishing boats.

It was too late, Deceptive was going to hit the quay head on. He made a last minute decision to head back out and swung the wheel hard to port. Deceptive's head came around fast and then, amazingly, she just drifted side onto the quay. There was a mild jolt as she buried the fenders in the concrete. Kevin and Sandy jumped off with the mooring lines and made Deceptive fast.

'There now,' said Fred , mightily pleased with himself. 'There now,' he repeated, not believing his luck. 'There now,' he repeated once more, wiping a bead of sweat from his brow.

The crowd was impressed and a few even nodded appreciatively. A spokesman stepped forward and offered his greetings.

'Welcome to Sardinia. It is a well, I see you hava done this before.' This was praise indeed, and Fred smiled graciously at the speaker. The rhino in the mud hole had just been satiated.

'Whera you comma from?' asked the Italian. Fred noticed the trim cut of the questioner's clothes. This put an entirely different slant on his questions.

'From Liverpool,' replied Fred proudly.

'Thisa explains how you are so good a seaman. But, why do you fly the Italiano flag?'

Fred hadn't realised that the Irish flag could be mistaken for the Italian one. Out of the corner of his eye, Fred could see another three customs officers advancing towards his boat, their suspicions aroused by his strange entry into harbour.

'Engine's knackered,' blurted Fred, by way of an explanation.

George and Nigel remained seated in the rubber duck trying to look unconcerned, despite the fact that they were embarrassed out of their brains. Here in Italy, where poise meant everything, they had made a stuttering, ungainly entry into harbour. It was something an Italian would never do, even if it meant running at full belt into the harbour wall. 'Eh Giovanni, the wall got in the way!' or some other valediction would be uttered as they stepped off their crumbled craft, blameless in the eyes of the beholders.

'Oh! The ignominy of it,' Nigel thought. 'How embarrassing.'

The customs officer repeated his question. Fred thought on his feet, his grey matter doing acrobatic exercise with the truth. When put to the test Fred could lie like the best.

'It's a courtesy flag, ' he blurted out finally. The customs officers huddled together like rugby players trying to turn a scrum. Something was bothering them.

'We think that this is da Irlanda flag and not the Italiano one.'

'It's faded?' tried Fred, lamely, but they wouldn't have it. 'I fly it out of courtesy for one of my crew who is froma Dublino,' muttered Fred, hoping that a smattering of Italian might ease matters somewhat.

'We wanna to see youra passports and papers and would like

to come ona board your a . . . sheep,' the customs officer replied dryly, motioning for Deceptive's crew to come back on board and join them there.

A thorough search was made of the boat. Fred proffered the ship's 'Bill Of Sale'. He was asked for his insurance documents, which he didn't have, as they were back in England.

'You need insurance in Italia. The yachtsmen here are not as good as you Anglish froma Liverpoole,' said the customs officer. Fred thought he detected a note of sarcasm, but brushed it aside. The one with the most spaghetti on his armlets did most of the talking as his three friends were still admiring the teak interior, and everything behind, under, and above it! He gave Fred a knowing look and a pronounced wink. Fred was going to wink back, but thought better of it.

'You speak very gooda Anglish, I mean English,' Fred corrected himself, finding it so embarrassingly easy to slip into the Italian's accent – especially when trying to hide the nervous edge in his voice, which was sure to give him away. Even though he'd done nothing wrong, Fred felt guilty.

'Mother of god,' Nigel swore to himself. 'Three minutes in the country and he's babbling like a half-wit. What's next?'

As time drew on, Fred became more talkative and an overt friendship developed between himself and the customs officer. The accompanying officers still admired the reverse side of the teak panelling. Obviously they were looking for something. All the usual questions were asked and Fred answered them getting more and more perplexed.

'He'll blow it,' Nigel whispered to George. They knew there was something far wrong; this was not the normal Sputnik. He was being far too polite, nervously ingratiating himself with the excise men, while smiling like a hyena with a bad cold.

After a while, the customs officers, tiring of their trifling little game, gave Fred the name of a diesel mechanic, where to get the weather forecast, where to get a new flag, and how to get to the nearest town, Antioco.

When the customs officers were gone, Fred let out a long sigh of relief. They decided to have some cool beer. It tasted good. They were once again in a safe harbour and were not about to move until the weather changed for the better, even if it took all week!

Kevin decided that here, at last, he would have time to get his hair cut.

The town of Antioco was a good hike from the port and by the time they got there, they were exhausted. Not because of the distance, but because of the oppressive humidity. The next time, they promised themselves, they would do the sensible thing and, instead of walking, take the tender.

'Beer time,' sang Kevin, who had lightened up noticeably since putting some distance between himself and Fred, who had stayed to wrestle with the engine, but not with any success.

After two hours Fred admitted defeat and went to find the diesel mechanic. The problem was the fuel. The mechanic emptied the contents of the water trap into a cup and there, sure enough, were minute globules of water floating within the lighter diesel. Water had somehow got into the tank and would have to be removed. Fred couldn't understand how it had infiltrated the system. He was always very careful when screwing back on the filler cap. The mechanic thought it was probably condensation. He told Fred that the tank should be kept full, especially if not using the boat for a while. Their only option now was to drain the system and Fred wondered how they were going to do that.

The mechanic found a tap at the bottom of the fuel tank directly below the chart table.

'German boat's good. No?' he observed, giving a smile of satisfaction. He drained over twenty litres of fuel from the tank before saying, 'Eet isa now okay. No more problem. Prego!' Next he checked the oil. 'I change deesa for you too, eet is far too thick and a . . . negro . . . black and a new filtro.

He removed the fuel injectors and took them away to be bench tested, with the three new tips that Fred had found among the ships inventory. He hadn't a clue what they were for until now.

Two hours later everything was finished. Deceptive's engine sounded sweeter than Fred had ever heard her before. She purred like a sewing machine. All the strong vibrations which had persisted since Fred had bought the boat had miraculously disappeared.

'I think da injectors no good long time. No?'

The mechanic only charged Fred the equivalent of forty

pounds, but in lira this seemed a small fortune and Fred was a little mean with the tip.

It was peaceful in the harbour and Fred enjoyed his time alone on his boat. He would eventually go and look for the others, but first he had to attend to a few breakages caused during the storm. He also had to work out how he was going to tell Kevin that he had decided that this was the end of the line. He would have to leave. Getting a flight back to Liverpool might be difficult, but that was Kevin's problem.

The talkative customs officer came around with the most recent weather fax.

'The wind she is camming round and perhaps you stay for a few days. It is going to camme from da sautheast and it is rough in the porto .Prego! You masta be ready to move youra sheep round next to da ponto. Capisco?' But Fred had no intention of moving his 'sheep' He was side on to the quay. Obviously taking someone else's place, and they were trying to move him for that, he decided. In any case he couldn't move the boat by himself. He would stay where he was and that was that!

The Anglish speaking customs officer went to help a French yacht which was just coming in.

'Probably needs to practice his froggy language as well as his Anglish,' Fred postulated, and thought no more of their unfinished conversation. Fred noticed that one of the fishing boats was leaving. 'Weather must be on the mend if he's venturing out. Maybe we can pull out tomorrow.' The French boat was going in ahead of Fred, which meant he would have to move back a little to allow her to go side on like himself. He really could have done without the bother of losening the warps and then re-tying them. He wasn't terribly enamoured of Frenchmen anyway, since his week of sailing lessons.

The Frenchman turned out to be a bouncy type and when he had secured his boat ambled up to Fred.

'Bonjour, l'Irlandais,' he greeted. 'Merci beaucoup.'

'Moi?' questioned Fred, incredulously, pointing to himself. 'Murky buckets to you too mate,' he thought.

Fred glared at him much as a rat would stare through a lavatory brush. He went to Deceptive's stern, removed the flag which was causing him so much bother, and, as he furled it, a wicked thought crossed his mind. He offered the flag to the Frenchman. 'I'm not Irish. I'm an Englishman. Would you like to buy an Italian courtesy flag, going cheap. In fact you can have it for nothing.' He pressed it on the Frenchman who backed away, wondering if this strange wild looking Anglophile was slightly mad. 'Could always tell Nigel its been stolen,' Fred decided.

'Quoi?' said the startled Frenchman, not understanding Fred's intention, and now desperate to return to his own boat.

'Bloody typical,' muttered Fred. 'Can't even give the flaming thing away.'

13

Eat Your Tagliatelli, Fred

Fred had little interest in visiting San Antioco as he was perfectly happy aboard his yacht in Ponto Romano harbour. After the diesel mechanic had left, he attended to a few minor repairs about the boat. He tried to fix the navigator's seat but found that the bentwood former was broken on one side and only held together by its leather cover. It could still be used, despite looking a little lop-sided.

'No splinters in sphincters, at least.' he thought. One of the hatch entrance steps had also split down the middle. This made it dangerous to enter or leave as part of the hinged tread kept sliding out from underfoot. Fred re-glued the two sections together, using some white glue, and screwed a brass plate on the underside to hold them firmly in place. It read 'Nobody's perfect except the captain'. This had been given to him by Marge as a going away present with orders to mount it in a proper place. He had racked his brains for an appropriate spot, thought of many, none of which would have pleased his wife, or his humble spirit.

'She couldn't object.'

At last he had found the ideal location for it. 'And where better?' he asked himself. This was an essential repair, otherwise those descending in a hurry could find themselves sharing a compartment with the Yanmar or spreadeagle on the cabin sole. Neither option, Fred felt, was conducive to the well being of his crew.

By the time he had finished this task, George arrived back to collect the kitty, which they had forgotten, and which they now sorely needed, having exhausted their credit at a local tavern. He invited Fred to join them for a meal in the town.

'I think it would be better if we took yon rubber duck, Fred. It's a long walk. In the "quack" we can go under yon bridge, Poncee Romano, I think they call it.'

'There's a few of those around,' Fred thought, amused by George's intentional misrepresentation of Ponte Romano.

Fred noticed that George's brogue always seemed thicker after a few beers and sometimes had difficulty in understanding him. It never failed to amaze him what the Scots, the Welsh, and the Irish did to his mother tongue.

They got into the rubber quack, as George had recently rechristened it, and set off, taking a wide sweep past two moored freighters. George had become an expert at handling the inflatable and their progress through the channel between the mainland and the island was faultless. Fred glanced out along the bay and could see white horses where they had almost gone aground that morning.

'Wouldn't like to be stuck out there now. What do you think George, eh?'

'Could be nasty alright,' agreed George.

As the customs officer had predicted, the wind was gradually moving round to the South-East and would eventually blow right into the port. Fred recognised the fishing boat he had seen leaving earlier. It was now moored alongside the channel quay. The significance of this was totally lost on him as he marvelled at the construction and size of the old causeway they were about to pass under. Once through one of its large granite arches they headed across a wide expanse of perfectly still water to a cluster of lights, beckoning invitingly on the far shore.

Kevin, Sandy and Nigel were waiting patiently in the ground floor of a small, quiet, unpretentious restaurant. Empty wine bottles littered the table in front of three well tanked crew members.

'It looks as if it's been a heavy afternoon.' Fred observed silently. Fully understanding their need to celebrate their safe arrival after their three horrific days at sea.

They need some food, and quick, he decided. He beckoned the owner over, even before collapsing in their sprawling, relaxed, midst. Nigel introduced the owner, as they had become the 'best of friends,' as he put it.

'If this camaraderie was directly in proportion to the amount of booze sunk that afternoon, 'best of friends' is certainly not a misnomer, Fred thought, unkindly. 'Looks as if they've drunk the bloody place dry.' However, he had to admit that Nigel had the knack of making friends easily.

'Fred, this is my . . . my very good fren Lorenzo. Lorenzo, shake hands with Fred. Fred, ole salt o' the earth himself.'

Fred made a quick revaluation. It was worse than he had initially feared.

Down the Hatch

'They're legless, rat-arsed,' he thought.

'Can we see the menu, please?' he asked, tight lipped, wondering how he was going to get this lot into the rubber duck, let alone back on the boat.

The menu could have been in double-Dutch for all they cared. Nobody bothered to read it.

'Let's have a little of everything,' suggested Nigel, taking care not to slur his words. He had been in similar situations before. He could see that Fred wasn't too happy. 'Decisions, decisions, always desissccisions.' Oops! Fell at the last jump, he thought, smiling inanely at Fred. He tried again. ' At least this way we'll get something we'll all like.' Burppp! 'Excuse me. Lorenzo, ole pal, ole buddy, a bit of everything,' he ordered, making circular motions approximately where he thought the menu was.

Lorenzo looked to Fred for help and Fred shrugged his shoulders. 'Do as the man ordered, we'll leave it to yourself. Whatever you think best.' Fred said, passing the buck. The onus was now on the restauranteur to supply the best he could offer. He went off, slightly bemused, to attend to the task.

When the meal did arrive they found that everything was palatable. Even the sausages, which had a definite unfriendly pungency, tasted much better than their odour had forewarned. The salads were terrific and Sandy remarked that they could easily exist on those alone.

'Rabbits do, an you know how horny it makes, 'em,' said Kevin, coarsely.

There was a mountain of coarse lettuce -to go with the coarse language- huge tomatoes slices with chopped onions and garlic on top, and a local white cheese made from ewe's milk. A large, heaped plate of french fries took centre place on the table. A few more bottles of wine were consumed and afterwards they called for coffee. Lorenzo suggested they try some Italian liqueurs, with their five expresso coffees, to round the meal off perfectly. From a vast selection, they chose Stregga and relieved him of the full bottle after a few sample sips.

'What did you think of the saussaaggess, Fred?' asked Sandy, whose teeth suddenly interfered with her diction. She draped a lifeless arm around Fred's shoulder. 'Would you . . . would you have . . .' Her question was, obviously, of paramount importance, it was taking so long to come out. 'Would you have preferred bangersandmash?'

'They were pretty pungent,' admitted Fred, who was having as much difficulty with Sandy's train of thought, as he was with the limp wristed hand that kept flicking the edges of his scraggy beard. ' You do know that they use everything. Bits that we wouldn't feed to our dogs.' Fred was in the mood for gory details. 'Entrails . . . '

'I don't want to hear this,' protested Sandy, screwing up her face and withdrawing her hand.

'I do prefer good wholesome English sausages,' admitted Fred, wondering just how banal her next comment was going to be.

'Down the hatch,' said Nigel finishing another Stregga in one go, Sandy turned her attention to Nigel.

Down the hatch is right, thought Fred, wondering again, how on earth he was going to get this lot back, and down Deceptive's hatch.

They had now reached that level of inebriation where song comes easily to the performer, if not so pleasantly to the beholder.

Nigel began to croak in an Italian accent.

'Give Fred a bash at the bangers and mash his mudder useta mauke.' The others, remembering the words, were eager to butt in. Nigel elected himself master of ceremonies, percussionist, orchestra leader and lead vocalist.

'When I say bangers and mash you say minestrone,' he ordered Sandy, already banging out time on the empty Stregga bottle. 'And then, the next person in line, you George, will have to add another Italian dish.'

'Ping, ping, ping,' went the bottle.

'Bangers and Mash,' sang Nigel, in false cockney.

'Ping, ping'

'Minnestronnneeee,' sang Sandy.

'Bangers and mash,'

'Cannellonniiii,' screeched George.

'Bangers and Mash.'

'Macaroni,' sang Kevin.

'Bangers and mash.'

'Ping, ping . . .'

'Fred, your turn.'

Fred couldn't think of anything other than spaghetti, which didn't rhyme.

'Ping, ping . . .'

'Spaghetti' sang Fred, deciding he was not yet drunk enough to play this game coherently.

Loud guffaws followed Fred's effort, much as he had expected.

'Tagliatelli?' he tried again, sarcastically. He was beginning to have more fun than he'd expected. 'Tortellinniii, fetucinniii, linguinnii,' he croaked, getting into the swing of things.

'Eat your Tagliatelli, Fred. Fred, for goodness sake,' sang Sandy, 'and belt up for goodness sake,'she added.

They were now all thoroughly enjoying themselves, including Fred, and decided to search out the local night-spots.

'A bit of action, eh, lads. The local dishgo,' ventured Nigel.

After wandering the length of a wide, tree lined, deserted street, which, in this small town was the main thoroughfare, they found a large enclosed garden where people mingled with drinks in their hands.

'This must be it,' suggested Kevin, and without further ado made a bee line for the bar which, he thought, must be through the back. They all followed in single file. This was the only place they had come across with any semblance of activity. There was

a large house at the rear of the garden and people could be seen through the open windows, standing in groups and chatting quietly. The women, of all ages, were very conservative in their dress.

So unlike all the Italian women that she had ever met, Sandy thought, a little surprised and feeling a little under-dressed in her green shorts and plummeting purple vest. The men were also soberly dressed. In a corner, an old man played a soulful medley on a violin. Naturally, Kevin decided they should join the people in the house as the bar was nowhere to be seen in the garden. In the main front room they didn't find the bar either but as everyone had a drink in their hands, they assumed it must be near at hand.

'Miserable, bloody bunch here alright,' Nigel whispered to Sandy, and then wondered why he had kept his voice so low. 'Looks a bit dead around here,' he added loudly.

They hadn't noticed the derisive looks they were getting as they progressed through the rooms. George was amazed at how the Sardinians, young and old, kept together as a family, and mentioned this to Kevin.

'I'm impressed,' he went on. 'They have their priorities right

hereabouts. The whole family go out on the town together, including granny. There is no doubt about that.'

'Where's the flaming bar?' asked Kevin, who had more important things to think about.

They followed Kevin, who was getting more than a little frustrated, into the back of the house and found themselves part of a slow moving, shuffle of people entering a candle-lit room. As their eyes got used to the dim light, they saw an old man whose stiff stretched form was decked out in his best formal suit and collar and tie. His eyes were closed and rosary beads were entwined round his joined, wax white, gnarled old hands. He was about to make his final journey. His candle-surrounded coffin was supported on a large brass frame with large wheels, its ornate lid lay resting, foreboding, against the back wall.

She hoped it sounded like a cry of despair.

'Christ almighty! It's a wake,' exclaimed George, loud enough for the mourners to hear. Sandy had a sudden uncontrollable desire to laugh and snorted loudly through her trembling hands as she quickly covered her face. She hoped it sounded like a cry of despair.

Too late, they realised they had blundered into a family funeral. Nigel blessed himself. The others in their acute embarrassment tried to copy but, unsure of the movements, made clumsy foolish attempts with hands going in all directions. Sandy was about to make a bolt for the door but Nigel held her firmly. They couldn't retreat now. They would have to follow the mourners around the raised coffin and touch the corpse's head with newly kissed fingers as the real mourners were doing. Sandy had a fear of death and shuddered as she touched the corpse. Nigel was worried in case they had offended the family and stood patiently saying a private prayer.

Chastened by their stupidity, they set off for the other side of town. Trying to get as far away as possible from the scene of their sobering embarrassment. It had been a horrible mistake on their part. The only place still open was Lorenzo's restaurant and there more Stregga and coffee was consumed by all.

'They really know how to send off their dead, don't they,' Kevin remarked.

Suddenly, the humour of the situation became apparent to them and they began to laugh at the experience. Lorenzo, who had worked for many years in Birmingham, joined them for a drink and explained that, the older you are when you die around here, the bigger the funeral. People's assets weren't handed over until they passed on, so mostly their children had to wait in the sidelines, working for almost nothing, and sometimes, in total frustration, helping nature along!

'It's more of a celebration than a funeral then?' asked Nigel.

'The old man must have been in his nineties, so this was a particularly good funeral,' added Lorenzo. 'His son has just become the owner of a large estate at sixty-five,' he added sarcastically, 'and his son and his son's son are already waiting in line until it's their turn.'

Later, their party spirit regained, they all fell aboard the rubber duck to head back to Deceptive. They sang 'Volare' and bits and pieces of other Italian songs they knew. They even went through the bangers and mash, routine again. Every so often, a ripple of water lapped over the edge of the rubber duck, soaking the unfortunate person sitting in its path. They didn't mind. It had been a damn good day and even Fred and Kevin had buried the hatchet for once. Motoring along the channel they were unaware of the roar of the sea in the distance. Coming out from under the bridge, they noticed that the inner quay was now crammed with all sorts of boats. The two freighters had come around to join the fishing boat Fred had noticed earlier.

At long last the penny dropped. The customs officer had come to the yacht to specifically warn them that the harbour was unsafe in a blow from the South East. Fred couldn't believe he had been so stupid.

The waves crashing into the exposed port were immense. They broke over the quay, rising high into the air, and cascaded down in a torrent of white spray, flooding the whole area in front of the customs offices and silos. They would have to leave the inflatable at the mouth of the channel and walk the rest of the way back, otherwise they would be swamped.

Once ashore, Fred didn't walk, he ran like hell. In the distance he could see the odd wave breaking over Deceptive's gunwales. White, translucent spray shot clear over her deck and onto the quay, the bright port lights giving the whole scene an eerie appearance. Her fenders were taking a terrible bashing, almost flattening completely on each surge. They were barely managing to keep her off the wall. If he didn't do something soon he wouldn't have to worry about the rest of the trip. He'd have no boat.

Bad luck had dogged his path since leaving Villamoura and now this, in a safe harbour. 'Would it never end?' Fred asked himself, almost in despair.

The Frenchman wasn't having much fun either. He had also gone into town for dinner, not understanding what he had been told. Now he was trying to ease his boat out, but each time was swept back against the wall. His engine was not powerful enough to beat the waves and there was nobody to help him rig a springer to catapult him off the wall, head on, into the heavy waves.

Fred flung all his available fenders between Deceptive and the quay wall and ducked through the spray to the Frenchman's assistance. His and Fred's only chance of clearing the quay wall was to spring a line from the offside of the boat to the quay and motor against it, hoping that the bow would point out sharply, allowing them a chance to get away into the oncoming seas. The Frenchman would have to protect his stern somehow, as there was a strong possibility that the boat's near quarter would be flung against the unyielding concrete wall.

The Frenchman pushed the throttle forward hard and spun the wheel as far as it would go. Nigel held a fender in place between the boat and the wall should she fall back. It looked as if the spring was working. The boat's head pulled round and the stern was clear of the wall, but before the rope could be released, she was swept back again and hit the concrete with a vicious, crashing swipe that pulled the fender out of Nigel's hands. There was no question, the sound of ripping fibreglass told its story. She was holed. Somebody would have to go on board to assist the Frenchman. Nigel jumped on board, immediately after the next surge, and released the springer at the precise moment the boat's head came round. She went with the undertow and managed to cross the next wave. Nigel shouted over the crashing seas that he would come back immediately the French boat was safe.

Fred decided that he couldn't wait and, anyway, didn't know if the French boat would sink, or not, before reaching the channel. His sole objective was to get Deceptive safely away. She was bigger than the other boat and had a more powerful engine. It might be in her favour. He had learned from the other captain's experience and was going to utilise that hard lesson immediately. But what if the engine conked out? It had only been fixed that day.

Now that his path was clear, he would motor as fast as possible at forty-five degrees, hoping to get six or seven feet out before turning directly into the waves. He wasn't going to use a springer. He was sure he could do it if he got his timing right. The thought of the engine failing crossed his mind, but he had no alternative, he would have to go. George and Kevin had fenders at the ready in case Deceptive's stern was pushed against the harbour wall. They would let the lines go immediately on Fred's order, abandoning them on the quay. Sandy remained ashore and would meet them at their new berth.

'After the next wave,' shouted Fred.

He pushed the throttle full forward as the wave struck. The lines free, Deceptive was pulled away from the quay by the backwash. She was heading out three feet, four feet, six feet. Fred swung the wheel hard as the next wave was about to catch them. They were being carried back towards the quay, but Deceptive's head had begun to ride over the wave. But she had moved back fast, now only three feet from the quay. Fred sighed with relief as the wave passed under Deceptive lifting her stern and pushing her forward. He watched as the wave harmlessly crashed into the quay soaking Sandy who was looking on apprehensively.

Fred prayed, once again, that the engine wouldn't fail and it answered valiantly allowing Deceptive to motor well clear of the harbour. Soon they were heading up the channel towards safety. There were no spaces left to berth on the sheltered quay, so they were forced to raft up to one of the fishing boats.

The French boat had also made it. Luckily, her stern locker was separated from the rest of the boat by a sealed bulkhead and, even though it had filled almost immediately, there was no danger of her sinking. They understood from the Frenchman that he was delivering the boat single handed to Greece. Now he couldn't go on until the boat had been lifted out and repaired. They invited him on board for a nightcap. Utterly dejected, he shrugged his shoulders and accepted.

'Ziss is terrible. I had no idea ze harbour was dangerous. I hope ze owner 'as paid 'is insurance, if not . . . ?' He shrugged his shoulders in a typical Gaulish fashion.

Fred was in a pensive mood. Despite their drunken state, they were now safely tied up. Maybe their luck was about to change. If anyone ever mentioned again that the weather was changing he would think a little harder. He would make sure he never get caught out like that again. He also promised himself that, in future, one of them must always remain sober. He assumed, rightly, that this would fall to him.

The Frenchman left after thanking Nigel once again for his help. Kevin and George decided it was time to turn in. Sandy went to her cabin and a few minutes later put her hand out and beckoned with her index finger.

Nigel smiled at Fred on his way past and said, 'Goodnight, Fred, that was a nice bit of work this evening. I thought we'd never have managed it after the disaster with the French boat. We weren't much help, with the drink and all, but we made it, Didn't we?'

He gave Fred a final nod and joined Sandy in their cabin. Fred smiled to himself as he put the last remaining light off.

Early the next morning, Fred went to the port office to inquire about the weather. An improvement was expected that afternoon, but it was advisable to wait until this was confirmed. The quay was no longer awash, even though the sea was still a little rough. Fred returned to the boat and helped Sandy with the breakfast. As they were all eating he mentioned that they would probably leave that afternoon for Cagliari. Kevin gagged and almost stabbed himself with his fork.

The crew decided to have lunch in Lorenzo's and return at about two o'clock. Nigel and Sandy would get the groceries and Kevin and George wanted to send some postcards. Fred's relationship with Kevin had improved somewhat and he was unsure of his feelings. Kevin was a much nicer person on shore than in difficult seas. The others might have something to say if he asked him to leave. He still couldn't gauge George's reaction and certainly couldn't afford to lose them both. Fred decided to phone home and consult Marge.

They needed diesel. The pilot showed that there should be fuel on the quay right where they were berthed, but none was available. Water was close at hand and the tanks were replenished before they left for lunch.

Fred made his telephone call from the port offices and Marge advised him not to be a silly fool. If he did get rid of Kevin, he would alienate himself with the others. She also told him she was missing him, but only after he had asked twice.

'I'm very busy,' she had complained. 'The shop's chock a block with customers. You're gallivanting half way round the world and all you're worried about is whether I miss you or not!' But he knew she was pleased he'd phoned.

Sandy, George and Nigel returned at two thirty, but Kevin was missing.

'He'll be along in a minute . . . haircut.' Nigel assured Fred. 'Don't worry.'

Fred now had an up-to-the-minute weather fax and it seemed prudent to leave immediately.

He had decided not to go to Cagliari as planned, but to head straight across to Sicily to try to make up some time. George had found a petrol station, but it was a fair distance away. As they only needed about three containers full, each would make one trip. An hour later the tank was full and everything stowed ready to leave, but Kevin hadn't returned. Fred sent George to find him. They arrived back at four thirty. It was obvious that Kevin had been drinking again, even though he didn't appear drunk. His hair looked exactly as it had been that morning and certainly was not cut. He clambered on board making no effort to explain himself, and went straight down below to his cabin. Fred watched his progress, like a fox watching a lame chicken. He was ready to pounce, but remembered Marge's words and bit his tongue.

Kevin really had gone for a haircut, but as the hairdressers didn't open again until four, he decided to wait. George would come for him in the rubber duck if they really were about to leave. He had spent the next few hours nursing a few beers, wondering if he should go on with the trip or not. He was going to leave, but might as well get a lift to Cagliari. It was only a short sail away. There he would get a flight to London, regardless of the cost. He was relieved now that he had made his decision, and would break the news to Fred when he got back. At four o'clock he had found a hairdresser, but, on seeing the pile of unswept hair on the floor and the standard of hygiene, thought better of it. On the way back he met George who briefed him on Fred's mood and suggested the best thing to do was say nothing and lie low.

Kevin lay on his bunk, safe in the knowledge that soon he

would be going home. George hadn't mentioned that they had decided not to go to Cagliari, but to carry on to Sicily. The effects of the beer had made Kevin drowsy and even before Ponto Romano was firmly in their wake, he was fast asleep, happy that this time tomorrow he would be back home in Liverpool.

14

Egadies! Here We Come

Fred was far from happy as he set a course directly for Capo Teulada, a remote tail of land that marked Sardinia's extreme south coast. Kevin had once again delayed them needlessly. He would have preferred to be on his way three hours ago. That way they would have been well clear of land by nightfall. The sky was already darkening as they hugged the shoreline. In the shelter of the bay the wind wasn't strong enough to push them along unaided. It merely glanced off the sheer mountainous terrain towering above them, ending in mild flurries at sea level. With the help of the now, sweet running engine they were doing a vibration free six knots. Fred had decided to motor-sail until they reached the headland. There he hoped to catch the full benefit of a strong wind which was leaving its unmistakable dappled patterns outside the shelter of the bay. Here the paltry, hesitant wind barely filled the open sails. Soon they would feel its full power.

The sky was completely overcast as the night closed in and wrapped itself around Deceptive's plotted path. Soon it was pitch black. Sandy was enthralled by the sharp black outlines of the closer outcrops of rock backed by greyer more distant shapes. She thought she could pick out an island ahead, but it soon merged with the shoreline and vanished.

'It has a beauty all of its own,' she mentioned to Nigel, captivated by it all. She hadn't seen the shore from a slow moving sailing boat at night and was gazing enraptured at the slowly changing silhouettes. Up ahead, she could clearly hear the sound of the sea breaking on the shore and moved forward along the deck to get a better view. The sea was suddenly rougher, much rougher! George was at the helm. Nigel was leaning against the guard-rail contemplating the long journey ahead, Fred was below working on the charts and Kevin was sleeping like a baby.

Nobody was prepared for the sudden change as Deceptive left the shelter of the high cliffs. The full power of the wind hit the sails before anyone even realised it they were in open water. The mainsail filled instantly with the wind's sudden violent impact,

She watched in horror as Deceptive disappeared into the darkness.

whipping the boom round towards Sandy standing amidships. It caught her sharply on her left temple. She faltered for a moment on the guard-rail and then disappeared over the side. Nigel, horrified, tried to find her in the yacht's wake. He failed to do so. She was already lost in the dark, troubled water. He plunged in after her.

In the split second before he dived in he wondered if she was badly hurt. Was she knocked unconscious by the crack to the head? He had to get to her before she drowned! How would he find her in the dark? Once in the water, he shouted her name, hoping she would hear him above the pounding of the waves as they crashed against the nearby rocky headland. No answer came. He struck out to where he thought she would be found.

The strong wind grabbed Deceptive and hurdled her through the troubled, chaotic sea at an ever increasing pace. Soon Nigel and Sandy were left far behind.

'Why did that stupid bastard jump in after her?' Fred shouted as he charged up on deck in answer to George's frantic shouts. He snatched the helm from George. At all costs he must remain calm! As they turned the light from the Cape Teulada lighthouse came into view, and then just as suddenly disappeared behind a black mass of rock. Fred recognised this as an island from his interrupted chart work. He quickly got his bearings and headed back towards the headland.

Kevin staggered on deck completely disorientated. Fred shouted to him to let the halyards go and ease the sheets. They would have to get the sails down somehow without wasting precious minutes heading up into the wind.

'For heaven's sake be careful!' Fred roared at Kevin, who seemed unusually unsteady on his feet. He staggered drunkenly as Deceptive bucked and crashed in the rough exposed sea.

Kevin let go the genoa sheets and the sail immediately flew off at ninety degrees. He followed quickly with the halyard and the sail dropped half way, trailing its lower section in the water. He had to use the winch on the reefing lines to lower the main, but eventually got it down.

He clambered on deck and roughly tied down the mainsail while George dragged in the wet foresail and lashed it to the guard-rail. Fred could see they were getting drenched in the process, but he had no intention of slowing down until he was back, as far as he could judge, to where Sandy had gone over.

George dashed below and brought up the powerful ship's torch. With Kevin peering ahead on one side, and himself on the other as he swept the waves hoping to catch the flash of a white face, or a raised hand.

Fred was heading back towards the headland in what he thought was a true reversal of their original course. He hadn't been at the helm when Sandy was knocked in and didn't think to look across the compass for a reciprocal bearing. The little island was once again behind them and they lost the comforting sweep of the lighthouse's lamp.

George could see the sea breaking over rocks to starboard and knew that Sandy and Nigel had to be around here somewhere. It was here, as they had cleared the headland, that the wind had caught him off guard and it must be here that he would find Sandy.

'Must be around here somewhere!' he shouted back to Fred.

They had already passed too far to the west of where Sandy had fallen in. George noticed a black rod silhouetted against the sky behind him and to his right. At first he thought it was a marker for nets, such as they had seen many times in otherwise deserted expanses of ocean, but then realised it was the Danford he had thrown overboard shortly after Nigel had leapt in after Sandy.

'We're too far over!' he shouted to Fred. 'Change direction and head closer to the shore.' Fred couldn't hear him. He handed the torch to Kevin and clambered back to Fred pointing to the marker.

'That way Fred! Over that way!' he shouted excitedly.

Fred knocked the engine out of gear to listen for a yell or a shout but all he could hear above the engine was the roar of the sea as it crashed into the nearby cliff face, drowning out every other sound around. Fred cut the motor completely to see if that would help but only the sound of the breakers could be heard.

'If they're swept towards that, they're in worse trouble than we thought,' he yelled at George. 'We'll have to head in towards the rocks.'

Fred turned the wheel and drifted further in, using the boat's momentum for steerage.

Up front, a sweep of the powerful ship's torch picked up a distant white flash. Kevin brought it back, cutting a swathe through the darkness, missed and tried again.

'There! I've got something!' he shouted back to Fred, never taking his beam off the distant waving blotch of white. 'Over there! Head that way. I'll keep the light on them.! George relayed the instruction from half way along the deck, fearful that they would lose sight of whoever Kevin had picked out in the water.

Fred hoped that Sandy was alright. He thought he had heard a sharp crack, above the sound of the main swinging across the deck when the accident happened and expected the worst. He couldn't understand why the well tried procedure of putting harness on after dark hadn't been followed. Their late start had a lot to do with it, but it was his responsibility to check and he hadn't done so. He dreaded to think what they might find as they drew nearer.

'They're drifting towards the cliffs!' George shouted. Fred could see for himself that time was now of the essence. He fired the engine. He had to get to them before it became too dangerous to pick them up. The shore was jagged and dangerous. He could clearly see sharp pinnacles of rock sticking out of the waves, highlighted by the white, thundering spray as it rose high into the air.

George dropped the stern ladder and secured a mooring line around a cleat, just in case Sandy might have to be lifted out of the water.

* * *

Nigel had no thoughts for his own safety when he launched himself into the water after Sandy. He had assumed the worst. The blow from the boom must have, surely, knocked her out. He had to get to her before she drowned. Would he find her in time? He couldn't bear to think of the consequences and swam as fast as he could in her direction. He was surprised at how choppy the sea was and, frequently, his mouth filled with water, causing him to splutter and choke as he accidentally inhaled a few drops. Within a few minutes he was breathless and realised that he had little chance of finding Sandy unless she could keep herself afloat.

When the boom swung in her direction Sandy, anticipating its jolt, had instinctively tried to duck. Fortunately for her, it had almost reached the limit of its swing and much of its force was spent, but its blow was still strong enough to tip her over the side. The cold water had the immediate effect of concentrating her thoughts. She watched in horror as Deceptive disappeared into the darkness, instantly fearing that she would never be found. She hadn't seen Nigel jump in after her and wasn't even sure if she would be missed until much later. Her first priority was to save herself. She immediately struck out for the nearest landfall, which was the worst action she could have taken. She had never swum in seas as big as this and, like Nigel, was finding it much more difficult than she ever would have expected. She could clearly hear the breakers in the distance and used their sound as her guide. After a few minutes of strong, exhausting swimming she thought herself no nearer land and was gripped by a sudden fear that, maybe, she wasn't going to make it after all. She began to panic. Her breathing came in short painful gasps as blind terror froze her diaphragm muscles. She couldn't even scream. She was gasping for life, and began inhaling water as she flailed madly trying to keep alive. All rational thought disappeared. Her wild frenzy destroyed any chance she had of survival.

She thought she heard Nigel's frantic voice calling her. Was it her imagination? Yes, there it was again. She mustered every last ounce of breath she had and called back. He was coming for her. She was going to be saved after all.

Now she could hear his soothing, calming voice close to her, encouraging her. She grappled with his body holding him in desperate vice-like grasps, climbing, trying to keep her head above water. But he kept breaking her grip and pushing her away and then, finally, under. She released her hold. She was drowning. Suddenly he was behind her, his arm under her chin holding her up. She could breath again, she was safe. His voice was telling her to relax, not to fight.

Only moments later the light from the torch swept across their path and she knew they would both be rescued.

'Thank God! thank God,' she kept repeating, not believing that her ordeal was almost over.

* * *

'A bit further over, Fred. They're both there,' Kevin shouted, waving his arms, barely making himself heard above the terrific noise of the crashing waves. Fred couldn't allow himself a sigh of relief yet, not until he knew how Sandy was, and they were both safely back on board. They would have to get away from here fast. He had no idea what was directly below the hull and half expected to hit a rock at any moment. The depth gauge was reading the bottom at only three metres. The beam from Kevin's torch seemed to stick like glue to the two, close knit, figures in the water. 'A ray of hope,' he thought. 'It's their only road to safety.'

Fred, once again cut the engine and Deceptive drifted slowly towards Nigel and Sandy. The depth gauge now read two metres. If it got any shallower they would have to head out again.

'What kept you?' shouted Nigel, breathlessly. 'It's bloody freezing in here. I thought we were going to get swept onto the rocks.'

Deceptive rose and fell with the waves as she drifted ever closer to the nearby rocks.

'How's Sandy?' Fred called fearfully.

'I'm fine, Fred,' Sandy answered for herself from within Nigel's grasp, her panic now gone.

Fred offered a silent prayer of thanks and exhaled deeply. She was safe, that's all that mattered. George threw in an end of the rope for them to grab and then walked them to the boarding ladder. Sandy was first on board quickly followed by Nigel. They both stood shivering on deck while George fetched some towels.

'Took your bloody time,' Nigel remarked to George, not realising that Fred had been at the helm all along. 'Why did it take you so long?'

His question remained unanswered as Fred pushed the throttle forward and headed away from danger.

Sandy was not badly hurt. She had not been knocked unconscious, so Fred wasn't worried too much about concussion. She would have a headache and a few bruises, but nothing more, or so he hoped.

Nigel had other ideas. He would watch Sandy for any signs of sleepiness or blurred vision. At the first sign he would suggest heading straight back to Ponte Romano.

Fred still wanted to know why, despite all the practice they had on their first day, Nigel had jumped in risking his life as well as Sandy's..

'What were you thinking about, for heaven's sake? You know the drill! We've been over it often enough.'

'I thought Sandy had been knocked out, I thought she'd drown! I knew that you'd find us alright,' Nigel answered quietly, trying to calm Fred down.

'What if we hadn't?' asked Fred, quieter, the hidden intent in his question not missed at all.

'I knew you would! Fred,' Nigel added patiently. Can't you wait until we've dried off before having a bloody post mortem!'

Fred turned his attention to Sandy handing the helm over to George. He asked her, how she was, unable to conceal the concern in his voice.

'Just a little wet Fred,' she answered, flashing him one of her most beguiling smiles. 'And bloody frozen to boot.'

Fred was so relieved he couldn't hide his emotion any longer and wrapped his arms around Sandy, giving her a big, reassuring hug and a kiss on the cheek.

While Nigel and Sandy were changing into dry clothes Fred decided they should search for the Danford, which they had already seen, and also for the lifebuoy that George had tossed in after Nigel and Sandy had gone overboard. The Danford was located quickly, but the lifebuoy remained elusive and wasn't found.

'It's in amongst those blasted rocks and, sure as hell, I'm not going in there looking for it!'

All was well, Fred decided. No lives lost. A lost lifebuoy was a small price to pay. They had been lucky once again.

Kevin returned to his cabin still unaware of their destination. It would only be a short sail, comparatively speaking, to Cagliari, and then it would be all over. He could put up with all the pitching, heaving and tossing that one more night could fling at him and then . . . home. Burying his head in a pillow, he burrowed deeper into his sleeping bag, almost happy at last.

The sails were re-set once again and they were on their way to Sicily.

Fred decided some food was called for, put some beans on the stove and opened a tin of sardines. The fresh bread purchased in San Antioco almost made up for Fred's lack of culinary expertise. Sandy wasn't allowed to do anything. She turned her nose up at Fred's effort, but downed some beans heaped on lumps of white, crusty bread just the same.

'Ah! some real food at last!' Nigel yelped, stuffing a bean butty down his throat. Sandy hit him with a cushion for being so smart.

George decided that she was none the worse from her ordeal, and that he too wouldn't need to watch her for signs of concussion any more. He could revert to his former ogling with a clear conscience.

Back on the helm Fred wondered who was really to blame for their near-tragedy.

'It was all Kevin's fault,' he decided unfairly. 'If he had returned on time we would have rounded the cape in daylight.'

The real problem was, that despite all his pious attempts to sail by the book, most of the crew wanted as little hassle as possible. It had been far more fun on deck watching the night close in, than pulling down sails and snapping on the deck harnesses. Fred, to give him his due, had already made that connection. He had finally realised just how unprepared they all were for such a demanding voyage. His reading and all his previous experiences were mere pointers when it came to dealing with the devastating, combined power of the sea and wind.

'Those unpredictable, untamed forces have led many an unsuspecting sailor to the final test,' he thought. He reflected on their near misses. There were far too many, and all created by his ineptitude. So far they had been very lucky.

'The luck of the Irish,' he thought, 'maybe those two Irishmen on board have brought their own kind of luck. Damn bad luck!'

Not for the first time, Fred, found himself considering whether or not he should abort the trip. 'It's really only a matter of time before one of us gets badly hurt. It really is just a matter of time,' he repeated out loud.

That night the weather returned to what they now considered normal. Rough seas and violently strong winds dogged their every movement. They were on a beat, mainsail reefed and the working jib earning its title. Frequent gusts of thirty-five knots hammered their salt encrusted craft, testing the strength of the cloth and the sailmaker's skill. The distorted, tortuous sea stretched ahead, glistening like scrunched silver paper in the eerie pale luminosity of a corona encircled moon. Moving around below decks was only possible with the help of the conveniently placed teak hand rails as Deceptive listed sickeningly, first to one side, then the other.

It would be forty hours before they reached Palermo, Fred worked out, as he wedged himself precariously on the boken navigator's seat. George was now at the helm. Fred was already searching the chart for a closer landfall in case they had to make a run for cover. He drew a circle around the Egadie islands with his pencil and then, with eyes closed, stabbed what he guessed was the centre. A wry smile crossed his lips. This was how he had picked last year's winner in the Grand National with his annual five pound flutter. He knew what the stakes were out here, but didn't dare bet on their shortening odds of arriving unscathed.

The reassuring lights of Sardinia's Costa Del Sud had been on their port side for four hours but now they were alone with only the wind and the crashing sea for company.

* * *

Fred couldn't sleep in the pilot berth as Deceptive heeled. He kept rolling on to the edge of the bunk. To remedy the situation he put one leg on the floor, but as he was in a sleeping bag, the other leg soon followed and he rolled off. He tried bracing one foot against the dining table across the aisle, but as soon as he relaxed, he found himself sprawling on the floor once more. There was no other choice, he would have to make up the double bed in the saloon. This meant dropping the table-leaf and putting the two specially made cushions on top. Comfortable at last, he fell into a deep sleep.

Nigel didn't wake Fred, but continued on watch with Sandy until dawn.

'The poor bugger looks like a limp lettuce. If he keeps punishing himself like this he's going to be a prime candidate for the happy farm,' observed Nigel. 'And besides it'll give us a chance to see the dawn together.'

'A couple of extra hours might do him the world of good,' Sandy said, pulling on an extra jersey to fight off the early morning chill. Nigel helped her to put her harness back on with one hand while trying to protect the newly made cups of coffee with the other.

They had seen a few ships in the distance and Sandy was amazed at how far off they could be seen at night. Their coffee finished, they clung together at the wheel, Nigel with his arm firmly round Sandy's shoulder and she seated with her two arms joined firmly around his waist. Conditions had improved and Nigel lazily moved the wheel keeping Deceptive's bow pointing to the compass heading Fred had worked out earlier. He could have switched on the Autohelm, but preferred to steer himself.

'It was really nice of you to jump in after me last night,' Sandy said earnestly.

'Well I'm kinda getting used to the idea of having you around.' He kissed her on the forehead and she snuggled in even closer. The sun rose above a dappled, flame and black sea to glow wearily in a partly overcast sky.

'Red sky in the morning is the shepherd's warning.' Nigel whispered, remembering the childhood rhyme.

Dressed in T-shirt and boxer shorts, Kevin emerged from his cabin, his hair sticking up, and eyes caked from a too long, drink induced, sleep. His tongue was coated in a thick white fur making his mouth taste awful. He imagined that his breath must be equally nauseous. 'Badger's breath.' He needed a cold drink and some headache pills fast. He had been aroused once or twice during the night and wondered why they still hadn't arrived in Cagliari but had drifted back to sleep. He opened the fridge and stared at the contents for a full thirty seconds before they became clear to him. This seemed rather long to Fred, who was keenly watching the proceedings from his curled up position on the couch. Kevin selected a can of coke, pulled the tab, and popped two Anadins in his mouth. He took a long swig, now regretting the late night drinking session he had succumbed to in his cabin. The black lifeblood flowed down his gullet and triggered a reaction in his solar plexus causing a bellyful of stale gas to make a noisy rush for the surface. He belched loudly and took another mouthful of coke. Fingers bent, left hand scraped his distended stomach and then scratched under each arm, his eyes firmly fixed, blindly staring through the galley porthole. His actions were completely involuntary.

'Positively bloody primordial,' thought Fred, smugly, conjuring up pictures of man's nearest relative.

'Should be in Cagliari any minute now,' Kevin mused.

'He'll scratch his left buttock next, and then drop his right hand to check that his love jewels are still in place,' predicted Fred, who had seen the same performance at least a half dozen times already. But Kevin decided he'd better have a look to see where they were. He leaned over the sink to get a better view through the porthole.

'The silly bastards are going the wrong way,' he exclaimed out loud, on not seeing the expected shore line. He rushed to the heads and peered through that porthole, but there was no land on that side either. A quick glance at the chart confirmed his worst fears. 'This can't be happening,' he told himself. 'Its a nightmare, I'll wake up in a minute, ... screaming.'

He ran up on deck and saw Nigel and Sandy at the helm. He took a slow look around. Nothing! 'Shit!' he swore under his breath, 'They've decided to go on to Sicily.'

Kevin went below. Life had been dealing him some strange hands recently, instead of heading home he was on his way to Palermo. He thought of tackling Fred. He was sure he'd done this on purpose. No! He wouldn't give him the pleasure. He dressed and then took the helm for the next four hours, only drinking a cup of coffee given to him by Sandy for sustenance. There was no turning back now. He decided to make the best of a bad job. He still wanted to see what Deceptive could do and today the conditions were ideal. The sea had levelled out and the wind was perfect for the full main and the No 3. He tightened the backstay, creating a backward incline to the mast. Fred worried about their fixed rigging, but thought it better to say nothing. From a canter Deceptive broke into a smooth gallop, clocking up eight and a half knots: this was what sailing was all about!

Later that day, Nigel, seeing what he thought was an improvement in Kevin's attitude, took him aside for a quiet chat. He told him that the decision to go on to Sicily had been taken by Fred and accepted by them all. If he had remained with the others, instead of going off on a wild goose chase, and, more to the point, not kept everyone waiting, he would have known of the change of plan as well.

'I've known you for, what? Five years!' he continued, reprovingly, 'And I have never seen you behave like this. I think it's high time you pulled yourself together and became part of the group, Kevin. I'm surprised Fred didn't sling you off in Ponte Romano. If I had been skipper I would have!'

Kevin accepted Nigel's criticism without a word, never once mentioning that he had intended leaving anyway. He would still leave all right: it would have to be Palermo now, but today he was going to continue with some real sailing.

Early in the afternoon as the wind steadily gained strength they took in a reef in the genoa. This was the first time they'd attempted to do this. Leaning far out over the pulpit George took up the slack. But even then they were overpowered as the wind continued to build. They were forced to substitute the working jib. Throughout the afternoon the wind continued to blow hard The Autohelm worked well, allowing the crew time to settle down and relax as best they could before the night watches commenced.

Again Sandy was unable to cook, so they settled for soup and sandwiches.

'No more sardines or beans! Please!' George begged, causing a few well needed raised smiles.

The incessant resounding thump of Deceptive's hull as she crashed heavily through the waves was beginning to have a wearing, wearisome effect on them all. They wondered if they would ever get a full day's pleasant sailing. Their moods matched the weather: when the sailing was good they were happy, when conditions deteriorated an impenetrable gloom descended on their spirits.

What they didn't know was that this sea area was notorious for high winds at this time of the year. It had been christened, *the windiest hole on earth*. The seas were often worse than they were experiencing now. Even in the height of summer winds would whip up from nowhere, buffeting everything in their path. They would sweep up from the Sahara or down from France with such regularity that many ships' crews couldn't remember an easy passage through here.

Fred wished it was all over. This state of despondency had continued since Sandy's accident. He seemed to be on his feet the whole time fretting, worried in case something would go wrong. He decided to try to push on without any further stops,. In future, they would only visit ports for provisioning and then, perhaps, they might have a few more days to enjoy the sheltered waters of the Ionian. Goodness knows, they deserved a break. Two thirds of their allotted time was already spent. So far it had been like an obstacle course, battling with the sea, wind, ignorance and each other. It would be another four or five days before they arrived in Argistoli on the Greek island of Cephalonia. Fred wondered if he could hold everything together until then. He doubted he could.

*   *   *

Night had just closed in when disaster struck again. For no apparent reason the sails luffed up suddenly, creating a fearsome racket as they flailed threateningly, no longer full. The Autohelm whined like a masonry drill going through butter, trying to get Deceptive back on course. George rushed to the helm as Deceptive went through the wind and grabbed the wheel before she started her customary waltz. He noticed the severed drive-belt from the Autohelm lying, useless, on the cockpit gratings.

'Fred!' he shouted, over the noise of the flapping sails, 'The flaming belt's snapped.'

He disconnected the redundant machine and pulled Deceptive back on course.

Within seconds all was quiet and they were once again on track, the sails full. Fred picked up the broken belt and went below to get a replacement. He had noticed that the previous owner had a few stashed away in one of the saloon cupboards. The first one he picked out was too big and the next too small. Fred's depression hit base, the thought of their having to steer by hand for the remainder of the journey was daunting. They were already tired and despondent, twenty four hours a day at the helm would finish them. But there was still hope, there was a single, solitary, belt left. Would it fit? It was the right size! Fred could breathe again. All that was needed was to slip it over the wheel and they would be back in business in jig time.

Fred picked up the ship's torch on his way back to the helm. He tried to slip the belt over the wheel, but the wheel was too big.

'It doesn't fit, the bloody thing doesn't fit!' he roared, trying to hang on with one hand and slip the belt over the wheel with the other. 'We'll have to take the bloody wheel off.'

Fred had no idea how to dismantle the wheel and neither did anyone else. On other boats he had noticed a large retaining nut; when that was unscrewed the wheel lifted off but on Deceptive there was only a circular chrome section in the middle which looked part of the wheel.

Fred remembered the emergency tiller. Remembered is the word, emergency denoting it should be near at hand. Another of Sod's law of the sea was just about to come into play.

'If you urgently need something, it will be at the very bottom, or at the end of, whatever or wherever you are searching.' (N.B Trying to circumvent this rule, by searching the most unlikely places first will only reverse the above rule.)

Fred finally fished out the emergency tiller after burying himself for ten minutes, upside down, in the stern locker. He had dumped everything else onto the cockpit sole; the skeg anchor and line, three Jerry cans, half a dozen coiled ropes, brushes and cleaners, a plastic bucket, cans of oil, spare chain, a portable generator, diving equipment, -a lady's bikini top! How did that get in there?

Everything was replaced, the tiller fitted and they still didn't know how to remove the wheel. Worse still, the whole operation had to be done by torchlight and in a madly heaving boat at that.

'A text-book example of Sod's law of the sea No.3, if anybody cares to check!' whispered George, out of Fred's hearing.

'Why does everything have to happen at night?' Fred moaned. Nobody answered, feeling it much safer to keep their opinions to themselves, having already heard a few of Fred's muted growls.

Ideally, the conditions should have been a sheltered quay, calm dry weather, daylight, and an experienced mechanic. In this case it was dark and wet, and each one of them would have to think twice before even changing a light bulb at home. Mechanics they most certainly were not! Nevertheless, they set about trying to dismantle the helm. Fred tried prising the chrome off with a screwdriver, but was reluctant to use any force in case he broke something. There were metal rings at each side of the wheel with six retaining bolts, which seemed to hold the spokes in place.

'That'll do it,' said Fred, removing all the bolts. The wheel still wouldn't come off even though now all the spokes were loose.

'Maybe the doodah is connected to the thingmajig and can be screwed off,' ventured Nigel, who was, surprisingly enough, understood by Fred and pointedly ignored. Fred next tried to unscrew the chrome part with a chain filter remover, leaving pitted teeth marks on the metal, but still it wouldn't budge.

'Maybe it can be knocked off with a solid whack,' suggested Nigel, pushing his expertise to the limit. He'd seen a British Gas fitter do precisely that to his heating system on a particularly black bank holiday Monday, even though he'd come to fix the cooker.

'Stick to television, Nigel, I don't think engineering is your thing,' George added, struggling with the ridiculously short emergency tiller, which he was straddling, using both his legs and hands to maintain their course. 'Look, either reduce sail or get that flaming wheel fixed, one or the other. I can't hang on here much longer. I'm getting friction burns in my balls.'

'I think Nigel's right,' Kevin ventured, taking the hammer and placing the tip of a heavy screwdriver on the back edge of the chrome section. Before Fred could protest, he hit it a mighty belt and the chrome cover flew over the guard-rail and was lost in the sea. There, sure enough was the elusive centre nut.

'Looks as if someone used Superglue to stop their wheel from being nicked,' Nigel observed.

They now had a formidable job on their hands. They would

have to re-assemble the sections they had already removed, before they could take the wheel completely off. This meant replacing all the bolts and centring the Autohelm gearing wheel, which they had also loosened. If the gearing wasn't exactly right the Autohelm wouldn't work properly. However, they did manage to get all the bolts back on without dropping any. The wheel now had a peculiar elliptical movement. They undid the main bolt and lifted the wheel off, replacing the broken belt within seconds. They re-aligned the wheel a little more by loosening and tightening the nuts holding the various spokes in place. Then, replacing the wheel, they made sure that the retaining bolt was tight.

Fred gave the wheel a practice turn. It wasn't supposed to spin, but it did! It no longer turned the rudder, just kept spinning. They had done something wrong. Fred was flummoxed.

George swore loudly as the emergency helm became too heavy and jammed his leg against the side of the cockpit. They tried to free him, but the force was too great.

'Drop the sails fast,' Fred shouted, firing the engine.

George suppressed another yelp of pain as Deceptive leaned further into the wind.

The sails were down in a jiffy and George's leg was instantly free.

It was still difficult to steer Deceptive with such a useless tiller, even with the engine on, but George soldiered on. He rubbed the bruised area around his calf, still holding on to the tiller with one hand while Fred tried to get enough headway to keep them in a straight line. Without the sails to steady her, Deceptive was yawing dangerously from side to side, the contents of the bookshelfs and open cupboards falling once more onto the saloon sole. Fred had no option, he would have to take the wheel off again.

On removing the wheel, they noticed a slot on the axle with a corresponding one on the inside of the hub.

'Looks as if a wedge has fallen out of the groove on the shaft,' said Kevin, who had sharp eyesight. 'I remember seeing something fall as we pulled the wheel off. Thought it was a lump of grease.'

Kevin had been extremely helpful since his earlier chat with Nigel, and now added, ' It must be under the grating. I don't see it lying on top.'

Fred was hit with another sudden sinking feeling. 'Oh no!' he exclaimed. The scuppers that he had been so glad of a few nights before were directly under the wheel.

'It'll have fallen down the bloody cockpit drains,' he moaned.

'Sod's law of the sea No.4,' added George, who was compiling a list.'

Fred's fatalism never failed to amaze the others. He needn't have worried. The grating was lifted as gingerly as possible in the circumstances. The pin was retrieved by Nigel who dropped a coin through the drain at exactly the right moment to give Fred an apoplectic fit. It took him a few moments to realise that Nigel still had the pin in his hand.

'Bloody fool,' he thought, but couldn't help smiling.

They fitted the pin to the axle and the wheel was replaced with its new belt intact.

Once again wheel and rudder worked in unison.

George removed the emergency tiller and Fred turned the wheel. It felt strange in his hands, its weavering arc was very unfamiliar.

'The wheel's balance is gone. It feels like a bicycle wheel run over by a ten ton bloody truck. It'll have to do until we reach port,' he declared, 'then we can get someone to do the job properly.' He feared that it would take more than their combined talent to rectify the evening's handiwork.

Later that night the wind reached force nine. It lifted the spray straight from the waves in a white foamy rain, blinding whoever was at the helm. Fred decided to drop the foresail, and take in the last reef in the main. They hoisted the storm jib to keep them steady. They would motor until the weather eased a bit.

They were still motoring at eight the next morning, hardly sleeping all night, having remaining huddled together in the saloon. The scene before them was spectacular. Pelting spray reduced visibility to one hundred metres. An uneasy, jade green sea was partly hidden amid a mass of stretched marbled foam. The waves were surprisingly small as the wind appeared to whip the crests off before they could develop. Its roar through the rigging drowned the sound of the engine, adding further to the anxiety below decks. Surrounded by this barrage of white, lashing spray, Deceptive lurched and staggered as she was hit by squall after squall. Wind, strong enough to uproot trees, howled

*It lifted the spray straight from the waves in a white foamy rain,
blinding whoever was at the helm.*

deafeningly about their ears. Hanging on below decks, it felt as
if the hull would split open at any moment. The crew had
donned inflated life jackets on Fred's instruction. The hatches
were firmly shut, as were all the portholes. What they had been
through before could be considered a picnic compared to this.

Fred, at the helm also wondered if the hull could take the
pounding. If they had to abandon ship would the life raft survive
these conditions? he asked himself. He honestly didn't think so.
He had already been at the helm for over three hours and was
now extremely weary. He glanced behind him at the life raft and
noticed for the first time that the heavy locks were still in place.
He must have looked at them a hundred times but it had never
registered before. He shouted above the din to Kevin, who was
sitting harnessed under the wind ripped spray-hood, to take
over the helm. As everything was battened down and secured
from inside, Fred had to knock on the hatch cover and, once

open, quickly clamber over the duck boards. He had to be fast, otherwise the whole place would be flooded with sea water as the waves now continually broke over Deceptive's deck.

'Is it getting any better up there Fred? Nigel asked.

'I believe it is.' Fred lied. 'Anyone seen the spare keys?'

'What do you need those for,' asked a very shaken Sandy.

'The . . . ' Fred paused. 'The life-raft. Might be better if we remove the locks.'

'Are we going to abandon ship?' Sandy asked.

'Naw, just a precaution!'

Fred found the keys and went back on deck. The locks hadn't been lubricated since their trip from Falmouth and were badly rusted. He tried first to unlock one then the other but they wouldn't budge.

He went below for a hammer and the W.D.40. He squirted the fluid through the keyholes and around the bolts, tapping each with the hammer until they unfroze. Next time he inserted the keys they clicked open. With an inward sigh of relief he fought his way forward again, giving Kevin a reassuring squeeze on the arm as he struggled past.

Below deck, he quickly readied the flares and filled a grab bag with essentials. He placed them all next to a fifteen litre container of drinking water. Sandy watched him, wondering what was going on.

'If we have to leave in a hurry grab those,' he instructed.

His earlier decision to use the rubber duck in an emergency now seemed illogical. This wind would lift it like a paper kite before anyone could get on board.

'Palermo is too far away,' Fred announced. 'We'll have to find shelter closer than that.'

Sandy held on to the table white knuckled, thinking that every minute would be her last. Nigel tried to comfort her as best he could but he wasn't entirely without fear either.

Fred examined the chart and the Italian pilot as best he could, hardly able to keep his eyes on one spot due to the bombardment Deceptive was getting. He couldn't believe how often the cumbersome pilot manual slipped from his grasp and crashed to the floor as Deceptive lurched and lunged onward. There it joined all his other navigational bits and pieces which had slid off the chart table. He decided to head for the nearest safe port, once he had found the flaming page again.

'Favignana in the Egadie Islands, about eight miles off the west coast of Sicily. It's more than fifty miles short of our intended destination. And it looks as if it's the only port that will give us a sheltered entrance, and it'll take ten hours off this leg,' he announced at last.

This welcome news was received with cheers and a burst of applause from Nigel, even Sandy released her grip on the furniture to give a few claps. There was an immense sense of relief below deck.

'Feels like remission for good conduct, Fred. Great! I felt as if I was adding a year to my life every mile we've done in this weather,' George added.

But the journey wasn't yet over. Again and again, the wind hit Deceptive with such force that she went over on her side and sheered ninety degrees. It looked to Kevin as if the mast was about to come down. The windward shrouds took the full brunt of the wind causing those on the leeward to slacken and belly out. The storm jib and the fully reefed main worked hard to bring Deceptive back on track each time she veered off. Kevin didn't have time to be scared. He hung on with a rigor mortis clutch keeping her on course. The short time since he had taken over from Fred had already strained every muscle in his body. He was mentally exhausted after the long sleepless night. He couldn't think straight any more. His eyes were sunken in his head and his face ashen. Kevin's thoughts were murderous. It was all Fred's fault. He was trying to get them all killed. He was going to have to pay dearly for this.

*　　*　　*

Their first fleeting glimpse of the misted shore was disconcerting. Visibility was still less than two miles and no distinguishing marks could be picked out. Fred was uncertain of their position and couldn't decide whether the island that kept appearing and disappearing on his port side was Favignana or its sister Lavanzo. For all he knew, due to the ferocious conditions, he might even be looking at one of the smaller islands in the group, miles off course.

During the night and most of the morning he assumed that they were being blown off course and had brought Deceptive's head up a few compass points at regular intervals. If the island ahead was Lavanzo they had come too far east and would have to head further south. He had no option but to keep on going until he could identify some prominent landmark.

An hour later, he saw a larger island to starboard. This was definitely Favagnana, he could clearly see a large hill on its western approach. He set a course for what he thought was the entrance to the harbour. They were soon in the lee of the island and the ferocious battering suddenly stopped, but conditions were still far from ideal.

He couldn't find the entrance to the harbour. His way was blocked by a never ending line of nets. They continued East along the line of nets for three miles and Fred decided they had gone too far. At least they had found some shelter from the wind but they were wasting time. Both Sandy, who had quickly regained her composure, and Nigel started to clear up the mess below decks and put things back in their proper places.

Fred had never seen nets like these. A heavy rope with floats held the heavy mesh just inches below the surface. 'Would stop a bloody whale,' he thought. 'There had to be a break in the net somewhere which would be the entrance to the port. There must be.'

Fred began to wonder if in fact they were at the correct island at all. There weren't any ships about to act as pointers to lead them in, and he certainly couldn't see any of the large buildings clearly shown on the pilot. But it had to be the right island, the large hill to the west and the long low sound at its elongated eastern tip proved it.

They had run back the whole three miles again before he saw the entrance. How he had missed it the first time he didn't know, but put it down to the blinding, sheeting rain, and his tiredness.

The port was busy. Many other boats were sheltering from the storm and it was difficult to get a position side on to the quay. Most of the others were anchored with their bows to the quay. Fred had never seen this before, still unsure of his anchoring ability, he was relieved to find a spot big enough to accommodate them, adjacent to a long jetty reserved for the mainland ferry. They came alongside without any problems and tied up quickly. An intense feeling of relief was felt by all. No longer able to suppress her emotions Sandy was first to express her feelings.

'Thank God we made it,' she exploded, unable to conceal her

joy at being safely moored. 'I thought we'd had it out there, thought we'd never make it.'

'With Fred handing out life jackets and readying the life raft I thought our number was up,' added George, jokingly.

'If the Ibiza to Sardinia bit was bad, how would you describe that last leg Fred?' asked Nigel.

Fred's answer was succinct and to the point. 'Bloody awful,' he declared.

Kevin kept himself apart in case they glimpsed the mental turmoil he had been through. His hands were still trembling. He blamed Fred for everything: It was Fred's boat. Fred had organised this trip. And it was Fred's incompetence that had endangering his life. The sooner he saw the back of Fred the better he'd like it, but first he needed a double shot of something, and fast, to steady his nerves.

'Anyone going for a beer?' he asked, trying to hide the urgency in his question.

No further persuasion was needed. Within seconds they were off the ship, leaving Fred behind.

'They'd learned nothing,' Fred thought sadly. He resented the fact that they were up and away without stowing things properly. The sails were uncovered and the deck was caked with salt. He assumed, wrongly, that the main cabin was a mess, not knowing Sandy and Nigel had already tidied up below.

'All pulling together, everything's tidied in fifteen minutes,' he told himself. 'Take me a flaming hour.' Fred picked up the hosepipe he found lying on the quay and turned the water on. A half an hour later, the decks were clean and the sails were bagged.

George came looking for Fred and was surprised at the frosty reception he got.

'You could have waited, Fred. You knew that we would come back and help you clear up.'

'Well! You don't have to now, do you? So why don't you just piss off with the others? There's no excuse for leaving the boat in that condition. The sooner this trip is over the better I'll like it.'

George was taken aback. He had never seen Fred so unreasonable and wondered what was bugging him, other than the dirty boat. 'Maybe he suspects, must know something's afoot.' he thought.

'Fred, if you really knew what's been decided, tidying up

would be your least worry,' began George, tentatively.

'What do you mean, George? Out with it.'

'Well . . .,' George hesitated, he didn't want to further upset Fred.

'Go on man. Spit it out!'

'Well, I think you've a mutiny on your hands, Fred,' George continued, watching Fred's face for any reaction. 'They've had it, Fred. Look, I'm prepared to go on, I really am. I don't want to drop out and leave you in it. That's all . . . Kevin's adamant.'

Fred scratched his beard and looked away. 'Can't say that I blame them really.'

He wanted some time to think.

'Go back to the others. I'll catch up with you later. It's only a small town, can't be many bars around here.'

Fred wasn't surprised. He had more or less expected this. He too, felt that he had as much of a hammering as he wanted to take. The problem was that he couldn't leave Deceptive here, as it was a commercial harbour, not a marina. He would have to give this new state of affairs some serious thought. When he went below decks and saw that everything had been tidied up he couldn't help feeling a twinge of remorse. He shrugged his shoulders, picked up the Italian pilot, and began to search for a safe marina. 'Somewhere nearby. Could this really be the end of the trip?' He didn't know, nor much care.

Kevin examined his drink. 'Yeah,' he thought, not sure why he wasn't more pleased with his efforts, 'that's Sputnik fixed . . . good and proper! Let's see how far he can get without a crew.'

15

Love at First Slight

Fred gazed along the wide sweep of the harbour. He could see diesel pumps at the far end of the quay to his right and didn't relish the thought of making the six journeys needed to replenish Deceptive's fuel tank. To his left was the jetty for the daily ferry which had remained empty for the last two days and was likely to remain so until the weather changed. They were safe here from the south easterners which continued to blow unabated at force eight.

It was already dusk and he still didn't feel like joining the others. He had decided that, until he knew for sure how long they were going to be hemmed in by the wind, he wasn't going to commit himself to any change of plan.

'A day in harbour, time to get our breaths back ,' he thought. 'Might throw a different light on things.'

The depression was moving around to the south west and hopefully it would soon blow itself out. Fred looked at the barometer. It had started to climb again since early morning and was already at a high. But this meant nothing any more, as it seemed to Fred to be bouncing up and down like a dot on a Kareoke screen. Did he really want to jack it in? If not they had two options: they could travel North, past the Aeolian islands, through the straits of Messina and straight across to Greece, or they could follow the southern route to Siracusa and strike out from there to Italy and Greece. The real answer was to find a marina in the Sicilian mainland, dump everything and return to some kind of sanity.

'Get some sense at last and piss off home, about time too,' was how he felt. 'Captain Fred! What a joke. We've made it here by the skin of our teeth.'

He made out George's dim shape walking along the quay and was tempted to duck down inside and hide. He still didn't want to be bothered with company, he had too much on his mind, but there was no escape.

'We've found a restaurant and bar. Are you coming?'

Fred did feel some hunger pangs and relented gruffly. He could do with something substantial down his gullet. He thought of all the diesel that had to be hauled in the morning and felt it might not be a bad thing to have the others to help. He was over his earlier annoyance and with a little bit of the right kind of persuasion, George knew that, Fred would come out of his sulks and become part of the group again.

The restaurant was pretty basic, with the emphasis on the basic. Pretty didn't come into the equation at all. White emulsion walls, wrought iron tables and chairs, and an amateur mural depicting the harbour were unable to soften the threatening glare of the harsh, single fluorescent tube which lit a corner of the room.

'With a little imagination this could be brought up to the standard of a typical, grade three prison cell,' quipped Nigel.

'You'd know, wouldn't you,' added Kevin, who was in much better form than Fred had expected him to be.

'It's amazing what an afternoon of beer swilling can do to brighten things up a bit,' Fred thought. 'Maybe I need a little of the cure as much as this bunch of reprobates.' Fred made his mind up there and then to have a few with the lads, for a change. After all, they had all been through the mangle together, why should he be the exception? He didn't feel any less bruised than the others. They weren't going anywhere, there was no doubt about that.

In spite of the depressing interior, the food was excellent, cooked, served and billed by the same, fat, dark, balding, little man, who seemed engulfed in a dripping exudation of perspiration as he struggled to cope, single handed, with five starving, thirsty, dirty, unexpected travellers.

'His wife's probably gone off to the mother's due to the ferry's non arrival,' George supposed, intrigued by the owners efforts to serve them.

After the meal they decamped to a nearby bar. Fred had managed to remain sober despite his earlier intention and, besides, he had a lot of catching up to do. Too much, judging by the state of the others. He smiled politely at the barmaid as he paid for each round, having been entrusted with the kitty for the evening.

A large, old television showing endless soccer matches blared out a perpetual cacophony of roars, cheers and whistles which were echoed by the few residents in the bar. A grating announcer stretched out the only word distinguishable to Fred,

'Goooaaallll, goaaallll, goooaaalll,' almost driving him to distraction.

The waitress came back for some more money and Fred smiled again. This was becoming a habit. On her next sortie he smiled once more. This must have been an all time record for Fred. By now the routine was well established and it came almost easily to Fred. She showed him an English pound note that she obviously cherished but, as he didn't understand Italian, he couldn't quite make out the significance. He assumed that it had been given to her by one of his fellow countrymen as a token of his gratitude, or a memento. But for what? He could only speculate. Naw! Couldn't be for that . . . He chastised himself, his mind was getting as bad as Nigel's, like a sewer and that rhymed with . . .! 'Probably a tip,' he decided.

Her name was Berenice. To remember it he thought of 'bare' and 'nice' and gave her an embarrassed look, his face cracking into yet another smile. 'She's no raving beauty, but she certainly is easy on the eye.'

He could feel a bond developing between then. Eye contact was made and held, but for the life of him, he couldn't see what a young girl like that could possibly see in his ageing features. Why should she be interested in him when there was George and Kevin about, both a good ten years younger than himself? He looked away abashed, chastened by his thoughts. What an idiot!

It was two a.m. before they returned to the yacht. Nobody had brought up the subject of their leaving. Would they go on, continue their journey? Fred didn't know and to make matters even worse, didn't give a twopenny damn.

The next morning, after filling the diesel tank, Fred, Kevin, and George decided to go up Monte Sante Catherine and set off for the long climb at a brisk pace. The harbour police had informed them that the ferry still wasn't able to make it, in answer to their question about the weather. They followed a road for the first few miles and then started to climb through the rock strewn fields until they reached a craggy outcrop covered in gorse where they stopped to have a good look around. The wind was still blowing hard and they could see heavy waves breaking all along the windward shore. Sicily was clearly visible in the distance but they couldn't see any boats or ships out at sea.

The harbour stretched out below them and there was the white and blue speck that had been their home for almost two weeks. From up here she looked fragile and certainly no match for the huge breakers which seemed to start their run miles out, to pound and burst into thirty foot plumes as they made contact with Favignana's western craggy shore. Did they really come this far in that little yacht? Fred, for the first time, realised the enormity of what they'd already achievement. Since buying the boat he'd sailed more than two and a half thousand miles and he'd never been on a sailing boat before. Marge was right, he was a prime candidate for the looney bin.

The end of the trip was foremost in everyone's mind but nobody mentioned it. Fred wasn't prepared to bring it up yet but his resolve was hardened once again. The night in harbour had made all the difference. As far as he was concerned, they had set out for Greece and Greece it was going to be, by hook or by crook!

They descended again, carefully picking their way through the rocks and shrubbery.

That evening, after another meal in 'the jail' as it was now renamed, they made a return visit to the bar and were welcomed back like long-lost friends. Berenice gave Fred a hug, and a peck on the cheek which made the roots of his beard red hot. They sat down for another night of beer and soccer, or was it soccer and beer? Whichever it was, there was an over abundance of both.

Nigel and Sandy decided to return to the boat at ten thirty. As they walked arm in arm along the quay they saw a monstrous, ugly Italian yacht laying its anchor and going astern, with its gangway already lowered and aimed directly at Deceptive's unprotected bow. It reminded Nigel of a giant battering ram. There was no doubt in his mind, it was going to do untold damage to their boat. Nigel raced on board and tried to fend off the attack. He tried pushing the gangway sideways, but it kept coming, threatening to snag the forestay. The inevitable happened, the boarding platform struck Deceptive, scoring the gelcoat.

Aboard the Italian gin palace were two full crew members, along with the owner captain, his two friends and their wives. They'd just arrived from Sardinia and had taken a battering on the way as had Fred and his crew the day before. The ship's inexperienced owner was at the helm and not making a good job of controlling the two powerful engines. The water boiled as he reversed in fits and starts. There wasn't enough room, but he

It reminded Nigel of a giant battering ram.

obviously thought that he could push Deceptive along the quay, even though she was well secured. His tiredness was affecting all rational thought. He was going to get his stern in whether there was room or not. A dark, brooding crew member stood poised, boat-hook in hand, ready to push Deceptive aside when his master called.

Nigel pointed to the damage already done, clearly illuminated by the abundantly over lit gin palace, but he made no response. They went astern again, their propellers making a massive, whirlpooling jacuzzi of the formerly still harbour. Again metal met fibre-glass and another scrape was evident on Deceptive's previously untarnished coat and more seriously, the gangway had snagged the forestay. A forward thrust from those immense engines and the mast would be pulled down.

Nigel was getting madder by the minute. He had a part-share in Deceptive and it was being demolished right in front of his eyes. He threw his full weight on the gangway to push it off while trying to tell the crew member to throw him a mooring line. He would help them tie up. But there was a language difficulty. The strain of trying to keep the gangway clear was beginning to tell on Nigel. More pushing and shoving, and the language problem became a little more expressive as he gave vent to a few not too obscure words normally used in stressful situations.

'Throw me the line,' he yelled. 'Yeah, you Gioseppi, throw me the rope! Throw me the effing rope!'

The crew member, who must have thought Nigel was swearing at him specifically, replied with something that sounded like 'Batarde Allemagna,' to which Nigel objected on two counts. One, he wasn't German and, two, he wasn't a bastard.

'Hey Luiggi, don't you dare call me a German bastard! You . . . you Italian prick,' he retorted angrily.

The crewman shouted, ' Batarde Anglais!' Was this asshole never going to get it right? Nigel wondered, as he equally resented being called an English bastard. He was an Irish bastard and he was proud of it. The idea amused him and he couldn't resist shouting it to his antagonist.

'Oiii!, Alfredo,' he shouted, feigning indignation, 'I . . . meo . . . me batarde Irlandia.'

Sandy, who had been watching the whole episode fearfully, couldn't resist the desire to smile.

Now all the Italians were jabbering and gesticulating at him.

'Hell,' he uttered, 'Its worse than when they hosted the Eurovision song contest! Everyone's having a go.' Sandy shouted to Nigel to leave it, but now he wanted satisfaction.

He put his foot against the heavy guard-rail of the other boat and pushed with the strength of a maniac. It started to move away slowly, so he put more effort into it and it moved a little faster. He hoped he would gain enough momentum for the gangway to clear Deceptive's deck. The crewman with the boat-hook facing Nigel took a swing. It telescoped out and wrapped itself around Deceptive's forestay. Nigel saw red. This was war. He darted in and swiftly smacked the Italian on the cheek and quickly jumped back to safety on his own boat. The guy in the Tango advert couldn't have done it neater. The Italian went mad, blindly striking out with the twisted, broken, boat-hook. Its jagged edge ripped his own expensive canopy in three places, while his boat continued to move further away. Seeing the gap widening, he made to leap across the chasm, but was held back, wisely, by the other crew member.

'Come on jump, you bastard! Fall in and drown yourself.' Nigel was shaking with anger.

'For heaven's sake, Nigel, leave it, call the police,' implored Sandy. She turned to the onlookers.

'Can someone please go for the police?' Her request was met with incredulous stares. Go for the police! That was the best one they'd heard for years. This was Sicily after all!

Nigel had noticed that the gin palace's wooden gangway was held up by a fancy rope. If it came over Deceptive's bow again he would cut it and let it drop harmlessly. He couldn't risk the mast getting pulled down. He went below for a knife.

All he could find, in his haste, was a bread-knife, useless as a weapon, but would cut easily through rope.

The Italian crew member had managed to cast a line to shore and this was secured by one of the onlookers. He began to pull it in.

The captain had now come off his perch amidships and was busy examining the rips in his canopy. The crew member was pointing and having a heated conversation. Nigel suspected that he was the topic for their debate. Their boat moved away from Deceptive as their mooring line was tensioned. The captain's anger was building up and he too started pointing threateningly at Nigel. He saw the knife in Nigel's hand and thought that he was responsible for the slashes in their canopy. Nigel lifted his hand in appeasement and the captain completely misunderstood the gesture. What more proof did the captain need? There was the culprit, knife in hand. The very same knife that had slashed his very expensive canopy.

All hell broke loose on the Italian boat, the captain pulling the large engine covers open, while shouting hysterically, in a loud voice, 'Pistole! Pistole!'

Nigel shouted back 'Police, police.' but, evaluating his position, decided that discretion was the better part of valour and quickly disappeared down the front hatch to safety, and locked all the hatches from the inside, waiting, with Sandy, for the police to arrive.

Meanwhile back at the bar, Kevin and George were playing darts and Fred was sitting nursing a full glass. Compared to the previous night at this time, the bar was empty. Only a few locals were left. Either they couldn't match Kevin and George's consumption of beer, or maybe, they'd heard that there was about to be a shoot-out at the harbour and shouldn't miss it as there hadn't been one for a few months now.

Fred was having his usual rapport with Berenice. There was a lot of smiling going on as he once again paid for round after round. An unspoken intimacy had developed between them and he was enjoying the novelty. The television was off for a change and a sultry tape was oozing romance through two large, lop-sided speakers on the white-washed wall, the mandatory fluorescent tube playing havoc with the mood. He saw Berenice glance in his direction and then purposefully make her way through the tables towards him. He examined his glass. It was still full. He looked over at Kevin and George's, theirs were also full. He had already paid. What did she want? She stopped directly in front of him intently searching his eyes. 'Hell,' he thought, 'I'll have to smile again.'

'Dance witta me?' she asked simply.

As Berenice had approached the table, Fred had a feeling that she was going to say something ridiculous, he had seen her talking to George and Kevin earlier and suddenly realised that he was being set up. He could have kicked himself for mentioning, in a weak moment, that he had found Berenice attractive. He knew she had been put up to it. They were trying to make him look foolish. He hadn't seen anyone dance in the bar and now they expected him to rise in front of the remaining locals and shuffle around to the low intimate music spilling from the wall! Fred refused politely.

'No thanks,' he said, giving a look that implied he was aware of her ploy.

Was he imagining the look of pained rejection that flitted across her face? She turned on her heel and sidled back to the bar. Fred glanced quickly to where George and Kevin were playing darts. George had struck a double and was retrieving the dart, Kevin, his arm raised, was contemplating pinning George's ear to the board. They were both unaware of what had taken place. He glanced towards the locals and they too seemed engrossed in what they were doing.

She really had wanted to dance with him. He couldn't imagine why. Only then did he realise what it must have cost her to ask him. The moment was gone forever and now it was too late, a friendship had been needlessly lost. Throughout the rest of the evening, every time he looked at her, she averted her eyes.

When they got back to the boat and found it in darkness they assumed that Sandy and Nigel had gone to bed. They were surprised to find them cowering in the saloon and even more surprised to hear their tale. Sandy finished the story, telling how all the lights had been put out for a while and then they had seen a dark figure leaving the gin palace with a box under his arm.

'Nigel had threatened to call the police. We fully expected them to arrive at any moment considering the disturbance we were making' she continued, 'and I think they were afraid that, if searched the next morning, the gun would be found.'

'Are you sure there was a gun?' asked Kevin sceptically.

'What was the box shaped like?' inquired George, intrigued by the story. 'It wasn't by any chance shaped like a violin case, was it? After all, this is mafia country . . . Cosa Nostra . . . Omerta . . . And you threatened to call the police. Really!' he continued, laughing with the rest at his attempt at humour. 'Whose side do you think they'll be on?'

A motor cycle backfired in the distance causing Sandy to sit bolt-upright. They all laughed again.

'Who's going to pay for the damage, that's what I'd like to know?' asked Fred, seriously. 'Can't let them get away with that.'

'I don't think we've any option, Fred. I did hit the guy that was trying to impale me on the end of the boat-hook and could be charged with assault,' Nigel said, now concerned by the possible consequences of his action.

They talked over the situation further and Fred made his mind up.

'I'm going to take a walk to the far side of the island. It's twelve o'clock. If the weather is anyway clear, we'll slip out first thing in the morning, hopefully well before the police start work. There's no point in Nigel getting into a mess just because he was looking after the boat.'

They all agreed that this was probably the best plan. If the police became involved it might take days, or even a week, before they could move on, and it was Nigel's word against those on the other boat.

'What chance would we have in getting our point across?' added Nigel.

'None,' Fred decided, as he climbed up on deck.

Fred found, on reaching the far side of the island, that the weather had improved even though the seas were still rough. They could safely sneak out at five o'clock under cover of darkness, he decided happily.

The next morning they were all up and ready to go, except Sandy whose services weren't required. Nigel leaned over the side, precariously tying a line to the Italian gin palace. This would allow them to remove the mooring line blocking their departure while still keeping the other boat in place. Fred jumped on shore and released the Italian's rope, bringing it back on board Deceptive, making sure to keep it outside their rigging as he scrambled forward. He would take it right round their own bow and then re-tie it on the quay. This would allow them to slip out quietly once they'd released all their own mooring lines, leaving the gin palace firmly in place.

Fred took the mooring line forward, passing it outside each shroud, and then handed the coil to George who leaned over the bow to make sure it didn't snag on the stowed anchor.

It was pitch black and Sandy had opened the front hatch as she liked to sleep with plenty of fresh air in the cabin. Nigel had noticed this as he got up, but thought it better not to disturb her sleep.

George passed the rope around the front of Deceptive and Fred went to cross over to take the end from him. He didn't see the open hatch and stepped into thin air. His rib cage took the full impact of his awkward fall as he struck the hatch rim. He landed on a sleeping Sandy, winded, unable to move and in dreadful pain. There was no question of his not being hurt.

Once Fred got his breath back, he made up for his previous silence by moaning loudly.

'What stupid. . . . aaah! . . . left the hatch open?'

Sandy crawled out from under him, careful not to move his wracked body.

Someone suggested going for a doctor, but Fred, through gasps of pain, wouldn't have it.

'Give me a few minutes . . . aaaah . . .,' he groaned again as he fought the terrible, surging pain that jagged his insides. I'll be alright,' he gasped.

More than a few minutes later, Fred answered their unasked questions by crawling off the bunk and heading, body twisted sidewards like a used hair-clip, for the helm; he was in pain, but he wasn't dead, yet!

He didn't see the open hatch and stepped into thin air.

The Italian incident had been a godsend. They were leaving because of it. He couldn't lose this chance which he had until a few careless minutes ago regarded as a gift from heaven. Even if it meant crawling on deck, that's what he'd have to do.

One of the Italians appeared on deck, curious to know what was causing the commotion. Seeing that they were making ready to leave he asked Nigel who was going to pay for the damage to their boat. The captain appeared behind him and told him to be quiet as he now, obviously, had heard the full story and knew where the responsibility for the previous night's events lay.

George got a grip on the newly re-fixed mooring line and helped pull Deceptive around. The Italians also helped walk Deceptive forward until her stern was to the quay.

186

The captain elected himself spokesman. 'Everything okay, no? You are leaving early. I hope issa gooda weather for you. Hava naice day,' he finished, almost apologetically. If Fred had been fitter he would have nailed him for a few hundred quid to sort Deceptive's gelcoat, but instead he started the engine.

Things were indeed different now on the Italian boat, tempers had calmed down, they'd had a rest. Embarrassed by their behaviour of the previous evening, they just wanted to make amends.

There was no real reason for Fred and his crew to leave any more, but still, Fred hit the throttle and headed out without giving his crew the chance to change their minds.

Soon they were well clear of the Italian boat and heading for the twinkling red light at the harbour mouth. It was almost six a.m. and a faint glimmer was appearing in the sky to the East . . . Fred allowed himself a sigh of relief; now there was no chance of them turning back.

He gave the helm to a very unhappy Kevin and told him to watch out for the tuna nets. They would only have the shelter of the island for an hour and he still hadn't decided whether to head North or South.

Nigel helped Fred below decks and stretched him out on the couch.

'Looks as if you've cracked a rib, Fred,' he said, as if it were an everyday occurrence. 'Don't worry about it. Take a few painkillers and we'll try and find a doctor for you at the next port.'

Nigel, Sandy and Kevin still intended ending the trip soon. They would find a safe marina and then they could all go home. The problem was breaking the news to Fred, especially now that he'd managed to injure himself. But George knew something that they didn't, that Fred was fully aware of their intentions. What George didn't know was that Fred had decided that the journey must be finished as planned.

Nigel had made inquiries and knew where they could berth Deceptive, and also, where they could get cheap air tickets back to England. He would have to tell Fred sooner rather than later, otherwise they might head North. His intended destination, unlike Fred's, could only be reached from the South. Nigel knew that Fred's fall was a bad one. It would also be better, he decided, if in the next few days, Fred had an x-ray to establish the full extent of his injuries. This would be better attended to in England but he wouldn't tell him yet.

16

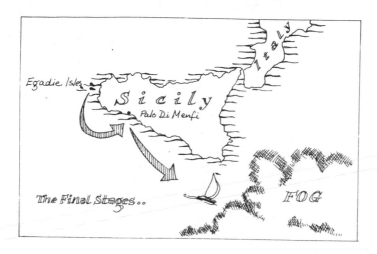

Kevin Spills the Beans

Kevin was feeling grim. Two days of heavy drinking had made his liver sluggish. This, in turn, affected his sense of well-being and now his whole system limped along in second gear. He would have killed for a cold drink but lacked the energy to call down to Sandy. He was tired, worn out, and had a mother of a hangover, but the helm was his and he would stay come hell or high water.

His only instruction was to head east and give the tuna nets a wide berth. The endless line of bobbing, black, markers warning of the danger that lay beneath the surface had a magnetic effect on Kevin. They kept drawing him towards them, waiting to snare him: like they were the run of tuna during the Mattanza. They were leaving Favignana, thankfully missing the wholesale killing that would very soon start, drawing tourists from far corners of the earth to watch the most horrific carnage imaginable, as these giant creatures were snared and butchered right along this very coastline. Kevin tried to shake the image of thousands of spiked, trashing, animals from his mind. He imagined the sea red with blood and gore and involuntarily shivered with the thought. The wind, in the lea of the island, was negligible but he felt deep down in his unwashed socks that the

189

weather was going to be really bad when they hit open water. It had after all to run to form, hadn't it? Why should it change now?

He couldn't help wondering how he was actually sailing again. Was it because last night he was too drunk to know any better and this morning his aching head hadn't allowed him to think straight? Circumstances had once again dealt him a rotten hand. He should have been on that day's ferry to Palermo and then home, yet here he was heading to God knows where and he didn't even know what direction he was going to take once they cleared the island. Sure, he told himself, they were going to ditch the yacht and let Fred stew in his own juice. But when? He was totally pissed off with Nigel and Sandy. They had agreed that Favignana was the end of their misery, yet here they were sailing along the same frigging line of nets that had so frustrated their entry on arrival from Sardinia. Nigel was only interested in saving his own neck, he decided, and didn't give a flea's fart for his feelings or those of the others.

'I suppose we do owe it to the old bastard to get the boat to a safe marina,' he reconsidered, feeling a tiny twinge of guilt considering Fred's most recent accident. 'I hope he isn't too badly hurt. Couldn't be,' he decided, feeling that Fred didn't deserve any sympathy after what he'd put them through, 'he has the stamina of a mountain goat, goes with the looks, ha!, even resembles one with that scraggy beard of his.

Nigel interrupted Kevin's daydream with a warning shout.

'Watch those nets. You'll foul the propeller!'

Kevin considered the distance between themselves and the nets and stubbornly maintained his course for some minutes before thinking better of it, then only moving out a few feet.

'I think we'll need more than that,' Nigel added, careful to make it sound as if it were an observation rather than an order. He knew Kevin's moods and decided that this was the only way to get results.

Kevin relented and grudgingly added a few feet more between themselves and the nets. Nigel still didn't think it enough, but thought it advisable to say nothing further and went below to help Sandy make the breakfast and check on Fred.

Fred was sitting up drinking a cup of coffee His side ached unbelievably and he had swallowed a few more Ponstan to try to take the edge off the pain. Nigel observed that his breathing was normal and that his ribs didn't appear to be fractured. A cracked rib could be damned sore as he'd found out once or twice on the rugby pitch. Sandy was boiling eggs for breakfast. Fred had suggested they might as well eat while they were in calm waters. Nigel thought this was another good sign. If Fred wanted to eat, he couldn't be all that bad.

When the eggs were ready, Nigel took his breakfast and a cup of coffee to the chart table. He studied the chart for a few moments before addressing Fred.

'What's it to be, Fred, which way, left or right?' He hoped that Fred would say South.

'We'll wait and see where the wind is. That'll decide it for us. Whether we go. Ohhh . . . you bas . . .!' Fred had tried to turn round to face Nigel and now regretted the move. 'Whether we go North or South,' he finished, careful not to move again. He wondered how on earth he could have fallen through the bloody hatch.

'Need to get my bloody eyes tested. Down the bloody hatch right enough.' But he hadn't been drinking that much, he told himself. 'Kevin and George yes, they were rat-arsed, but not me!' Life was cruel he decided but they were once again on their way and that was all that mattered. It had been touch and go back there. There was no turning back now.

Thirty minutes later, Kevin could clearly see a large, makeshift, buoy marking the end of the tuna nets way out past the headland. As he had expected, the sea was rough out there, even though there was hardly any wind.

As they got closer it became evident how the danger to shipping mark had been improvised. A metal frame with a flashing light was mounted on an old forty-foot wooden fishing boat which was well past its sell-by date. The high rusting metal pillar replaced the wheelhouse. If they were going to head South they would have to steer well clear of it not knowing what might be under the surface. The sea was now piling up in short corrugations with tops of two metres, or more, and some could be seen breaking over the unyielding hulk.

'Wind's south south-west, Fred. I think its make your mind up time. Which way do we go?' Nigel crossed his fingers, not relishing the thought of a battle with their injured skipper at this very moment. Fred would know of their intended mutiny soon enough.

Fred glanced at the wind speed gauge from the couch. 'Nine knots and we're probably making most of that ourselves.' He paused in deep concentrated thought, giving it serious consideration. It didn't make any difference which way they went. But around the bottom of Sicily was a little shorter and Palermo on the North was too risky; they might want to stop there, jump ship. That would be yet another obstacle in ever reaching Greece. No! They would head South.

'We'll go South.'

Nigel also gave a sigh of relief, the confrontation was off for a little longer.

'Nigel,' Fred called. 'Would you mind plotting the course for me. I'm going to lie down in George's cabin for a bit.' He could only lie on his good side and, with a few hours undisturbed sleep, he'd probably feel a whole lot better.

Sandy got some extra pillows and helped him remove his shirt. A large purplish black bruise had already developed on Fred's lower rib cage. She handed him a few sleeping pills from the emergency kit, which he took gladly, swallowing noisily with a long drink of cold water.

'I don't think I'll be much good to anyone today,' he said, thankful for her sympathetic help. 'If I get a few hours . . .' He hoped fervently that the sea wouldn't be too choppy. He didn't think he could bear being bounced around with ribs as sore as this.

Nigel studied the chart and drew a line in pencil from the tip of Favignana to the south-western edge of Sicily. He was surprised at how shallow the waters were around the coastline.

Fred was already sound asleep long before they reached the yellow wreck marking the end of the tuna nets. Deceptive was once again being tossed about by remorseless, rolling waves. She staggered up their glistening slopes causing spray to break over her bow, adding colour to her teak deck. Cabin doors swung on their hinges noisily banging until they were properly secured, but Fred still slept on.

Nigel shouted up the proposed heading to Kevin, who looked at the compass and then at the vanishing west coast of Sicily. He looked back and saw that they were well clear of the headland. Ahead stretched the remainder of the nets for which he had formed that fatal mesmeric attraction, not having moving one inch further out than he thought necessary. He was quite pleased with himself. He had run the gauntlet, stuck to his decision and they had made it. He could relax now.

Here the seas were different. They no longer had the shelter of the island and the line of nets was no longer straight, but bent with the sea in a zig-zag pattern, unable to cope with the large waves rising and falling over and around them. He was steering too close. Far too close! Shortly they would be rounding the heavily moored buoy. Immersed in his befuddled, brooding thoughts he couldn't see their obvious peril.

Nigel came on deck. Immediately he saw the danger.

'Watch out!' he shouted. 'Take her out Kevin, take her out, damn you!'

Kevin, startled by Nigel's yell, spun the wheel rapidly to port and they seemed to gain some necessary space. But they were too late. There was a sudden clunk and a deathly silence as the engine stopped. A stray piece of mooring line had wound itself around the propeller and they were firmly attached to the heavy hulk marking the end of the nets and very possibly the end of the voyage.

They moved closer, then drifted away only to be snatched back again as they see-sawed on the large waves.

'We'll have to get that line off, and fast,' roared Nigel, 'or we'll be wrecked!'

Deceptive was poised on top of a wave and about to fall towards the much lower boat. George had no doubts what the resulting crash would mean. He would have to keep her off. He sprung to the rail, putting one leg over the side to fend off the fast approaching disaster. Nigel saw him just in time and scrambling after him, pulled him roughly back. There was a jolting crash as the boats collided.

'Get a fender. Don't ever do anything as stupid as that again, you'll loose your flaming leg!' screamed Nigel.

Kevin stood frozen at the helm. This was all due to his stubbornness. He felt impotent, drained out, resigned to the fact that, shortly, Deceptive would be smashed to little pieces. Anyone could see that their fibre-glass hull was no match for the twenty-ton ,wooden monster that was going to batter them to smithereens.

Fred was off his bunk, but unable to help. He held on to a hand hold, head groggy, trying to resist the nausea surging up from deep inside his chest.

Sandy passed some fenders to George, but not quick enough to prevent another sickening jolt as the boats crashed together once more. The teak rubbing strake split open, its jagged edge marking their point of impact. Sandy pulled out the life jackets. It wasn't far to shore, a few miles, she judged, and she could easily swim that distance if the others were with her, but what about Fred?

'He'd never make it in his condition: not without help,' she decided

George, leaning over to fix the fenders to the guard-rail, could clearly see the heavy rope holding the boats together.

'Like a huge umbilical cord,' he thought. 'Get a knife!' he shouted to Sandy.

Deceptive was like a harpooned whale in the last throes of its life. Her stern was being pulled down with such force by the attached rope that anyone brave enough to enter the water would be risking their life. As she would crash down after each receding wave, those in the water below her trying to cut the rope could be forced under or end up being ground to pulp as she met the other boat side on.

Nigel couldn't risk it. He wasn't going to jump in himself and wouldn't let anyone else either. He would have to think of something else. There was another searing crash throwing them all off balance. Deceptive's teak rubbing strake was crumbling like balsa wood.

Sandy rushed on deck and handed George the knife.

'The fool's going to jump in!' Nigel thought. 'Wait, we'll try something else first!' he yelled, roughly pushing Kevin away from the wheel. He didn't know if it would work, but he would have to try it. He thrust the throttle into reverse and gave the starter button short jabs, but not enough to start the engine. He was trying to unwind the rope by reversing the propeller. It was their only chance.

George, leaning over the side, shouted excitedly. 'Its working. A little more!' Then as the rope dropped below him harmlessly, 'Its free!'

Nigel waited a few cliff-hanging seconds before starting the engine to make sure they were well clear. He didn't want to catch the rope again. He gave her full throttle and quickly distanced them from the 'yellow peril' as George had already re-christened it.

194

Kevin Spills the Beans

The whole incident had only taken minutes. Nigel was furious with Kevin and was about to give him a good tongue lashing but, sensing his distress, thought better of it. He went below and assured Fred that everything was once again okay.

Kevin, back on the helm, decided to forget his earlier intention of tackling Nigel about their change of plan. What did it matter any more? The near calamity had sharpened his thinking. Twice already he had almost caused a disaster, each time the result of a binge the night before. He wondered if he had a drinking problem and realised instantly that he probably did. He decided, not for the first time, that he was finished with drink. He would dump the unfinished bottle of whisky he had stashed in his cabin at the first opportunity.

They now entered what they would remember as the bleakest period of their journey. Nigel was in a bad mood because of Kevin. Kevin was suffering from a rare mood of self disgust. Sandy was bothered because she felt responsible for Fred's injury, having left the hatch fully open. George was upset because they weren't going on to Greece as they'd planned and he felt he as if he could sail forever.

They followed the Sicilian coast line past the towns of Marsala, Mazara del Vallo and on to Cape Granitola. They had been motoring for eight hours unable to put the sails up due to a total lack of wind. The sky was murky and overhung, the seas choppy and lumpy, ideal conditions to make even the most hardened sailor sea-sick. Nobody felt in the mood for conversation. They simply gazed sullenly at each other for much of the day.

No one was inclined to eat so they made do with soup and crackers. To Nigel's surprise, Kevin offered to take the soup cups down to the galley. As he went below George had a startled look on his face and both Nigel and Sandy anticipated his coming remark.

'Is Kevin not feeling well? Must be running a fever, that's the first time he's ever offered to wash the dishes,' George commented.

'Let's check his cabin later. If he's cleared up in there, we have a reformed Kev. on our hands,' added Nigel, knowing, only too well, that this particular leopard couldn't possibly change his spots as quickly as that.

'As much chance as a wasp in a microwave,' added George.

195

Fred had slept all day and was feeling much better, but still didn't feel inclined to join the others. He thanked Sandy for the soup and went back to sleep.

From Cape Granitola they were to head south-west across the Bay of Marinella and that night would be spent in the port of Sciacca.

They had no sooner rounded the cape when the weather worsened. Large black clouds blocked their path and the water began to boil. They had only twenty miles to go, but the rising wind was on their nose. This, combined with the large dappled waves, slowed down their progress to a snail's pace. After six hours of getting nowhere they headed for the nearest port.

Nigel had noted a small harbour below the historic monument of Menfi. There they would seek shelter. But, they would have to move fast in order to avoid an ugly, squall-ridden cloud that rose up from the sea like a giant anvil. It was slowly heading their way and could cut them off from safety. George noticed, in the distance, something that looked like a grey, inverted ice cream cone. It hung suspended from the clouds and seemed to rest on the sea.

'What the hell is that?' he yelled.

'If it comes our way we could be in trouble.'

Nigel realised at once what it was. 'Its a giant water spout! If it comes our way we could be in trouble.'

Even Fred ventured, painfully, on deck to see the spectacle. They watched it for some time, marvelling at its immense power as it sucked tons of water into the heavens, weaving its erratic and potentially destructive path through the sea.

'It's heading out.' Sandy's words confirmed their unspoken observations.

An hour and a half later they entered the small harbour called Palo Di Menfi, which was sheltered by a high sea wall, the inside of which was used for mooring purposes. The sea was crashing against this makeshift quay with tremendous force, sending spray right over the top. The impressive white Roman columns on the hill above the harbour had been visible for an hour but now faded in the failing light.

Fred was once again giving orders. He examined the pilot and didn't want to go bows to the harbour wall as recommended, which was not surprising, considering the water sweeping over the top. The large rocks forming its base also couldn't be trusted and he didn't want anyone breaking a world record, or something else, trying to jump ashore.

'Kevin, you drop the hook when I give you the go-ahead,' he ordered.

He took the helm from George. The buffeting had stopped. Immediately they motored behind the shelter of the wall. Other boats were also riding on anchor and Fred carefully picked his spot.

'Let her go!' Fred gently went astern as the anchor was laid. 'Tie her off,' he shouted continuing to reverse. He cut the engine and went forward to see if the anchor was set. Everything was in order. He was sure they would be safe for the night.

It was now pitch black and once below decks, switched on the anchor light. Nigel opened the drinks cupboard.

'Anyone care for a sundowner?' he asked. The moment of truth had arrived and he needed a stiff drink before breaking the news to Fred.

Drink in hand, he was about to speak, but Fred got his oar in first.

'Look, lads, I don't think I feel like going to a restaurant tonight. I'll just make myself a snack here. Just go on without me.'

'I don't think anyone's interested in going out, Fred,' commented Nigel, putting off once again the fatal moment. 'We're all shattered anyway. What do you say lads? We'll make a snack and turn in early?'

'I don't mind cooking something,' piped up Sandy, going to the galley and lifting the cover off the sinks. She called Nigel over. 'Would you believe this!' she exclaimed.

Nestling in the sink were the unwashed soup cups that Kevin had taken down that afternoon.

'For heaven's sake, Kevin, couldn't you even wash a couple of cups? You've done eff all this trip but moan and make life difficult for everyone!'

They were astonished at Nigel's outburst. This was not the normal Nigel who could be expected to throw oil on stormy water.

'I'm totally pissed off with your attitude and so is everyone else,' he continued. The others looked away embarrassed.

'I think Kevin should make the evening meal,' Nigel continued, quietening down.

Kevin was suitably chastened. He had conveniently convinced himself that being second mate freed him of the more ordinary chores.

'I'll make the supper. It's no big deal,' he offered shamefacedly.

'Good,' pronounced Nigel, and turning to Sandy. 'Sit down and enjoy your drink, Sandy. Be our guest for the evening.'

Kevin started to rummage about the cupboards, desperate for inspiration, but all he could see were tins of beans and sardines.

Nigel decided to drop his bombshell, carefully watching Fred's reaction.

'Fred, we've decided to call it a day. I don't think any of us want to go on. The trip hasn't been what any of us expected, including yourself. We've had bloody awful weather thrown at us and now we just want to go home.'

'We can't leave the boat here,' protested Fred feebly, and added quickly, 'There's no way I can take her to Greece by myself.'

Fred was beaten, and he knew it. He had tried to fool himself all day, desperately wanting to believe that they had had a change of heart.

'I'll help you get to Greece, Fred,' George offered, seeing the look of utter desolation on his drawn face.

'No, Nigel's right,' Fred admitted, manfully 'We've just about used up our allotted time. And in any case, I think we would have been hard pushed to find a marina in Greece in the short time we have left. There's also the problem of flights home.'

Fred was making the best of it. He knew that he was finally beaten. Pride wouldn't allow him to show his bitter disappointment.

'Defeated within a stone's throw of our destination!' he thought. 'Marge was right. His whole life had been one long line of failures. He was just running true to form.

'Any ideas about where we can leave the boat?' he added dejectedly, unable to keep a brave face on things any longer. 'There must be some safe marina around here or you wouldn't have decided to break the news just now.'

'Yes, there is, Fred,' answered Nigel, seeing him lose the struggle to make the best of it and now wishing that, maybe, they should have gone on after all. 'I think Malta is the answer.'

'Malta?' Echoed George. 'Where the hell's Malta from here?'

'It's a full day's sail from here.'

What do you mean? Twelve hours or twenty four?' questioned George.

'Twenty-four,' added Nigel. 'I know that there are regular flights to England. Cheap too.'

'When did you find all this out?' queried Fred 'You're a mine of information, all of a sudden.'

'I met a chap in Favignana who winters there regularly. He said it's the best spot. Safe.'

'You're not too surprised, are you, Fred?' asked Sandy, comfortingly.

In his book, it was bloody mutiny, he decided, but he had to put a brave face on things.

'Naw, George had already warned me.' The others shot George a surprised look. 'To tell you the truth I'm surprised we got this far. The weather an all.' He brightened, 'Well Malta it is then. That's settled.

Kevin had selected a tin of beans and was now rooting noisily for a tin opener. After much clattering of cutlery, they watched as he awkwardly plunged the point of the opener into the can and began to cut around the rim. The jagged edge slowly rose as he circumnavigated its unfamiliar edge, then suddenly slipped.

'Blast it,' he swore, dropping the can onto the floor. Blood streamed from a cut on his index finger.

'That's twice the beans have been spilled today ' Nigel said, looking at George, who didn't miss the intended barb.

'Looks as if he'll need some stitches,' Fred decided, after examining the deep wound.

'Let's see what's in the medical box first,' suggested Nigel, knowing full well that he had brought some special preparations for just such an emergency.

'Ahhha! 'He produced a large sailmaker's needle and wagged this at Kevin, who suddenly paled.

'Get away from me, you're not going to use that on me!' he burst out, a trace of panic in his voice.

'No,' said Nigel, exchanging the needle for a small packet.

He put four butterfly sutures neatly across the wound.

'There,' he said proudly, 'Knew my boy scout training would come in handy sometime.' It was really his first aid training, but he was desperate to liven things up a little. 'You're not going to lose the finger after all, Kevin,' he continued.

'And I don't think he'll be able to make the meal either,' said Sandy, cleaning up the mess of tomato sauce and white squashed beans lying on the floor.

'Bloody did it on purpose. Cut off his bloody finger to get out of washing the dishes,' added Fred.

They finished their drinks, some happy, some sad. The end to their misery was in sight. They had a few drinks more, all except Kevin, who hadn't touched a drop.

Kevin had kept his earlier resolve to quit drinking and couldn't quite get into the swing of things. He was happy to be going home, but now wished he hadn't alienated himself so much from the others. Sandy procured ingredients as if from mid-air, and cooked a wonderful meal which they ate hungrily. Later in the evening, when they had all bedded down, a plop was heard, which sounded like a fish jumping, but it was only Kevin's still unfinished whisky bottle hitting the water outside his cabin porthole. Kevin really had turned over a new leaf. He had, on too many occasions, he decided, taken them to the brink. This morning's episode was, by far, the worst for him – far worse than falling asleep on watch. He realised drinking at sea was not on, especially not to the excess that he was used to in

Liverpool. It was finally brought home to him. Fred had been right. Kevin now wished that he had respected Fred's views on that first day. Things might have worked out so much differently.

17

The Last Resort

No matter which way he turned, Fred, couldn't alleviate his torture. He curled himself into a tight ball to see if that would ease the pain, but it was no use. He had taken a few more Ponstan. They didn't seem to work any more. At first light he tried to get on his feet, but found the effort too much. He dozed off again.

George was the first to get up. He made some coffee and took it up on deck, marvelling at the freshness of the morning. The dew made little trails on Deceptive's salt-encrusted brightsides. Finishing his coffee, he began to dry off the dew, leaving the gelcoat white and gleaming in the early morning sun. If this were his boat, he thought, he would look after it properly.

The Roman ruins on the hilltop glowed a faint pink and slowly turned brilliant white. Inside the harbour there was hardly a ripple on the surface, but outside he could hear the angry waves dashing against the quay wall. He wished it all wasn't going to end so soon. By midday tomorrow he would be in Malta. He didn't want to return to his office in England any more. He had found, he honestly believed, what he had been searching for all his life. He wanted to go on to the Greek islands, to Turkey. He imagined an Atlantic crossing, Antigua, Panama, the Pacific. He loved this boat. She was a brave lady, well able to withstand what nature and incompetence could sling in her path. He wondered if Fred wanted to sell her? Perhaps he would make an offer. His business was well-established and could run itself for a few years.

He was aroused from his daydreaming by the sound of the others moving below. Fred had at last managed to get up and was leaning over the chart table, his body tortured by unrelenting nautious pain which grabbed his every breath.

'We'll have to go to Sciacca first to clear customs. It's not far. Then on to Malta,' he said gruffly. 'The sooner we're on our way the better.' Fred was being foolishly brave. He knew he required medical treatment, but that would have to wait until Deceptive was safely berthed.

Within fifteen minutes Deceptive was riding over the large

breakers, bucking like a steeplechaser on fresh grass. By the chart it would take them two hours to their first stop. They would first have to head out to Cape San Marco and then head back the same distance on the far side to Sciacca before heading out once more for Malta. The two hours were already up even before they saw the Cape lighthouse perched high on the cliff face. Deceptive was being stopped in her tracks by short confused waves. Fred knew that the further they sailed from land the tamer the sea would become. Here the waves piled up on themselves as they struck the shallow shelf which extended well out to sea. Another four hours of this would be more than he could handle.

He noticed that the log had begun to act up and was reading much lower than their estimated speed. He would have to find the manual and see what could be done about it. He assumed that a piece of weed had got trapped in the impeller, but thought that the only way to clear it was from underneath the boat. 'Who needs one anyway,' he thought, remembering American Jimmy's technique. Jimmy could tell their speed simply by spitting over the side and counting the seconds before it was lost in the wake.

The waves looked more foreboding around the point. Fred tried to call the coastguard on channel sixteen, but received no answer. He then called the port of Sciacca to see if there was any way he could avoid clearing customs.

'Sciacca port, Sciacca port, Sciacca port, this is the yacht Deceptive. Over.' There was no answer, so he tried again. Still no answer.

'Why not post the transit log back from Malta?' Sandy inquired, more aware of Fred's condition than anyone else on board. 'I'm sure it will be alright.'

Fred wondered how she could possibly tell if it was alright or not. She seemed to know too much about these matters for a mere accountant, but he had to admit, nevertheless, that she probably had a valid point. He decided to head straight for Malta. They would save time and he could blame the decision on his medical condition.

For the next two hours Fred kept giving furtive glances behind them, expecting to see the coastguard cutter on their tail. Deceptive was clearly visible to the large lighthouse on the cliff and he imagined they were being watched through powerful binoculars. 'All they have to do is telephone and we've had it,' he thought, wishing fervently that Deceptive's name wasn't so prominently displayed along her sides. Fred, as usual, was prey to all kinds of irrational fears and was, once again being haunted by his over-active imagination.

A half tank of diesel still remained despite the continuous motoring of the previous day, but this was barely enough to get them the one hundred and fifty miles to Valetta. To be on the safe side, Fred decided that the sails should be set. They would have to tack. This would make the journey much longer, but the purpose was to save fuel.

Fred spent a painful half hour working at the chart table and then issued his latest instructions.

'A starboard tack for one and a half hours and then to port for one hour, this to continue throughout the rest of the morning and well into the afternoon.'

The wind was a steady fifteen knots and, with the full main and tacking jib, they would average five knots.

'We must keep rigidly to the plan,' Fred advised severely, otherwise I won't be able to work out our position once we've lost sight of land. Fred had reason to worry. Malta was a small target, only eighteen miles long and, from the point of their approach, a mere three miles wide.

As Fred had predicted, the sea flattened as they left the shore far behind. There was also a distinct change in the weather. The early morning sun was replaced with high, even cloud cover.

Once the sails were up and Deceptive steadied, Sandy made a breakfast of scrambled eggs. Spirits were up this morning and they really began to enjoy the sailing. Later in the day she made lunch, each taking a glass of red wine, with the exception of Kevin who stuck to his guns and drank coke.

They had noticed Fred spitting into the sea at regular intervals and mumbling but none dared question this unusual behaviour.

Today everything continued to run smoothly. The sea had flattened even more and the wind remained perfect. It was as if the elements were apologising for what they had already put Deceptive and her crew through and were now trying to make amends, to be given another chance.

Throughout the day they kept rigidly to plan. At dusk the wind died completely and Fred was forced to start the engine. Thick black smoke shot out from the exhaust surprising Fred but she ran sweeter than he could remember and he soon forgot about it. Fred estimated their position and set course directly for the lighthouse on the island of Gozo: Malta's little buddy.

Their evening meal was made from the remnants of the various packets of pasta Sandy had already opened. Provisions were getting low but, with only a night and a morning to go, there was no problem. They also finished the last of the wine and wondered how they had managed to drink so much in such a short time.

Nobody wanted to sleep as this was their last night aboard ship. Conditions were so smooth that Fred's recently re-inforced rule about deck harness was forgotten. They sat in the cockpit for, what seemed like hours, chin wagging, reminiscing. Their trip was already taking on a new perspective. Memory was dulling reality and some were even remarking on how they had enjoyed their trip.

Sandy and Nigel excused themselves at one thirty and went to their cabin, this would be their last night together and there was some unfinished business to attend to. George and Kevin were relaxed and happy to keep watch. But Fred was anxious. He had to see the Gozo light. They had made good time and he expected to see its first feeble glimmer any time now. His features had taken on a haunted drawn look and his palour looked anything but healthy.

At four fifteen, a now frantic Fred still hadn't seen the light from Gozo. Something was far wrong, but he couldn't work it out. He racked his brains looking for an answer. He puzzled over the chart, calculating and re-calculating until he became confused with his figures. There was only one possible explanation. They had forgotten to reverse their tack at one point along the way. So instead of running off for an hour, or an hour and a half, they had, maybe, strayed from their course by either seven or five miles. Enough to miss, not only the light, but the entire island of Gozo. But which way? Had they gone too far to the West or too far to the East?

Another fifteen minutes passed before Fred gave up working on the chart. He would have to question each in turn to find out who had not changed tack at the required time. He remembered vividly telling them how important this was. Another horrible thought struck him. Supposing on of them had transposed East for West and instead of going for one and a half hours in one direction had only gone one hour, the error repeating itself all day? That would also have taken them miles off course.

If only his side hadn't been giving him gyp he could have concentrated better, kept a watch on things, but he had lain down for a few hours, given in to the pain. Fred punished himself unnecessarily.

'Have any of you seen that bloody light yet?' he shouted through the hatch, unable to hide the frustration in his voice.

'For heaven's sake Fred, you've been asking the same question every five minutes for the last three hours. Nothing! If we see it we'll let you know,' George answered back, getting annoyed with Fred's persistent request, and beginning to feel uneasy about the whole situation. He went forward along the deck and peered into the distance, but still couldn't see anything. The sea was like glass and he could hear the soft whish as Deceptive's bow cut effortlessly through the perfectly still water. Up front he could hardly hear the sound of the engine as it now ran so smoothly.

Fred questioned George and Kevin and they both assured him that they had stuck rigidly to his instructions. A sleepy Nigel also confirmed that he hadn't deviated for more than a minute and could he please be allowed to get a bit of peace and quiet in the middle of the night. Was it himself? Fred also couldn't remember a single moment when he could have incorrectly changed course.

At five they still hadn't seen the lighthouse. If they didn't get a glimpse of it soon, its light would be lost in the rising sun and useless to Fred. He desperately wanted its reassurance. There would be no other way of telling where they were unless the Sat. Nav. decided to lend a helping hand. He had to face the bare, solitary conclusion that screamed at him from the chart. They were lost!

Fred went over the scenario carefully in his mind. Their approach was from the North therefore Malta would stretch out ahead of them in a straight line. They were surely running along its coast, but too far off to see the lights Should they turn to port or starboard? He decided to go thirty degrees to starboard.

At first light it looked as if the day was going to be overcast and grey. The early morning glimmer had taken on a vitreous luminosity that didn't go unnoticed by Fred and his crew. They were in more trouble than they had imagined. They were engulfed in thick, impenetrable fog.

So this was why they hadn't seen the Gozo lighthouse, Fred realised, totally exasperated by the revelation. The last thing he had expected was fog.

'Fog was an English thing. You don't get fog in the Mediterranean! Travelling all night through bloody fog and didn't know it,' Fred moaned, still not believing his eyes.

They peered into the gloom, certain that they would run aground at hardly a moment's notice. Grey, spectral images now threatened to wreck their ship.

Fred couldn't help thinking of the irony of the situation. Less than an hour ago he was worried about not finding land, now he was desperately trying to avoid it. He remembered that he had changed his course by thirty degrees and, knowing that in all probability his original calculations were correct, he was heading straight for the rocks.

'Put the engine off!' he shouted to the exhausted Kevin and George, who now were regretting their decision to stay awake all night. He wanted to see if he could hear something, anything: the lapping of water on a nearby shore, or the throb of a distant propeller. But there was only an eerie silence. It was as if the fog was blanketing out all sounds.

George was in the mood for fun. This was their last day so he thought he might as well liven things up a little. He went below and got the fog horn. Signalling to Kevin to be quiet, he crept up behind Fred who had gone forward. There was a harsh disturbance of air and then a hoarse rush as the horn gave a loud 'Blawwwwwwwwaaa'. Fred would have left his skin in a heap on the deck if his body had leapt as hard as his heart just had. For an instant he thought they were being run down by a freighter.

'You could give someone a heart attack, doing that, you stupid fool!' he shouted, very startled.

'Caught you there, eh!, Fred? Almost peed yourself, didn't you, what?' cried the highly amused George.

Kevin, was creased with laughter.

Sandy and Nigel poked their heads through the front hatch, bemused looks on their faces.

A smile flitted about the corners of Fred's mouth and then broke into a sheepish grin. He wanted to laugh, but the pain would have been too much.

No answering blast was heard so they assumed they were alone.

Fred still had no way of confirming his position and decided to try the radio. Consulting his Reed's Mediterranean Navigator he tuned into Valletta harbour. He could hear voices speaking in what he hoped was the Maltese dialect, but they kept breaking up and fading. 'Still too far away,' he said. 'We'll give it another shot later.'

Subsequently, Fred did hear a voice with a strong accent warning, in English, that no ships were to anchor off Valletta harbour due to the fog. He also heard other ships calling in, giving their positions, and getting instructions. Fred couldn't call in as he didn't have a clue where he was due to the tardy log. All he was sure of was that Malta must be somewhere to his immediate right.

At ten o'clock they saw a sharp, black, immobile shape outlined against the still dense fog. Fred decided to head straight for the stalled ship. When he was close enough to read its name he called her up on channel sixteen but received no answer. The ship began to move away and he followed and was soon lost again in the fog. They could clearly hear her engine even though she was nowhere in sight.

Fred assumed, wrongly, that the ship had been anchored.

'There must be shallows further in, where she had been,' he decided, but didn't feel inclined to check further in case they ran aground. He looked at the chart and saw that the only place a ship could anchor away from Valletta harbour, as instructed by the heavily accented voice on the radio, was an inlet five miles north of the town.

'We must be right here,' he informed Nigel poking an extended finger at the spot on the chart, pleased with his deduction. Nigel didn't disagree. After all, Fred had brought them this far and by now his navigational ability was way beyond dispute.

They had estimated that visibility was about a quarter of a mile, judging by the distance they had travelled to the other ship. Fred suggested that they take a gradual right and head in towards land. He was going to try and get back to England that night if possible, he decided. He couldn't put up with this pain for much longer, something serious was wrong.

They motored gingerly for another hour, but land failed to

appear. Fred increased his angle of approach and they continued for another hour. Sandy decided that it wasn't worth her while making anything to eat as they would be in harbour soon, and anyway, there was barely anything left to assemble a reasonable meal, so she settled for coffee.

Fred was puzzled, but continued nevertheless. They should have seen land ages ago. Surely they must be heading directly for it? Also worrying Fred was the sense of being alone again. Earlier he had almost felt the land, knowing that it was near at hand, but now it was different. It seemed further away, more distant. The reception on their V.H.F. had finally given its last spurt of spoken gibberish and now all that could be heard was the loud static burst of vacant airwaves. 'Time of day,' Fred speculated.

An hour later he gave up his futile effort to find land.

'We must be well past Valletta now,' he confided in Nigel.

'End up in bloody Libya if we're not careful, Fred,' Nigel answered, missing completely the significance of Fred's statement.

Fred didn't think this at all funny. He remembered the arrest in France of an Irish cruiser full to the brim with deadly weapons. Gun running was synonymous with Libya and it wasn't something he could joke about any more: not since the questions that were asked by the official on the dock in Gibraltar. Neither was the helicopter incident that the others had found, oh, so, so, amusing.

'You don't joke about such things,' Fred added, sourly. 'You never know what certain people may think and Libya is not that far from here.'

Nigel looked at Sandy who had been listening attentively to every word. 'Lighten up Fred its only a joke.'

Fred realised he was being silly. 'I think we'll have to stop the engine and drift for a while,' he muttered, changing the subject. 'At least until the fog lifts. Land might be close at hand and we're just barely missing it.'

The seriousness of their situation suddenly struck Nigel. 'Supposing that when the fog finally lifted there was no land in sight. What then?' he wondered, looking concernedly at Fred.

Fred was really tired. His ribs ached badly when he moved and he could hardly keep his eyes open. He felt drained, worn out. He needed to lie down, relax, settle his nerves. Kevin and

George had already given in to their tiredness from the long sleepless night, and now lay dead to the world in their adjacent cabins. Fred stretched out in the pilot bunk and was instantly asleep.

18

Missed Chances

The weather had changed. The lows which had dogged their
path for the last three weeks were heading off towards the Urals
leaving behind a permanent high. The weather for the next four
months was going to be settled, much as it was every year. The
Llevantades had blown itself out off the coast of Spain. The
Sirocco had become a local breeze along the North African
coast. The Libecco and the Mistral had decided to take a rest
until the end of August, and the Gregale, off the coast of
Greece, was just about to pack it in until September. If
Deceptive's crew had started the trip now it would have been
effortless. Summer had arrived at last. Just one day earlier and
they would still be on their way to Greece.

Nigel looked at the clear blue sky. 'Somebody up there
doesn't like us,' he decided, and returned to the more
immediate task of locating Malta.

Fred had intended to sleep for an hour. He looked at his
watch and couldn't believe that it was already six o'clock in the
evening. He had slept all afternoon! He could hear the confident
hum of the engine and faintly recollected that he had heard it
start earlier, but had been too exhausted to investigate.
Obviously, the fog had lifted and Nigel and Sandy could see
Malta. He had relaxed then for the first time in twenty four
hours, knowing that all was well and had fallen back into a
blissfully deep sleep. He examined his watch again, could it
really be six o'clock? He was surprised that it was taking them so
long to head in. He had estimated that they should have been
approximately two hours off, at the most three, but definitely no
more than that. He carefully climbed out of the pilot bunk to
avoid jolting his aching ribs and looked out through the hatch.
Sandy and Nigel were sitting in the cockpit, both looked drawn
and weary.

'Kevin and George must still be asleep,' he decided, not
surprised, considering their long vigil of the previous night. The
pain in his side had eased off a little with the rest, but it was still
far from comfortable. It wasn't going away. To make matters
worse he appeared to be getting a cold. He could feel the

congestion building up in his lungs making him breathless. He was feeling a little peckish after his sleep, but quickly realised that they were pretty low in provisions and consoled himself with the thought that shortly he would be sitting down to a slap up meal in a quayside restaurant.

Fred slowly mounted the steps leading up to the cockpit. Nigel and Sandy watched his every movement silently. They had a lot on their minds as Fred was about to find out.

'How much longer then, Nigel?' Fred asked, unconcerned.

Nigel looked away before answering, and Fred's heart hit his boots. He didn't have a chance to formulate his answer. Fred, knew the awful truth. Nigel hadn't seen Malta after all.

Nigel explained that shortly after Fred had crashed the fog had lifted, replaced by bright, glaring sunshine. They found themselves in the middle of a calm empty ocean. There was no land in sight and, reluctantly, Nigel made the decision to motor, in what he thought was a reciprocal course, adding thirty degrees to make sure they met land. He had believed that they must come upon the island of Malta soon. They couldn't have missed it by that much.

Fred didn't say anything, anticipating correctly what was coming next.

The brilliant sunshine had brought its own problems as a heat haze had now replaced the earlier fog and visibility was only three to five miles. Nigel had mistaken a distant cloud bank for their intended landfall and had once again changed direction. Not familiar with the usual navigation procedures, he hadn't written a single entry in the log, trusting the whole lot to memory. He had returned to his earlier course when it became evident that the land they had seen in the distance was an illusion. He then began to understand his earlier mistake and once again changed course. Later still, he had seen a ship in the distance and, now desperate, had assumed that that would lead him back to Malta, but after following it for half hour that too was lost in the distance. By now Nigel was totally confused and, reluctantly, had to admit to Fred that they were well and truly lost.

Fred couldn't believe Nigel's stupidity. Why hadn't he woken him instead of going around in circles all afternoon? When he had bunked down he was confident that they were somewhere in the vicinity of Valletta. All that was required was to wait until the fog had cleared and, if they still couldn't see land, just hang around until nightfall and the lights from one of the many lighthouses must surely be visible.

Fred had a sudden bout of harsh, lung-wrenching coughing, causing Sandy to throw a startled look at Nigel.

'Put the engine off. There's no point in wasting any further fuel,' Fred advised brusquely, as soon as he caught his breath, unable to hide the frustrated edge in his voice . 'Why didn't you wake me up before going off on a bloody wild goose chase?

Nigel didn't answer.

'I'll have a look at the chart and see how far off the lights from Malta can be seen,' Fred relented. 'Just pray that we don't get another foggy night to-night.' Fred went below decks and had a quick look at the chart. 'No problem,' he shouted up. 'Everything's okay.' He read out loud from the pilot. 'Marsamxett, Dragut Point Lighthouse, that flashes twice every four seconds. There's also Valletta and that can be seen twenty three miles off. We'll just have to hang around a bit longer, then we'll know exactly where we are,' he concluded, confident, now, that their difficulty was merely a temporary one.'

'That's good news Fred,' Sandy answered, relieved that there was an easy way out of this particular mess.

Fred looked at the fuel gauge and saw that the needle was bouncing on the red. 'Only enough fuel left for six hours at the most, that's thirty miles.' he thought angrily. 'What in the name of blazes was Nigel thinking about? He used up precious fuel and we've still no frigging idea where we are.'

Fred could see that Sandy and Nigel were upset. There was little point in belabouring the facts so he decided to rummage in the food cupboards for something to eat. They still had plenty tins of beans and more than a few cans of sardines. There was no bread, just a few packets of Ryvita. 'Cardboard,' Fred muttered out loud. He found a few sachets of 'Cuppa Soup' and a hardly used caterer's pack of instant mash. He would have to make the most of it. They weren't going anywhere until after dark, that was for sure. Fred made some coffee and heated a tin of beans which he served with some instant potatoes. He had to add a large lump of butter to enhance the flavour of the starchy stodge, but it wouldn't be wasted. The other very hungry twosome on deck would see to that. There was no point in rousing Kevin and George until later as they would be needed to bring Deceptive safely into Valletta harbour in the early hours of the morning.

Fred convinced himself that they must be at least ten miles out for no other reason than that Nigel had been unable to see land when the fog had lifted. He switched on the V.H.F. expecting to hear some traffic, there was nothing. He had a slight feeling of unease. Could he be wrong? He brushed it aside, as his frame shook with another racking, chest bursting, bout of coughing. The pain in his chest was unbelievable fierce and he had to curl in a ball on the pilot berth to try and get a little relief. Sandy looked again at Nigel, a worried look creasing her brow.

'Fred certainly isn't on the mend. The sooner he sees a doctor the better,' she whispered to Nigel, both now very concerned.

'Only a few hours to darkness and everything will be alright,' Fred managed to get out, once he had recovered his breath, realising that Nigel and Sandy must be feeling really bad about the whole thing. He couldn't help adding, 'Its bloody ironic, but, if we'd kept on going, instead of heading for Malta, we'd probably be more than half-way to Greece by now.'

Time dragged frustratingly slowly as they waited anxiously for darkness. Fred struggled on deck. Nigel kept glancing at his watch, but only a few minutes had passed since he had last looked.

They watched the sun sink slowly below the horizon and, to ease the monotony, took bets as to who would see the lighthouse first. Sandy reckoned that she was sure to be the first as she had grabbed the only pair of binoculars on board. Both Fred and Nigel called her a cheat, but she wasn't going to hand them over.

'And, besides,' she joked, 'nobody mentioned that they couldn't be used. Nothing in the rule book says one can't use a little female cunning,'

Nigel made a grab for the glasses, but she was too fast for him.

Sandy scanned and re-scanned the horizon with the binoculars, but the lighthouse failed to appear.

'Give it another half an hour. It isn't dark enough yet,' encouraged Nigel.

When they couldn't pretend it wasn't dark enough any more, they had to admit that they had lost their last hope of finding Malta. Fred went over, time and again, the directions that Nigel thought he had headed in that afternoon, but it all didn't make sense.

'That bloody lighthouse is visible for twenty-three miles and we can't see it. Where the hell are we?' Fred demanded, angrily bouncing his clinched fist off Deceptive's hatch cover. There was no question of fog as the night was crystal clear and they could already see a multitude of stars lighting the heavens.

The Sat. Nav. was turned on, but Fred no longer gave it a second thought. It hadn't worked before when they were in trouble, why should it work now.

Nigel and Sandy threw each other worried looks. The magnitude of their stupidity was slowly becoming dumbfoundingly evident to them.

Fred had to make a decision. They couldn't hang around here all night. His mind was easily made up. To the south was Libya, to the west was Tunisia, there was only one option open to them and that was to head for their original destination, Greece. To return to Sicily was going to take them at least a day and a half, maybe more, depending on where they actually were. Why not go on to Greece? It would only add one more day to their journey.

'It's got to be Greece,' he announced. The only other alternative is to return to Sicily and that's not practical as there are no marinas to the south. Food's a little short, but we'll manage. Can't do anything else. What do you both think?'

The question of fuel didn't come into their calculations. There wasn't enough no matter which way they went. There was now no way of finding Malta, so that as a choice was no longer feasible. If they saw a ship within calling distance they would ask for assistance, but Fred didn't have much faith in this method of deliverance, considering their previous experiences. They would have to depend on the sails and their sailing ability to get them wherever they were going. 'Deceptive is a sailing boat after all.' he argued.

Sandy and Nigel agreed.

The question of whether or not there would be enough wind didn't even cross their minds. If they were going to succeed, an initiative would have to be taken and Fred had just done that. George and Kevin had no option but to agree to the plan. They too couldn't think of any alternative course of action.

'Could do with a few pounds off anyway. Done nothing but eat and drink on this trip,' was George's only comment. For him the real adventure was about to begin in earnest. A whole new scenario had opened up before him. They were no longer playing games, this was the real thing. He was almost happy.

Fred was now coughing more frequently, and much longer, making it painful for him to breathe properly. He blamed it on the damp night air to the others, but deep down he knew he was in trouble and wondered if he would ever make it back.

That night Fred's right lung hurt like hell, and the more so when he coughed. And this despite the handfuls of pills he kept shovelling down his throat since his unfortunate fall down the hatch three days ago. George and Kevin were on duty, but they were going nowhere, there was no wind.

Next morning, engine on, Deceptive was once again moving north-eastwards. They had little fuel left, but Fred decided it must surely be enough to bring them into some wind, going by the experiences of the last three weeks.

Four very disgruntled and worried crew members huddled together in the cockpit, not at all happy. Their boredom could no longer be lifted in anticipation of Sandy's culinary inventiveness, she'd have to be a magician to make anything palatable of what remained on the shelves. How were they going to manage for two days or more without proper meals? Already their optimism of the previous evening was beginning to fade in the realisation that they were on, as Kevin put it, 'A very sticky wicket!'

Their landfall was Greece. But where in Greece? Fred hadn't been specific, he couldn't be, they were unfamiliar with one of the fundamentals of navigation: you have to know where you are to begin with and this Fred did not know. However, he felt they would be able to identify any island they came upon from the chart. That is any island from Zante right up to Corfu, he didn't have a chart of southern Greece.

Nigel blamed himself for their present misfortune. He should have taken more interest in navigation from the start, instead of leaving it all to Fred. If he hadn't gone off half-cocked they would, by now, all be back in England. He also tortured himself, remembering that the decision to go to Malta had been his and his alone. Sandy tried to cheer him up, but couldn't convince him that anyone, given the same circumstances, could have missed Malta. He could already imagine the comments back home. 'You actually missed Malta!' There would be no end to the ribbing once this got out.

There was also the worry about Fred's health. His injury wasn't getting any better and for long periods now he sat with his body bent in pain, not speaking to anyone, staring into the distance, unseeing.

The diesel ran out that afternoon and still there was no wind. Throughout the rest of the day the sun beat down relentlessly with not a breath of air filling Deceptive's hopefully erected, but sadly redundant, sails. Perfect weather for sunbathing if anyone had been interested, but not on this boat. Already every effort was being made to conserve any food they had. Repeated and urgent requests were made on channel sixteen for assistance, but no answer was received.

Throughout that day and the following night not another vessel was seen. Fred made fewer and fewer attempts to leave his bunk as his condition steadily worsened.

They consoled themselves that they had thirty gallons of drinking water on board, enough to last them for weeks. However, the frequent usage of the V.H.F. was draining the ships remaining power, the consequences of which had not yet dawned on them. Once the batteries were dead the pump used to draw water from Deceptive's water tanks would be inoperable, and to all extent and purpose their water supply would have dried up.

Temperatures rose to the high eighties that afternoon and remained there throughout the next day. Deceptive had hardly moved, other than turning slowly through all points of the compass as the feeble currents dictated.

Already, the crew looked gaunt, having lost pounds on their enforced starvation diet. A few spoonfuls of beans or a couple of sardines was all that Sandy would allow to alleviate their hunger pangs. The instant mash was now treated with unusual favour as Sandy dished it out sparingly spiced with; tomato sauce, mayonnaise, or even pickled mustard. George began to fish with some hooks he found in a cupboard, but still hadn't caught anything. When they remembered their recent past it was hard to imagine that they had already been becalmed for two days.

The batteries finally died that afternoon as did their water supply. Fred was now unable to raise himself from the pilot berth at all. The, hidden, internal damage to his chest was causing excessive fluid to build up in his right lung and this was playing havoc with his breathing. Sandy allowed him a little more food than the others, but he was struggling to finish even that.

It was hours before George worked out a simple method of drawing water from Deceptive's innards. He had first thought of puncturing her stainless steel tanks, but then thought of syphoning it as had once been demonstrated by a thief he'd disturbed emptying petrol from a car in Liverpool. He inserted a length of hose into the water tank through the filler hole on deck and dropped the other end through the hatch. Using a hand pump, which Fred had purchased to remove the engine oil, he laboriously extracted the air from the pipe and the water began to drain slowly into a flat pan held in the bilges. He had to get below the level of tanks otherwise the water wouldn't syphon off.

'Water always finds its own level, remember that when we're sinking,' he quipped.

Precious water was lost until they got the hang of it, some was stored in the sink in case the weather changed and they wouldn't be able to use George's innovation. They now had plenty drinking again, but very little food. Things were looking bleak, but they still had spirit left, despite the realisation that nobody was out there looking for them.

'If only we'd introduced ourselves to the radio operator at Valletta harbour, when we knew we were within calling distance, they could have picked us out of the fog on their radar and led us safely into harbour,' Fred gasped to Sandy, struggling to breathe through the ever thickening mucus filling his lungs. Now, he kept punishing himself, blaming himself for their present predicament.

'It's all my fault, I've done nothing right this trip . . . and . . . now we could all die.' The others blamed themselves too. If it had not been for their desperation to end the trip they would now be safely in Greece. If only he had had the sense to inform people of their progress, someone would be out there searching for them. The 'if only's' were coming fast and furious, but the milk was long since spilt and no amount of wailing was going to get them out of this mess.

Nigel couldn't believe it, but they were praying for some wind. Changed days indeed.

George had studied the instructions on the flares and was ready, the instant he saw a ship, to set one off. It now seemed their only hope. George, unlike the rest, had really come into his own. He was continually taking stock of their condition and sometimes chided Kevin and Nigel for getting so depressed. He regularly got them to jump into the sea for a swim around the boat to keep cool. He had stretched a sail over the boom to reduce the build-up of heat below decks, and this had kept the temperature below decks to a bearable eighty-three degrees during the day. He read sections of the many sailing books that Nigel and Fred had brought on board, which dealt with survival at sea and had learned how to hand-start the engine should they get diesel from a passing ship. Throughout the blistering hot days he organised Scrabble or Trivial Pursuits sessions and card games. Anything to pass the time and build morale, but the minutes had still dragged into days and the days seemed to be endless. Time was standing still. The unrelenting heat was slowly draining moisture and strength from their unsuspecting bodies.

The fourth day passed since leaving Sicily. The wind came up on a few occasions, building up their hopes, only to die almost immediately. Nigel and the others could hold out for weeks if necessary and didn't doubt about their ability to survive. George had finally caught some fish which seemed to be using the boat as some kind of shelter and now Kevin and Nigel were becoming enthusiastic fishermen as well. Sandy had cooked the fish in oil careful to conserve gas. Dolphins had swum around the boat on two occasions creating much excitement on board as they leaped into the air. It was almost as if they were showing off. They too seemed thrilled by this mid-ocean meeting.

Fred was a different proposition. His condition was steadily worsened and the others were already beginning to fear the worst, wondering amongst themselves what to do. He had become delirious, mumbling aloud in his troubled dreams.

Sandy was now dosing Fred with the remnants of the drinks cupboard as there were no pain killers or sleeping tablets left. To try to allay his irrational fears Sandy helped him to drunkenly drag his saliva lubricated pencil over pages torn from a notebook and stuff them into an empty brandy bottle. He watched as she replaced the cap tightly and cast it through the porthole above the galley. He relaxed and seemed to breathe a little easier, happier that now the world at large would hear of their journey if they didn't make it. Others would learn from his mistakes, he assured himself.

Sandy was beside herself with worry over Fred's condition and tried hard to hold back the tears that frequently filled her eyes as she watched his slow but certain decline. She felt helpless. All she could offer was her tender loving care. Fred should have been treated in hospital immediately after the fall, a few anti-biotics, she assumed, and he would have been well by now. It was all so frustrating, they had been within hours of a flight home and because of silly mistakes, a man's life was in jeopardy.

Her heart jumped to her mouth as Fred slumped back on the couch. His now familiar, continuous and racking cough grabbed and shook his tortured, failing, body. A tiny trickle of blood oozed from the corner of his mouth. He lay still. Sandy looked at him sadly, lifted his lifeless arm, once again feeling for a reassuring pulse. There was nothing else she could do. She found it. It was feeble but steady. 'If only we had some wind,' she thought for the thousandth time.

Nigel had exhausted his little knowledge of first aid a long while ago and now, with the rest, watched Fred's spiralling decline helplessly, hoping for a miracle.

George continued to be their life and soul and had more or less replaced Fred as leader. He seemed to be in far better condition than the others and was still careful to wash and shave.

That night a faint wind ruffled the sails and Deceptive began to move, painfully slow at first, but then gradually building up to what George estimated to be three knots. He scrambled on deck praying that the light breeze would continue. He dropped the working jib and hanked on the No.1 genoa. Deceptive's speed increased to about four knots and remained steady at that. By the morning the wind was higher and Deceptive was fairly creasing along. But where to? Heading north-east they hoped it would take them to the Ionian, that's if they hadn't already drifted too far south. George was becoming an expert at reading the wind speed by the state of the sea, and at midday predicted that it was blowing at twenty knots.

He hardened the sails, refusing to heed Nigel or Kevin's warning to reef down. They were in a race against time and he was going to make full use of what he had. He was throwing

. . . but still George did nothing to slacken their momentum.

caution to the wind and would much prefer dying this way than starving slowly to death. They were heading into a thunder-storm ahead, but still George did nothing to slacken their momentum. He would use the onward impelling force of the storm to gain even greater speed. Deceptive's rigging groaned protestingly under the unaccustomed strain but continued valiantly on. The thought that the mast could go never even entered his mind. The sky grew darker and then the squall hit. George brought Deceptive closer to the wind to reduce some of the excessive force and shouted to Nigel and Kevin, at last, to reef the main. George's prayers were being answered and already a new hope was instilled in the others. They might get Fred to hospital in time after all.

They pressed on through flashing thunderbolts, as bad as anything that had been flung at them before, but remained resolute. They were sailing as never before, taming the elements to suit their headlong dash for survival. One hour, then two, then three passed and still they raced on. Sandy looked at Fred's still body and could hardly feel his pulse now. He wasn't going to make it. Blinding pellets of ice cold rain began to fall hurting George's unprotected skin, but he still held on.

The sky was now a brooding, sinister black, the sea perfectly reflecting its melancholic tint, lit only with the necklace chain effect of lightning rushing to earth. George had already spent five hours at the helm. Soon he would have to hand over to someone else, but not just yet. A light flashed in the corner of his eye. It looked different, man made? He searched for it again. There it was in the distance and far to his right. It was a ship. All his prayers were being answered today. He must try to stop the ship. But how was he going to get their attention?

George decided that he would have to match their angle of approach to try to head them off. He had to judge their direction carefully to make sure that their paths intersected at the right moment. Deceptive was a much slower vessel and to try to close with the other ship from the rear would be futile. They only had one chance, otherwise they would fail and any hope of Fred surviving would be lost.

He held, what was now obviously a large ship within the triangular frame of the centre and middle shroud. Any divergence from there would tell him that he was going to lose the race, either passing too far forward or too far behind. The other ship began to move imperceptibly forward and George was having difficulty holding the angle.

'Shake out the reef,' he screamed. 'We're losing them!'

Deceptive groaned under the strain of the extra canvas and increased her speed. George hung on to the wheel not allowing her to deviate one inch. He had it cracked. They were going to cross exactly in front of the other ship. Any loss of wind and they would lose it.

As they closed they saw that she was a massive, luxury passenger liner. They would have to stop her, but how? The radio was out of the question due to the flat batteries. By crossing their bows, even at close range, would tell their captain nothing.

'The ships torch! That's it!' It came to George almost without thinking.

He remembered a recently read Morse S.O.S.

'Quick, start flashing dot, dot, dot, dash, dash, dash, dot, dot, dot,' he shouted to Nigel, who had picked up the torch on his hurried instruction.

Nigel started to flash the code aiming the light where he assumed the liner's bridge would be.

'Will they see our flashes against their brightly lit decks?' Kevin wondered.

As they got closer, the size of the liner completely overshadowed Deceptive. George couldn't tell if they had been spotted or not. 'Keep at it, Nigel!' he encouraged.

Nigel was trying to lean out under the sail so that his flashes wouldn't be obstructed and was having difficulty hanging on with one hand.

The ships were on a collision course and George wasn't about to give up this close to success. He would stop her alright, he decided, even if it meant going right under her massive bows.

'Kevin, let off a few flares!' George instructed. He had forgotten all about them in his haste to catch the other ship.

Two red flares in quick succession lit up the night sky.

'They surely can't miss that,' Kevin yelled, rubbing his hand where the badly held first flare had scorched his skin.

'Nigel, keep flashing S.O.S,' George encouraged.

Sandy was holding Fred's limp hand and gently cooing, 'It'll be alright soon Fred, it'll be alright soon, we've seen another ship,' like a mother nursing a sick child. They were so close now that George could see the immense wash being created by the liners bow wave. They were still under full power.

Two red flares in quick succession lit up the night sky.

'They aren't going to stop,' Nigel shouted from under the sail.

This was crazy, they could clearly see people moving about the bridge. Passengers were pointing at them and waving and yet the liner wasn't going to stop. They were so close they could actually smell the fumes from the her stacks as it was carried towards them by the wind.

A light started to sparkle on the bridge. They were answering! But nobody on Deceptive knew the Morse code.

'What are they trying to tell us, why don't they stop?' shouted George.

Sandy looked at Fred. 'The only chance the poor bugger has is going to slip away,' she thought, not wishing to upset Fred by showing her fears.

They continued to close with the liner. George wasn't about to give up as easily as this. He would run right under her bows if he had to. A man's life was at stake here. They could survive, they must reach land soon, but Fred probably would not.

Suddenly the air was shattered by five short blasts from the liner. George didn't know what that meant either, but realised the liner was coasting. At the last possible minute George brought Deceptive's head around and ran along the lee side of the liner. He knew it was a mistake the moment he had done it and now hoped that they had enough headway to carry them safely along the line of the ship without colliding. He didn't have to shout to Nigel to keep flashing. He kept it up even as he slithered across Deceptive's deck.

The liner was like a ten storey skyscraper. It seemed to go up and on forever. Even if they did stop, Nigel wondered how they were going to get Fred on board such a large ship.

A voice on a megaphone, somewhere far above them, told them urgently to, 'Stand off, stand off, keep off! We'll come to you.'

Even before the liner had stopped, one of her enclosed ferries was being lowered from the top deck with quiet precision. It had no sooner hit the water when her lines were released and she was heading back towards the stalled Deceptive who's sails were already down.

The ship's doctor was on the tender as the captain had rightfully anticipated some kind of accident. One quick look at Fred was sufficient to have him transferred to the tender. When told what had happened, the doctor informed them that there was a fully-equipped operating theatre on board and that, if necessary, they could treat Fred with minor surgery. They would X-ray Fred's chest. It was obvious that his lung had collapsed. If his injury was too severe they would get a helicopter out to the ship and have Fred transported to hospital.

'It looks as if we've just got him in the nick of time. You fellows should consider yourselves extremely lucky,' the Scottish doctor told them, between giving Fred an injection and requesting, on his hand set, that his team on board should get ready for their 'latest customer.' His captain wanted a few words with them and he handed the handset over to Nigel, who briefed him fully on what had happened.

'Our next stop is Corfu. Will you be able to follow us there?' the captain asked, concerned that, without their skipper, they might be in further difficulty.

George took over the handset and requested their present position, explaining that if they had some food and diesel, getting to Corfu wouldn't be a problem and finished by saying, 'Captain Fred has trained us well. Look after the old bugger for us, will you?'

The captain assured them that he would and not to worry as his team on board were second to none.

Sandy would go along with Fred. They were surprised to learn that they were only two hundred miles out of Corfu and could make it in two days. George assured Sandy that they would catch up with her there as Nigel gave her a final hug.

'Thanks for everything and especially for what you've done for Fred.' Sandy hurried onto the tender, the tears welling in her eyes.

In less than forty minutes after it had come to a halt the Cunard liner was disappearing fast into the darkness and Deceptive was holding a new course directly in her wake, her engine once again re-charging the batteries. They kept in touch with the liner until the radio reception broke up. Before losing contact they were informed that Fred had had a minor operation for a ruptured lung. George, Nigel and Kevin were chomping into one of the most enjoyable meals they had ever tasted, compliments of the Cunard flagship's captain. The other Fred was on duty at the helm. George had re-christened the autopilot Fred.

Down the Hatch

'Told you there was nothing to this sailing lark,' mouthed George through his stuffed happy face, a glass of fine white wine clutched in his greasy hand. Nigel and Kevin eyed him strangely, but thought it better not to comment.

19

The Epi-Log

Fred had finally arrived in Greece by luxury liner. It might not have been the way he had intended to complete his journey, but nevertheless, here he was in Corfu battered but safe, his mission accomplished. The fact that he was in a private ward in a local hospital with a tube protruding from his arm pumping Dextrose into his body was neither here nor there. He'd arrived and that was all that mattered. As a result, Fred was on the mend and fast regaining his strength. He was very much alive and should have been thankful for that, but Fred, being Fred, had other complaints.

'The bed's too bloody short, my legs are sticking out,' he had protested to a severely uninterested, horse faced nurse. He couldn't for the life of him understand why they opened all the french windows at night to keep the place cool. They allowed hoards of hungry mosquitoes to enter and feast on those self-same legs, instead of switching on the bloody air conditioning.

Marge had been contacted by what she assumed was a sassy young tart who rolled her r's, and who couldn't give a plausible reason for being aboard Deceptive, but had been perfectly well able to give a concerned, long, and painful account of her husband's accident, and of how she had travelled with him aboard a cruise ship to an hospital in Corfu. After finding out that Fred was out of danger, Marge asked Sandy again what she was doing on board her husband's boat. She obviously had not been informed by her husband – which she emphasised – of any young women taking part in the trip. Sandy decided not to make her any the wiser.

Marge, her suspicions aroused, decided to take the first available plane to Corfu to investigate for herself, not waiting for a cheaper charter flight! She was going to put an end to her husband's gallop, once, of course, that she'd seen for herself that he was truly on the mend.

'It's all that announcer fellow's fault,' she decided, 'Far, far, too much charm for his own good, leading my husband astray like that.' She would stay on the yacht, she decided. 'Might as well get some benefit from it.' She thought of the fortune her daft husband had thrown away on that stupid boat and shook her head. 'And now women too! It'll be drink next!' she told herself. 'I'll have to take an interest in that damn thing after all.' That afternoon she purchased a few essentials one of which was a rather expensive, too revealing bikini. She had the figure for it she convinced herself and wasn't too sure of the competition.

Nigel, George and Kevin were welcomed on their arrival at Gouvia Marina by a delighted Sandy. She had stayed at a small taverna with the unusually appropriate name Takis in the adjacent village of Kontakali. There she met Woody who'd been around boats even longer than he cared to remember, first fishing boats in the North Sea and now sailing yachts in Corfu. He assured her that himself and Topdeck Brian would keep their eyes peeled for Deceptive as they were always up and down the coast with charter boats. Brian had seen Deceptive coming through the straits between Corfu island and the mainland while trying to get six reluctant Aussie-manned yachts to form a circle so he could bring them in to the tourist village of Murtos one at a time.

'Cara one, two, three, four, five, and six form a circle,' he cajoled patiently on channel sixty. Cara four, cara four, cara four a clockwise circle. Suddenly noticing that he now had seven yachts, he shrugged his shoulders, 'You lose some you find some,' he thought. The seventh yacht was Deceptive. He gave George, Nigel and Kevin a heading for Gouvia, over a few glasses of wine in George's quayside restaurant, and later radioed ahead giving their approximate time of arrival.

Sandy was fetched by Woody and she quickly informed them of Fred's condition. They were relieved to hear that old Sputnik was well and truly on the mend.

'He's a hardy old basket, knew he'd make it!' said Nigel.

Meanwhile Fred had more than enough time to think of his future. He tried telling himself that the trip had been worth while, but knew better. The yacht had cost him more cash than he was ever likely to see again. He should have taken Marge's advice and put the lot into a pension fund. That way they would have had security in their old age and would have been able to enjoy life. Then he had second thoughts. After all, he was only forty-three. At sixty he wouldn't be able to do the things he could do now. No, he reasoned, life was far too short. You only have one nibble at the cherry. Better make the most of it while you can.

He had learned a lot about sailing in the last three weeks. 'Not many people could boast of having sailed across the Med. never having skippered a yacht before. He was certain, of course, that he would never brag about it! Well maybe just a little.

Fred was delighted to see that Nigel, George, and Kevin had arrived safely in Corfu. They told him about the remainder of their trip, putting their safe arrival down to his good training. Nothing out of the ordinary had occurred in their two and a half day journey since he had been carted off. With a steady wind from the Southwest they had made reasonable headway. Their first landfall had been the little island of Paxos which they identified by its tiny neighbour, Anti-Paxos, just off its southern coast. From there it was only another six hours to Corfu town.

A large bottle of Metaxa brandy with more stars than a Michael Jackson movie was produced. On Fred's whispered instruction the door was secured from the inside by a chair firmly jammed under the handle.

'Just in case that old battle-axe of a nursing sister turns up.'

'We couldn't leave without a farewell drink with our skipper after all we've been through together, now could we?' Nigel said, making an extravagant gesture with the plastic beakers he had produced from thin-air.

It was to be their last sundowner together before Fred's crew caught their flight home the following afternoon. Fred wasn't supposed to touch alcohol.

'Ah well! It's our last night together and as long as we keep that stony-faced old bag of a nurse out it'll be okay. Don't want her coming in here telling me what I can and I can't do,' Fred exclaimed.

After a few drinks a nostalgic mood overcame Fred. This was the end of the line. It was all over. His freshly flushed system couldn't cope with the combined effects of the Dextrose and the brandy as was soon manifestly discernible by his actions. He was becoming maudlin, almost likable. This was not the Fred they knew. He thanked them profusely and invited them to sail with him again in the future, anytime. He spoiled it all by saying that he hoped they would know what to do next time.

'Gentlemen,' he continued, Sandy caught him before he fell out of the bed. She swiftly propped him up with a few well placed pillows. 'Gentlemen,' he continued, amused by his temporary inability to sit up straight. 'I have to shay . . .' Did he really say that? he wondered. He couldn't go on like this. He bit his index finger to help pull himself together and gave an embarrassed cackle. 'I have to say that with one notishable exception, you were all, aaaahhaaa.' He hadn't meant to make any exceptions, '. . . you were all terrific.' Everything was coming out wrong. The Mataxas were too much for his still weak body and he couldn't shut himself up.

They all looked at Kevin, who suddenly busied himself looking out of the window. An element of panic was creeping into the proceedings. Whatever was he going to say next? They wondered if they should call a doctor. It would have been better to have left the celebration until his safe return to Liverpool. Now it was too late and they would have to bear with him.

Fred too was panicking, he had to change tack immediately, or else. 'Some of you started off as boys, but you all ended up as men, and I'm proud of you.' This was better. 'I'm including . . .' He fell over on his side and had to be helped up by Nigel. 'My good friend Kevin,' he continued, struggling to say what he felt.

'We may not always see eye to eye, but I love him,' he lied. Kevin, Sandy, George and Nigel all knew he was lying. There were smiles all around. 'I love Kev. like I love the rest of you.' He spoiled it with another cackle. They regarded each other in bemused silence and then burst out laughing.

'It's the drink Fred, it's gone to your head,' George said.

Fred's own sentimentality was becoming too much for him and he had to wipe a tear from the corner of his eye. He pulled himself together. 'Kevin may know absolutely noshing about washing dishes, ah ha ha ha!,' he was off again, 'but he is bloody good with the sails just the same. I've learnt a lot from him.'

This sudden show of affection was too much for the others and loud guffaws burst from their throats. Even Kevin couldn't suppress his laughter, the thought of Fred's suddenly disclosed love was impossible to take with a straight face.

It was George's turn next. 'George, what aboush George? He was terrific too,' said Fred. Everything was terrific to Fred tonight. 'Learned more about sailing than I've forgotten!' he continued 'An we'd have starved to deash if Shandy hadn't come on board, .. ha ha ha! and she's so beautiful, so very.... A round of applause for Shandy.'

The Epi-Log

The others agreed whole-heartedly and gave her an embarrassingly loud show of approval by hand clapping interspersed with a few wild cheers, so much so that Fred put a finger to his lips to denote silence.

'You'll have that old bag down on top of me like a ton of bricks if you don't keep quiet and I don't particularly want her on top . . . or under for that matter aaaahaaa.'

Fred was well gone now, they decided, giving each other knowing looks, between snorts of suppressed laughter.

'And last but not least, Nigel. Without him this trip could not have taken place. He had to dig often into his pockets, but he never complained. Pity about his flag though, hate that bloody flag with a vengeance.'

Fred was about to finish. They could see this by the effort he made to be serious 'This time the weather was crap, but next time.. It'll probably be aaaahaaaa,' he failed miserably,'be worse,' he continued. 'But you're all welcome back to ol' Defective, I mean Deceptive any-time.

'He's in form tonight,' whispered Nigel to Sandy between laughs. Maybe that's been our mistake? We should have got him plastered more often.'

They were genuinely touched by Fred's speech and Nigel answered in return.

'Lady and gentlemen,' he began. 'Can you be upstanding for a toast to our esteemed captain. He may be a crabbed old bugger at times, but he got us here.'

'Almost!' Fred interrupted.

'I speak for the rest when I say that we will never forget this trip, Fred. Cheers.' They lifted their glasses and toasted Fred with the remnants of the Mataxa bottle. Kevin, true to his word, toasted Fred with a pretence swig from an empty bed bottle, saying 'Down the hatch, Fred'.

At that moment a starchy, matron type nurse broke in and, seeing the drink, cleared them from the room, admonishing each in turn while screaming for a doctor to examine the still amused Fred, who kept pointing at her, wagging his finger, and telling her not to come near or else!

As they walked down the hall they could still hear his chuckles and ended up helpless themselves. This was a new and far more interesting Fred.

THE END